Unplugged

Joe Barrett

Black Rose Writing | Texas

ISBN: 978-1-68433-492-6
PUBLISHED BY BLACK ROSE WRITING
www.blackrosewriting.com

Printed in the United States of America
Suggested Retail Price (SRP) $19.95

Unplugged is printed in Baskerville

*As a planet-friendly publisher, Black Rose Writing does its best to eliminate unnecessary waste to reduce paper usage and energy costs, while never compromising the reading experience. As a result, the final word count vs. page count may not meet common expectations.

This book would not have been finished without the relentless badgering and brutally honest criticisms of my son, Joe, who was twelve-years-old when I wrote it. I love you so much, bud.

Unplugged

UNPLUGGED

CHAPTER ONE

"Baby!"

And I cringe. I have developed a Pavlovian response to the term of endearment "baby." Instant dread.

"Baby, it's me!"

She doesn't know I'm here. How could she know I'm here? I don't move a muscle.

"Come on, baby! Open the door! It's me!"

I hear a fistful of pebbles smack onto the lower windows of the building. It's probably just the second-floor windows. Clancy hasn't got much of an arm. And since the second-floor is divided into two apartments directly above the front door, I'm not sure if she's strafing Marc's apartment or Linda's apartment or both. But it only matters if she cracks the glass because Marc and Linda are single young professionals who work normal Manhattan hours and it's not yet three p.m.

I exhale slowly. Weigh my options.

"Baby! Are you home!? Baby!"

More pebbles hitting glass. Who stands on a sidewalk in the middle of the afternoon throwing fistfuls of gravel at the windows of a brownstone? After all these years, Clancy still has the ability to mortify me like nobody else in the world. That must mean something.

"Hey, there, cutie-pie!" I hear a window slide open, one floor below me. Sluggo. He shouts from his third-floor window, "You want me to buzz you in?!"

"Oh, hey, Sluggo!" Clancy shouts back sweetly. His real name is Mike, but everyone calls him Sluggo because he looks exactly like this character from an old-time comic strip called *Nancy*. The fact that it's such an esoteric reference speaks to how much he looks like this Sluggo character. And it's not a good look. Go ahead and Google it.

"Cutie-pie, when are you gonna forget that bozo upstairs and start taking the elevator to floor three?!"

"Sluggo, you rascal!" Clancy shouts playfully. I could vomit.

And now I have to get involved because Sluggo has no problem engaging in a full-on third-floor-to-street dialogue at high volume. And that's not fair to the neighborhood moms. I walk to the front of my apartment and slide my window open.

"Oh, there you are!" Clancy shouts, all cutesy-like, as if she's talking to a kitten. "Hey, baby!" She's bouncing up and down, waving at me from the sidewalk. What Clancy looks like is a nineteen-fifties movie star, updated for the new millennium. Think Marilyn Monroe or Jayne Mansfield, re-scaled for two-thousand nineteen.

Take how she's dressed right now. You lay Clancy's clothes out on a bed and you'd think someone was screen dressing a right-wing television personality. You've got two strings of pearls. You've got a wide-collared white knit sweater with short sleeves. You've got a Laura Ashley lightweight skirt, dark blue with big white polka dots. You've got snow-white tights - not stockings, like a normal woman would wear. She's wearing tights, like a child who's dressed up for church.

But you put these clothes on Clancy and it's a wet dream come true for any guy who struggles with repressed mommy fantasies, which — keeping it real – is probably all guys in some shape or form. Clancy's two strings of pearls hang just a bit too tight, not quite a choker, but definitely not country-club loose. And they do just enough to attract eyes to the neck of her knit sweater, the collar so wide as to allow clear and frequent visibility of a lightly laced, sheer white bra that strains to contain two of the most spectacular breasts in the world today. The Laura Ashley lightweight skirt, which no one would ever confuse with a miniskirt, is just short enough to billow with the slightest breeze or twirl, revealing the opaque whiteness of her tights and panties with a frequency that you would think is intentional. And it probably is. Maybe it is. I've never gotten up the nerve to ask her, because asking would make me feel like I'm the pervert.

Anyway, intentional or not – almost definitely intentional, I think – what Clancy does to grown men is make them feel the way puberty-aged boys would feel about a middle school teacher that's Disney princess hot and remarkably careless in terms of keeping her private parts covered.

When we first started dating, this whole accidental exposure schtick bothered me. After a couple of years, I have to admit, it kind of turned me on. But lately I'm just over it. And even though we dated for four years and were engaged for eight months, I never spoke to her about it.

Makes me wonder if we ever had the slightest clue what real intimacy is all about.

"Aren't you going to buzz me up?!" Clancy shouts.

I look down at her, slide my index finger across my neck in an aggressive throat-slashing gesture. Clancy's mouth drops open. Score. Then she smiles at me, as if we're sharing a joke. Take back the score.

"What's that supposed to mean?" Clancy yells, oblivious to how many innocent, well-to-do mothers are negotiating nap time with their toddlers on this high-end Jersey City waterfront block.

"It means we're not on Staten Island," I reply, my voice loud enough for her to hear but still an octave or two below an actual shout. "We don't scream at each other from streets and windows around here."

"I got no problem with window-to-street dialogue, cutie-pie, if that's…" Sluggo shouts and lets the balance of his sentence hang. He's got the same view of Clancy that I do – her wide collar hanging so loose below us that, even from our height, you can see the outlines of pink nipples pressed tightly against her sheer bra. Honestly, I've known no other woman so adept and consistent in doling out the cheap thrills.

Sluggo has freely admitted to me that he is deeply in love with Clancy. Just like pretty much every repressed male is in love with Clancy. Every repressed male except for me. The irony is not lost. I point down at Clancy and then point to the front door, shut the window, walk to the buzzer.

All the other tenants in the building have video buzzer tech that lets them see who's in the vestibule, talk back and forth, open the door – all from their smart phones. My buzzer, it's a custom job. Restored, actually. From the building's original buzzer system, installed at build in the nineteen-fifties. Fortunately, contractors never tear out old wiring systems when buildings are updated, because… why bother? So I just had my contractors patch up some of the prior electrical work and, bingo, it's as good as old. The buzz is so loud that I can hear it clearly through my open fourth-floor window.

Clancy takes the elevator to the third floor, walks down the hall and then up the stairs to my door. The elevator no longer goes to the fourth floor. Another of my custom jobs.

"Open up!" Clancy shouts.

"It's not locked," I shout back, my voice echoing off the exposed brick walls of my enormous apartment.

"Come on. O-pen up," Clancy whines. She can't figure out how to work the crossbar handle mechanism on my giant, industrial steel front door. Or she's afraid of getting her hands dirty while trying. Either way, she continues to stand in the hallway, banging on the door, while I deliberate just letting her bang-away until she tires out and goes home. Clancy making a scene in my hallway bothers me so much less than Clancy making a scene from the street. But I'm fooling myself. She's not going anywhere. Eventually I open the door.

Like a Japanese anime character, Clancy's face is a hyperbole of joy when she sees me, but her wide-eyed look quickly collapses into a hyperbole of misery when she looks past me, into my apartment. And like any hyperbolic cartoon, I'm pretty sure neither of her looks reflects any deep feelings going on inside of her. I mean, cartoons don't have deep feelings, right?

Chapter Two

I'm going to digress here to give you some back story…

My name is Dan Johnson. Some people call me Daniel, which is fine. Just don't call me Danny, because I'm not a six-year-old.

If you work in the app development space, you've probably heard of me. If you work in any other field, probably not. And even in the app development space, you haven't heard of me for over a year. But if you want to go back to the archives, you can read about me in *Fast Company* or *Wired* or one of the other tech rags.

I bought this five-story Jersey City brownstone about eighteen months ago, right after I sold my app development company to private equity, outright, for a solid nine-figure sum. Nine figures for a half-assed app, a cloud-based platform, and over half-a-billion users. Hint: the half-billion users is what did it. A ridiculous world we live in, right?

Don't get me wrong. My tech solved a problem, and I'm proud of what I created. But between you and me, what I designed and built should have been worth maybe a million dollars. Maybe two. Definitely not nine figures. But, luckily for me, the problem that my app originally solved tripped over three additional problems. This happens sometimes. And when I adjusted the functionality to address these new problems, the app went viral and the user community shot into the stratosphere. And what do you do when a tech giant offers you hundreds of millions for a fortunate accident? Duh.

But to be honest, the whole thing was more surreal than real and I was in a kind of befuddled daze after finalizing the sale. Not necessarily a bad daze, but not necessarily a good daze either. A daze is a daze.

So, back then I'm twenty-eight years old and I'm engaged to Clancy, who happens to be everyone's ideal in terms of marriage. And all of a sudden, I'm filthy rich and retired and in this post-windfall daze. Sometimes, when everything you ever thought you wanted comes way too early, all the other stuff you ever thought you wanted can get a little blurry. And going through the same old motions can suddenly feel like you're trying to dance with no music.

So, anyway. This brownstone was my first big purchase after the windfall. I'd assumed it would be a tear-down and rebuild scenario, but structurally it was a type of solid that you could only get in mid-twentieth-century buildings, so it ended up being a strip-and-gut job instead. And, most inconveniently, Clancy's former college roommate and lifetime bestie, Gwen, had recently joined one of the hottest new architectural firms in Manhattan.

I'm going to digress from my digression and back up a little more here...

The first school that probably pops into your head when someone says Ivy League, that's where Clancy and Gwen went to college. Roommates, freshman year through graduation. Both graduated with highest honors. Both were virgins until their sophomore year.

And both were cheerleaders!!! In case you missed it, that's sarcastic enthusiasm!!!

I've always considered it oxymoronic for Ivy League colleges to even have cheerleading squads, considering the intelligence bar for acceptance at these schools. You'd think they'd screen out people who'd voluntarily join a team of miniskirt high-kickers that jiggle and jump in front of a live crowd of drunk collegiate sports fans. Objectify much?

Furthering the oxymoron, cheerleading co-captain Clancy graduated with a 4.0 average in Women's Studies. Women's Studies! So, tell me how that makes sense? Sorry, I'm off on a tangent. From my last digression.

And it's only fair to say that I didn't always feel this way, exactly. I mean, I dated Clancy for four years, was engaged to her for about eight months. I spent so much of my life thinking she and I would get married that I really don't know how to feel about her. A part of me still wishes that I was missing the same part of my brain that she's missing so I could be happy about the same stuff that makes her happy. Even though all that stuff that makes Clancy happy is now the same stuff makes me want to vomit.

And even though I broke up with her, my relationship with Clancy... it's still pretty complicated.

Anyway, Gwen is cut from the same cloth as Clancy, but she's more of a sidekick version. Like, Clancy is the brand name aspirin and Gwen is the generic store label, but the ingredients are essentially the same. Like, if they ever had pharmaceutical rep beauty contests, Gwen would always be first runner-up to Clancy's crown. Not that either of them is a pharma rep... they both just look the part. The only real difference between them, as far as I can see, is just that everyone perceives Clancy to be a little bit better than Gwen in every way imaginable. The only advantage for Gwen is that, like Avis Rental Cars, she tries harder. And this has made her an animal in the workplace.

So, designing my brownstone somehow turned into a fast track career builder for Gwen, while it represented absolutely no discount or other advantage for me because I had more than enough money anyway, according to Clancy. As such, my befuddled windfall daze wasn't so much replaced but distracted by the Gwen and Clancy brownstone project. The goal was to create the most ultramodern daily-tech enabled living environment outside of science fiction. And I went along with it because... why not? I didn't really have anything else to do, and I was shelling out mid-seven-figures for the building, anyway. It was, at the very least, a distraction from the blur that was then my life.

Because the floor plan of my brownstone is so enormous, the idea was to split each of the first three floors into two ultra-modern luxury apartments. Opulent near-city homes for the highest paid young professionals looking for a view of the Manhattan skyline, a ferry to work, and twenty-four-hundred square feet of voice-and-iPad-controlled automation that, in retrospect, totally takes the "living" out of "living space." But, to each their own.

I also built out a basement apartment where my landlord slash handyman slash new-stay-at-home-dad slash younger brother lives rent free. His name is Bill. He's got the same modern set-up as the six above ground apartments, minus the Manhattan view. He's also got a truly miserable, high-power attorney wife named Betsy and a two-year-old daughter named Bitsy. They landed on the name Bitsy after a whole year of indecision, during which the baby began looking more and more like my ball-busting sister-in-law. So they ultimately decided on Bitsy because it sounded like "a little Betsy," and they had been calling her Bitsy that whole time, anyway. Bitsy — sure, there's a name that's got legs.

My unit is where the top two floors used to be. I don't like calling it a penthouse because I don't think any top-floor apartment that isn't at least ten stories high should be called a penthouse, but this doesn't make it any less impressive. It is, in industry terms, a double-wide, double-high. Meaning it's the width of two apartments and the height of two apartments. Meaning the original brownstone was a five-story building, and I collapsed the fifth floor into the fourth floor to make a bigger box. Originally there were going to be several split levels throughout the unit. Until I opted for, what you might call, a more open format.

"I love it," I remember saying to Gwen — what was it, a year ago next month? We'd blown out the fifth floor, stripped the walls down to the original exposed brick, ground the floor to an ice rink of bare, polished concrete. Temporary wire-cage working lights were draped all along the high ceiling. No rooms, no stairs, no drywall or dividers. The place was an enormous, echoing twentieth century cave not yet touched by modern tech. Gwen, eyes glued to her oversized iPad, might as well have been in a Starbucks for all she noticed.

But there was something hushed and holy about the place, like some kind of ancient church.

And we were going to ruin all of it.

This is when I came out of the windfall daze that had been blurring my thoughts and vision since I'd sold my company. And this release was like I'd dropped a whole bunch of heavy stuff that I didn't even know I'd been carrying.

"This is good," I said.

Gwen continued to swipe through the interior designs on her iPad, enthusiastically pointing out how my unit would be the next gen of next gen daily tech living. Lighting, heat, sound, security, all activated via a central voice recognition system. Dozens of recessed lights and giant screens that would slide up from the floor or out from the walls on command. A lot of the furniture would be automated, too, digitally linked to the central system. It was going to have *five* Japanese toilets. If my downstairs units were *The Jetson's*, my upstairs unit was *Star Trek, The Next Generation*. Gwen made cute little shrieks, she was so excited, reviewing each design tech function. I've always hated Gwen. Which is funny, because she reminds me so much of Clancy.

Back then, Clancy was as jacked about five Japanese toilets as Gwen was, but she had nothing to gain in the bargain other than getting hot water and air blown on her crotch at twelve different speeds, in five different bathrooms. Don't get me wrong. A Japanese toilet is nice when you're, like, in Japan or if you stumble onto one at some rich dude's party. But it's just a novelty, not some kind of yardstick for finally having made it.

"This is good," I said again.

Gwen shoved the tilted screen of her iPad a little further in my direction, not wanting me to miss a single feature.

"Awesome!" Gwen replied, actually jiggling with excitement. "Great. That's great. Just give me a digital signature… here, and the contractors can get started on Monday."

"No, no. I mean *this*," I said, spreading my palms outward at the brick and concrete box surrounding us. "*This* is good. We're going to leave it just like this."

Gwen's eyes widened. And then she laughed. Which made me laugh. But I'm pretty sure we weren't laughing at the same thing. She smacked my shoulder. Hard. Like, good one, dude! And then our laughter slowly expired into a few hiccups and I explained to her, totally and completely serious, that I wanted to leave my unit exactly the way it was. Leave it a bare brick and concrete box. I have to admit I wasn't really considering anyone else's feelings when I made this decision.

That's when Gwen went all Tasmanian Devil on me.

It took my general contractor and five construction workers to pull her frantic, clawing, screaming self from my body and restrain her while we waited for the security guards to come up from the lower units. Since then, my relationship with Gwen has been a bit strained.

Chapter Three

"Baby, I know you don't want to talk about it, but all I can think about when I walk into this place is how you totally submarined Gwen's career," Clancy says in hyperbolic misery, glancing at my bare brick walls.

"How about we talk about why you're here?" I ask. "We did break up, right?"

"I mean, this project was going to get Gwen into the magazines, turn her name into a brand, give her the chops to make partner and maybe, eventually, even start her own firm."

"And I could be mistaken, going by the literal definition of a break-up and all, but doesn't that mean we don't just stop by each other's places unannounced?" I am not going to engage in a dialogue about Gwen right now.

"Gwen totally blames you, you know. But I tell her it's not your fault. Every time I see her, I tell her that."

"Yet here you are, despite our break-up, throwing rocks at my building and disturbing my neighbors."

"I keep telling Gwen that people have nervous breakdowns sometimes – like, that's life, you know? You sold your company. You made a lot of money in a very short timeframe. Something like that can take a toll on a person. But I think, deep down, Gwen knows that everything will eventually work itself out. Look, you haven't even changed the upper unit since the tear down. So, I tell Gwen that when things get back to normal, she'll be right where you left her, you know, career-wise."

"You actually think Gwen believes that?" As usual, Clancy has dragged me into her conversation, ignoring my own line of discussion about our break-up.

"Yes."

"Why?"

"Because that's what I tell her, and she trusts me. Even though she's all, like, 'I'm turning twenty-six next year and I wanted to be a partner by the time I was twenty-five and now that will never happen because there's no way to turn back the clock.' She thinks her career is ruined because of you."

"Because of me," I say flatly. A statement, not a question. Who makes partner at any firm when they're twenty-five? Millennials. I hate how these freaking millennials set crazy life goals and then convince themselves that they matter. Of course, that's easy for me to say now. I do realize that I probably was one of those people.

"But I just sit her down and I tell her we all have challenges," Clancy continues without missing a beat. "Lord knows I have my own challenges when it comes to you. But I always tell Gwen that getting through these challenges is what turns us into better human beings."

I feel a segue coming.

"Like, I tell her that waiting for you to come to your senses is making me a stronger person on my own. Just like not making partner before she's twenty-five will probably make Gwen a stronger person, too. Or at least a better manager... I mean, better in terms of being able to understand what people who don't make partner by twenty-five are struggling with, I guess."

"There's a population that needs more empathy." Clancy ignores my comment.

"Just like I'll be better at understanding what other women feel – like, when they don't get married before they're twenty-seven, too."

"You're twenty-five, Clancy."

"I'm twenty-six in eight months. And I want us to be engaged for at least a year."

"And we broke up."

"Yeah, for however long that's going to be," Clancy says, like she's talking about a delayed flight. "But you know what? I'm accepting it. I don't have to get married by the time I'm twenty-seven, just like Gwen doesn't have to make partner at twenty-five. That's what I keep telling her."

"I think we'd both benefit by really embracing our break-up, Clancy. Like, how about we pretend that we will be broken up forever and live our lives that way for a while? I think it would do us both some good."

"Don't be an idiot. I'm not the one who had a nervous breakdown."

"I did not have a nervous breakdown, Clancy. Cite for me the time and place that I had a nervous breakdown."

"September seventeenth, two-thousand eighteen, at four twenty-six p.m."

The day I halted plans for my apartment. The day that Gwen attacked me.

"No, Clancy. That's when Gwen had a nervous breakdown and put three fingernails through my cheek." I lift and turn my head so that the sunlight coming in through my windows can better light the scars. Truth be told, I don't really mind that Gwen did permanent damage to my face. It looks kind of bad-assed. "She had to be restrained overnight. Hell, she's lucky I didn't press charges."

"Don't you try to pin this on Gwen! She was trying to save you!"

"Save me," I repeat, flatly.

"Or at least help you. I mean, you'd lost your mind."

"Lost my mind." Maybe I can just repeat the last thing Clancy says for a while and this discussion will peter out. She'll get bored and go home.

"We all agreed on the design of this place!"

"The design of this place."

"We were a family!"

"A family."

"Have you been drinking?"

"Not today, no."

"Then quit repeating everything I say and just listen to me for a minute."

"Okay."

"What was I saying?" Clancy asks, in all seriousness.

"We were a family," I respond, flatly.

"That's right. We were a family. We were supposed to help each other out. If you didn't want Gwen designing your living space, you could have just told her at the start. You didn't have to let her present everything to her bosses and ramp up the PR engine before you nuked her dreams."

"Nuked her dreams."

"You said you would stop doing that."

"Sorry. Can I respond?"

"Please."

"First, I never actually agreed to let Gwen design my apartment. You did."

"We were engaged. It was our apartment, or it would be, at least. And anyway, you were, like, totally out of it at the time. Like a sleepwalker or something."

"I was reassessing."

"Well, the world doesn't stop just because you feel the need to reassess."

"No, but this world you're talking about did kind of stop when I finished reassessing and decided to re-prioritize what's important in my life. At least Gwen took me seriously."

"What's that supposed to mean?"

"It means she attacked me," I say and tilt my facial scars into the light again. "She understood that things had changed. She obviously wasn't happy about it, but she got it. You, you just…"

"Hey, is this a bad time?" Sluggo asks, standing in my open doorway for I don't know how long.

"Hey, Sluggo!" Clancy shouts, apparently okay changing the direction of our conversation away from where I was steering it. When Clancy spins around to face Sluggo, her skirt twirls high enough so he can see her panties. Sluggo's jaw drops and his eyes pop, but Clancy either doesn't notice, or she pretends she doesn't notice. I honestly have no idea what is up with this girl in terms of this whole unintentional sex show thing she's got going on.

"Jesus, dude. Really?" I sigh at Sluggo, more because he's been eavesdropping on our conversation than because he was so obviously checking out Clancy's panties.

"I would have texted you, but you know…" Sluggo lets the sentence trail with a tight-lipped grin. "Anyway, we're late."

"We're late," I say flatly. I have no plans with Sluggo today.

"Now you're doing it to Sluggo," Clancy giggles. "That's good. I thought it was only me."

"Doing what, cutie-pie?" Sluggo asks Clancy.

"Repeating what the other person just said. I think it's a new symptom," Clancy replies cheerfully. Clancy and Sluggo have spent hours discussing the symptoms of what they consider my condition. Or, at least Clancy has spent hours pontificating about my condition, while Sluggo probably just stared openly at her body, hoping for another accidental reveal, which is what he continues to do right now. Shamelessly, I might add.

"Anyway, I won't hold you guys up," Clancy says, smiling at me. "I just came over to let you know my parents are in town on Friday and they're so looking forward to seeing you, baby."

"You crossed the Hudson to tell me that?"

"I just found out this morning. Not enough time for the standard post and your answering machine has been full for more than a month. What did you want me to do?"

Clancy doesn't ask me to flip the tape on my answering machine. I guess she thinks if I'm going to live in relative isolation with regard to her, it might as well be the same with everyone else. Or maybe she just doesn't want to acknowledge the fact that there's a nineteen-eighties, analog cassette tape answering machine attached to my land line.

I actually like Clancy's father, Ben. He's always helped me to get some perspective on my life, albeit unintentionally. Clancy's mother – Amanda-call-me-Mandy – is a carbon copy of her daughter. I know, you'd think it would be the other way around, but it's not.

See, back when Clancy was twenty-three or so, her mom decided to abandon the personality she had been wearing for decades and adopt the personality that her daughter had constructed. When I first met Clancy's mom she was Amanda, a Connecticut-country-club wife. That's a thing. But a few years into my relationship with her daughter, Clancy's mother changed dresses, figuratively speaking. Amanda the Connecticut-country-club wife transformed herself into Amanda-call-me-Mandy and fashioned herself in the style of her daughter, complete with frequent and suspiciously unintentional reveals of her assorted private parts. Clancy's mom might be getting on in years, but she keeps herself in pretty good shape, so she can still shift some eyes. Especially, I'd imagine, among her husband's friends.

If Clancy's father, Ben, even noticed his wife's transformation, he never discussed it with me. In fact, he's only ever discussed two things with me. One is the fact that he hates his wife on a gut-level. Connecticut-country-club or call-me-Mandy, the version didn't appear to make any difference to Ben. According to Ben, his wife is the antichrist. The second thing he discussed with me, despite the fact that he really does love his daughter, is that I should immediately get as far away from Clancy humanly possible. As fast as humanly possible. He said this to me about fifteen minutes into the very first time we met. Back then I thought he was joking. Now, sometimes I feel like Ben is the only person who has ever truly understood my situation with Clancy.

"You still haven't told your parents we broke up, then." I state the obvious.

"Look, baby. I understand that you and I are in different places right now. But I honestly believe that what you're going through is just a phase. And while I'm willing to let this play out between the two of us…"

Really? I mean, that would sound a lot more convincing if she weren't standing in my hallway, right?

"… I'm not going to let this phase of yours do who-knows-what kind of damage to our entire social network, including, and not the least of which, my family…"

So, it's been ten months. And nobody knows that we broke up. I guess that makes sense. I mean, if Clancy isn't going to tell the world, then who would? Sluggo? Hell, no! Sluggo definitely wouldn't want anyone to know that Clancy is back on the market until he's exhausted every possible chance to be with her, or least stare at her apparently unintentional indiscretions while she discusses the various causes and symptoms of what she calls my "condition."

And who am I going to tell?

"… so, we don't have to get back together for good or anything. We just have to get back together for Friday, at the Soho House, at seven."

"There's no way I'm going to the Soho House." Either the inflection in my voice shuts down any hope Clancy's got of arguing, or she figures that yielding on this point also implies that I will, in fact, be meeting her parents on Friday. I think it's the latter.

"So, where then?" Clancy says demurely, swallowing what I'm sure is a victory yawp.

"Applebee's." No need to make this any easier for her.

"Seriously?" Clancy says with a smirk.

"Seriously," I say, seriously. "I'm in New Jersey. Let's do like the locals."

"You want to take my parents to Applebee's?"

"Actually, I want your parents to take us to Applebee's. I'm okay ordering off the two for twenty-dollar menu if you're worried about the cost."

"How about Nobu? You love Nobu!"

"How about Buffalo Wild Wings? I'm sure there's a game on Friday night."

"Fine, Applebee's. I'll tell them you're thinking about buying a few franchises."

"Do what you need to do."

"There's an Applebee's in Midtown, you know."

"There's also one at the Hudson Mall, by the Hackensack River Waterfront. I'll meet you there at two p.m."

"You want to have dinner with my parents at two o'clock in the afternoon."

"We could skip the whole thing, if you prefer."

"Fine, two o'clock," Clancy concedes.

"I'll meet you there," I say.

"No way, buster. We'll pick you up here at one-thirty."

"Why?"

"Why? Because I'm not dragging my parents out to an Applebee's at the Hudson Mall and then having no way to get in touch with you if something comes up."

"Okay, fine."

"Fine," Clancy says in a snooty voice. Then she walks over to Sluggo, gives him a friendly peck on the cheek. "Take care of this one for me, Sluggo," she whispers, placing her hand innocently on his chest.

"You know I will, cutie-pie." Sluggo has an erection, which he is taking no pains to hide because he knows that a lady like Clancy isn't going to glance down at his crotch.

"Well, I guess I'll see you Friday, one-thirty," Clancy says, walking over to me. She leans in to give me a kiss on the cheek, which I can oblige out of politeness, and then she shifts her head at the last minute, planting one right on my mouth. And I guess I'm so used to kissing her for so many years that I just start kissing her. But only for a second. Maybe two. Within which time she is able to deftly work her tongue into my mouth before I can pull my head back. Our faces separate for a just a second and then she flexes up on her tiptoes, gives me another kiss on the lips. Not a peck, a real kiss. Just no tongue this time.

"So, I'll see you Friday, then?" I say, dumbly.

"Sure it's not just a phase," she says, swaying her butt as she walks out the door. "You are so funny, baby."

Chapter Four

"You so stupid, man."

"Why are we here, anyway?" Where we are is at a cash-only bar called Mike's Place on the West Side of Jersey City. That's the side closer to the rest of New Jersey than it is to Manhattan. It's less than four miles from my building, Jersey City not being very wide. And actually, it's only a few blocks from the Applebee's at Hudson Mall, where I somehow made plans to eat with Clancy and her parents on Friday afternoon.

"Don't change the subject," Sluggo snaps. "What were we talking about… oh, right. You are so stupid."

"I assume you took me here for a reason? Seeing as you could have told me how stupid I am back at the building."

"You've sunk low, Dan."

"Have I?"

"Scraping bottom."

"Did Clancy put you up to this talk we're having?"

"She did not. We're having this talk because I care about you, dude. Also, there are some people I might want you to meet. Depending on where your head is at following our conversation."

"Oh." I don't bother to ask who are the people Sluggo has dragged me across town to meet. In a former life, I would have thought it had something to do with business. But, as I've divorced myself entirely from the world of business, I can only imagine that these people Sluggo wants me to meet are some variety of neighborhood freak show. Which is fine. It's not like I've got anything else to do this afternoon. "Where are they?"

"We have to go to them, if and when I think it's necessary. But first, let's talk. Just you and me, man. One on one, everything on the table."

"I'm not attracted to you, Sluggo."

"You know I'm not gay, Dan."

"Really? I wouldn't have a problem with it, if that's what you're worried about."

"You know I'm not gay because I am so totally and completely obsessed with Clancy."

"Ah."

"You know that I am fully rock hard almost every time I'm around her," Sluggo says with easy candor.

"I do?"

"Yeah, I've seen you check me out."

"You have," statement, not a question.

"Sure. But I'm not implying there's anything gay about it. You're just like, whoa, what's this guy with a full-on erection doing hanging around my girlfriend."

"Okay, yeah. That's accurate. But Clancy's not my girlfriend anymore. If you dragged me out here to ask me if I'm all right with you asking Clancy out on a date, the answer is yes. I'm fine with it."

"Don't be an idiot," Sluggo says disparagingly. "Clancy would never date me. I'm a pig."

"Your self-awareness is inspiring."

"Look, I got a good thing going with Clancy. And I don't want you to ruin it."

"Okay, you're going to have to explain that to me."

"Sure, let me spell it out. As long as Clancy is your girlfriend, I get to hang around with her solely because I am your best friend."

"You're not my best friend, Sluggo."

"These days, I'm your best friend."

"I'll concede your point to move this discussion along."

"Thank you. So, you called off your engagement to Clancy... what? A year ago?"

"About that, yeah."

"Well, I moved into my apartment around the same time, right?"

"I know. I leased you the space."

"You leased my parents the space. Let's keep it real." Sluggo's dad has so much money that he makes me look like a pauper. "Anyway, when I first moved in, Clancy was coming around… what? Five or six times a week?"

"Okay."

"And now she comes around like… what? Two or three times a week?"

"Give or take."

"Well, if you guys don't get your relationship back on track, eventually she's gonna stop coming around altogether."

"Yeah, Sluggo." I sigh, put my hand on his shoulder. "That's the way these things work."

"Well, that can't happen."

"Sorry?"

"Look, cards on the table, okay?"

"Sure, you can stop being so coy now."

"I need Clancy in my life, Dan."

"So, what? You have a relationship with her. Pursue it any way you want."

"Don't you get it, Dan? I don't want to pursue a new relationship with Clancy. I want what I've got right now. I want to be my best friend's girlfriend's best guy friend."

"Sluggo," I say haltingly, replaying his words in my head until they make sense, which they do. "Why?"

"Are you kidding me? Clancy and I can get as close as two people can be, but because of you she's always forbidden fruit! Do you know how sexy that is? And her body, the way she dresses – that weird innocent, accidental thing she's got going on? For real, every time she bends over or shifts her legs I'm worried that I'm gonna have an unassisted orgasm. It makes me feel so dirty when I look at her, man – like I'm some naughty thirteen-year-old kid again. I can't find porn like this on the Internet. It doesn't exist."

"Okay, first, please don't refer to yourself as a naughty thirteen-year-old kid. I'm not sure why, but that crosses a line for me."

"Sure, sorry."

"Second, are you sure there's no porn like this on the Internet? I mean, have you looked?" Sluggo rolls his eyes. Of course, he's looked.

"You can get anything on the Internet, dude. But it's not the same as having an intense, real-life friendship with a Disney princess babe, where you can look at her parts, but will never have sex with her because she's your best friend's girl. What's hotter than that? She's ruined me for even the most random, esoteric porn. And don't think I haven't done my research."

"Sluggo…" – how do I say this? – "you might be a very sick man."

"We said no judgments."

"We did not say no judgments. And you might want to talk to someone about this."

"I'm talking to you."

"I was thinking about someone with a little more training in the field of psychology. Actually, you could probably afford a whole team of psychologists, if you wanted to go down that path…"

"Stop it. I'd only need to talk to a shrink if I were ashamed of how I feel, which I'm obviously not, given that I'm talking to you about it, you being the main person who would have a problem with how I feel because you do have an intimate relationship with Clancy. An actual intimate relationship, I mean. Not the one-step-removed version like mine. Not that I would trade places with you. I like what I got just fine."

"Yeah, Sluggo," – this is so weird – "but I'm not with her anymore. And as much as I want to extend myself for you, I will not get back together with Clancy just to support your 'one-step-removed' non-physical, highly erotic relationship with her."

How is it I'm the one who feels like a jerk right now?

"Look, I get it. I would never ask a best friend to be in a relationship with someone just so I could be my best friend's girlfriend's best guy friend and perv on her. That's not the kind of person I am."

"Noble."

"Yeah. But, you know, obviously your life has imploded, right?"

"What? Not right. What're you even talking about?"

"You're in the middle of a crisis, dude. And I think, because you're in it, you can't recognize it as a crisis. But my point is, I don't think you should let this crisis – temporary as I hope it will be – destroy your relationship with Clancy. And, by association, my relationship with Clancy."

Am I the only one who recognizes the legitimacy of my break-up with Clancy?

"Exactly how am I in a crisis?"

"Dude, you don't live in our world anymore."

"I'm right here."

"Really? Because if I walk across the street and try to Facetime you, I can't. If I want to catch up on what you're up to on Instagram, I can't. If I want to friend you, if I want to add you to my network on LinkedIn, if I want to send you a freaking e-mail, if I want to call your damn cell phone – I can't!!!"

"I've got a land line."

"You know, you're probably the only person in Jersey City who still has a land line. Wake up, man. Forget about the conveniences of modern technology. You have to understand that we are social animals. And when the ways we communicate evolve, we need to evolve with them. Otherwise you spin out of orbit. Which is fine… your choice, right? Except you're not only hurting yourself. You're taking me down with you, and my one-step-removed relationship with Clancy, too. What kind of friend would do something like that?"

Chapter Five

Sluggo doesn't know what he's talking about. Or maybe he does. I mean, somewhere in all of that unfiltered honesty there may be a glimmer of substance. I don't know.

That day when I kyboshed the plans for my condo, I spent a couple of hours in the emergency room, where they removed three of Gwen's fingernails from my cheek and replaced them with eight stitches. I think they were fake nails, but Gwen and I haven't been in touch since the incident so I can't be totally sure. Anyway, I was bleeding pretty bad after Gwen blitzkrieg'd me, so one of the security guys scooted me out of the apartment and drove me straight to the emergency room. In all the rush, I didn't think to grab my iPhone.

The emergency room doctors got me in and stitched up pretty quick, but I had to stay put in the curtain-cubicle for fifteen minutes so the nurses could be sure I wouldn't pass out at departure. It was probably the first extended period of time that I hadn't had my phone with me since college. No calls, no e-mails, no Facebook, no Instagram, no Twitter.

I knew that life was going on outside the hospital. It was just going on without me. All I could do was sit in that curtain-cubicle and think about why I wanted to live in a big, empty, brick-and-concrete box instead of the next gen of next gen daily-living high-tech apartments, think about why that big brick-and-concrete box with exterior pipes and electrical wires seemed so right to me.

When the nurses released me, I walked back out to the waiting room and sat down there. If I'd had my phone, I would have probably just called an UBER. But instead, I held off from asking the desk nurse to call me a taxi and just sat there thinking. Tried to figure out what I was feeling. It wasn't the stitches or the anesthetic that were making me feel different.

Eventually I realized what I was feeling. I was feeling undistracted. Not distracted. Whatever the right word for it, I was experiencing it... right there, right then. Nothing was taking me away from the now of the hospital waiting room.

I sat there amazed at how rare that type of moment had become.

I looked around the waiting room and saw this kid – maybe seventeen or eighteen – lying on a gurney, waiting to be taken into the operating room. The kid had what looked like a vinyl floor tile sticking straight out the side of his skull. The kid was wide awake and didn't appear to be in any pain. In fact, he looked normal. Aside from the floor tile embedded in his head, I mean. He saw me staring and flashed a peace sign with his fingers. I responded with the same gesture.

After they'd wheeled him into the operating room, I got up and asked the nurse if I could pay the kid's deductibles, or whatever medical expenses were outstanding. I'm not sure why I wanted to pay the kid's medical bills, but money isn't an issue so I decided to just go with the impulse. The nurse said thanks and told me that the kid was fully covered. He needed nothing from me. Another superficial relationship. The kid is in and out of my life in a blink, even in the here-and-now of the hospital waiting room.

I asked the nurse to call me a taxi. I never found out if the kid with the vinyl floor tile embedded in his skull lived or died.

Instead of going back to my old apartment in Manhattan where all my stuff was, I took the taxi to my new, unfinished apartment in Jersey City where Gwen had attacked me earlier in the day. The security guards were very accommodating when I returned, not a huge surprise considering I own the building and had so recently been attacked on their watch. Not that they could have done anything to prevent it.

When I walked back into my double-high, double wide brick-and-concrete box on the fourth floor, the first thing I did was find my phone. I had six missed calls, which I thought was a little sparse considering the fact that a crazed interior designer had attacked and mildly disfigured me only a few hours ago. I had thirty-two new texts, seventy-four new e-mails (mostly junk, I imagine) and twelve of my apps were showing some kind of new update or message for me. I looked down at my phone, but didn't click on any of the icons.

Then I walked to the front of the apartment, slid open my huge bay window and side-armed my phone into the Hudson River.

As I watched my phone frisbee out towards the water, I thought about the kid with the floor tile embedded in his skull and answered my own nagging question of how the hell could something like that have possibly happened. Whoever frisbee'd the floor tile into that kid's skull must feel pretty bad right now.

I grabbed a block of wood and walked to the middle of the concrete ice rink that was my floor. I lay down, resting my head on the block of wood, and looked around at the giant brick-and-concrete box I'd saved from so much pointless technology earlier that same day. I wasn't distracted.

I didn't know exactly what would happen next, but I knew what would not happen next. I would not get a new phone. I would not retrieve my laptop from my old apartment. I would not update, post or like anything.

It's not that I have anything against technology. I mean, technology has been very good to me. But I felt like it was necessary for me to take a step back. A step even further back than kyboshing the voice recognition lighting, heating, sound and security that I'd saved my brick-and-concrete box from only a few hours earlier.

Then and there, I decided to divest myself of everything that is digital technology. For how long, I didn't know. Maybe a day or a week or a month. Maybe forever. But lying in my giant brick-and-concrete box, it seemed like the right thing to do. And that sense of right-here-right-now that I'd experienced in the hospital waiting room — that same feeling of experiencing right-here-right-now — seemed to grow as I made my decision.

Chapter Six

"You're an idiot."

Drunk, actually, is what I am. We've been at this bar Mike's Place for two hours drinking Irish whiskey. Whoever Sluggo wanted me to meet, it doesn't look like we'll be seeing them tonight.

I am worse for the wear, while Sluggo looks like he could competently drive a school bus full of kindergarteners on a field trip. I need to get drunk more frequently, raise my tolerance for alcohol.

"Just take a breath and try to understan' what I'm saying," I whine. I know I'm drunk because I never whine when I'm sober.

"I understand what you're saying. It's why I called you an idiot."

"It's an experiment, thas' all. Think about it. In today's world, only someone who's independently wealthy with no interdependencies could possibly pull this off. Think of it as an experiment."

"It's a stupid experiment."

"Why?"

"Because it's getting in the way of me and my once-removed relationship with Clancy."

"No, not true," I say. "I was done with Clancy before I decided to give up digital technology."

"No, you weren't. You broke off your engagement a month after Gwen attacked you."

"Ah, okay, yeah. If you're looking at it from a linear timeline kind of perspective, sure. But what I'm saying is, the same thing that made me want to give up dishital teshonomy is the same thing that made me want to split up with Clancy. I didn't drop Clancy because I gave up dishital teshonomy, I dropped dishital teshonomy and Clancy because of something else that happened in my head."

"Say digital technology again."

"Dishital teshonomy"

"You need a water."

"I agree, sir."

Sluggo waves for the bartender, asks for two waters. Both for me, I assume.

"Is he okay?" the bartender asks.

"He's got money," Sluggo replies. The bartender shrugs and walks away. "Okay, champ. I think I got you a little too drunk to introduce you to the people I mentioned earlier. What I think we need to do is get you home. I'll get an UBER… wait. You can take an UBER, right?"

"It's just a car, right?" I say drowsily.

"Yes, I assume that the UBER I call will be a car. I could try BLADE, but I don't think there's anywhere to land a helicopter around here."

"Yes, I can go with you in an UBER."

"Fine, now pay the man and we'll be on our way."

I reach into my pocket and grab a handful of bills, stick them on the bar, fairly certain that it amounts to two or three times our actual tab, unquestionably certain that shuffling through the bills to achieve a more accurate total isn't worth the effort.

When we pull up to my building, Sluggo reaches across the back seat and grabs my shoulder. "You're going to remember our talk, yeah?"

"I'll remember our talk, yeah," I say, still drowsy but more sober than I was at the bar, "but I'm not getting back together with Clancy just so you can perv on her at close range, dude."

"Selfish. But you're drunk and I'm not asking for any conclusions right now. I just want you to think about it. I also want you to think about this social suicide you're constructing by cutting yourself off from technology. You don't want to keep going down that path, man. You're not going to like where it leads."

"I'll think about it," I reply, wondering what exactly there is to think about. We exit the car, Sluggo takes the elevator to his floor and I walk up the four flights to my apartment.

Just because I saved my double wide, double tall, brick-and-concrete box from the techno travesty that Gwen had designed, it doesn't mean that I haven't made some old school adjustments to support my habitation in the space. In fact, I'd bet that anyone under the age of twelve would think my living quarters are super cool. That said, anyone over the age of twelve would probably find it reminiscent of Hooverville, the make-shift shantytown built by unemployed and destitute people in Central Park during the Great Depression.

My place is huge, so it's never going to look cluttered, but in each of the four corners there is a hodgepodge of dome tents and pillow forts, which is where I do my no-tech daily living. I have a maid service clean the place three times a week, for which I have to pay double the regular price, I think because of the creepy Howard Hughes vibe the place gives off – as opposed to the unconventional cleaning efforts necessary to address tents, sheets, sleeping bags and air mattresses. On the plus side, Clancy hasn't asked to spend the night at my apartment even once since we've been broken up.

Chapter Seven

I've been asleep for minutes, or maybe hours, when I hear the echoing clangs of someone struggling with the crossbar handle mechanism on my enormous, unlocked, industrial steel front door. I quickly hit a button that turns on all the temporary wire-cage construction lights that still hang from my ceiling, thinking someone might be trying to break in and rob me. Instead of fear or outrage, this thought is accompanied by an amped up sense of anticipation. I would be so jacked to see the expression on a burglar's face when he walks in on what he thinks is an ultra-lux penthouse apartment and finds this bizarro set up instead. If I still had my iPhone, I'd be positioning myself to capture a video of the intruder right now.

After about thirty seconds I realize that the person clanging around outside would have to be a fairly incompetent burglar because he still hasn't figured out how to open the unlocked door. I walk over, grab the parallel handles, flip the latch, and swing the door inward.

"Oh, good. You're back," says my brother, Bill, handing me his two-year-old daughter Bitsy. His trouble opening the door obviously has less to do with coordination and more to do with the toddler in his arms. He looks shaken.

"I'm drunk," I say, handing the toddler back to him.

"That's okay. I'm stoned," he says, handing the toddler back to me. Bitsy squeals, laughs like she thinks this is some kind of game. My brother gives Bitsy a look of utter disgust. I decide to hold on to Bitsy for the time being.

"It's almost midnight," I say, glancing at my wind-up watch. "Why's she up?"

"She can't sleep."

"Why are you up?"

"She can't sleep," Bill snarls at his daughter, her tiny head resting on my shoulder.

"I mean, why isn't Betsy taking care of her? You watch her all day, right?"

"Betsy's working late, some big corporate buy-out thing with a deadline."

"She's working past midnight? Are you sure she isn't, like, cheating on you?"

"Pretty sure."

"Why?"

"Because it's been two years and she hasn't lost her pregnancy weight. I don't want to sleep with her so I figure no one else does either," Bill says, matter-of-factly.

"Ah."

"And her personality doesn't much lend itself to attraction, either."

"Right. Okay," I reply, wondering whether I should be more concerned about Bill's negative opinion of his wife or the apathy with which he communicates it. But it's late, so I worry only about steering our conversation to some kind of point. "So, my happily married brother, is there a reason you and your daughter are at my door this late in the evening?"

"Yeah," he blanches, pulls a small tape recorder from his pocket – the type doctors and lawyers used to keep verbal notes in the eighties – and hits record. "I have a favor to ask," he says clearly.

"I'm not taking Bitsy for the night."

"That's not what I was going to ask."

"So, ask what you were going to ask and let me get back to bed," I yawn.

"Is there any way that you could walk the dogs tomorrow?" Bill asks hesitantly.

In addition to managing my building in exchange for free rent, Bill runs a side business walking dogs for my tenants. Ten dollars per dog per walk. Since Sluggo and I are the only people in the building without dogs, this adds up to fifty dollars a day for Bill, cash. And Bill's ball-buster wife, Betsy, knows nothing about this side business or the cash it throws off. Bill uses the dog walking money to buy pot. Betsy doesn't know that Bill smokes pot, either. So, she obviously doesn't know that Bill is stoned for at least five or six hours of his stay-at-home-dad workday. Whatever. I don't have a problem with Bill's lifestyle. Being stoned doesn't interfere with whatever minor fixes Bill needs to take care of around the building and we call contractors for all the major stuff, anyway. And if he's going to be pushing Bitsy around the park in a stroller anyhow, he might as well drag along some dogs and make a few bucks.

When I'd first figured out Bill's routine vis-à-vis the dog-walking and pot buying, I was a little worried about him being stoned all day with Bitsy. But Bill's proven to be a fairly reliable stoner and, if anything, it probably makes him a better day-to-day caregiver for Bitsy, who is not the easiest child in the world.

In fact, the only thing about Bill's whole situation that I do have a problem with is the fact that he is standing in front of me right now, thinking he can ask me to sub in and walk the dogs for him tomorrow.

"Nope," I say.

"Listen, Dan. Believe me. I wouldn't ask if this wasn't, like, an emergency situation." He seems genuinely rattled. Nonetheless, I maintain my position.

"Remember when I agreed to let you have the basement apartment in exchange for managing this building, how we discussed the potential awkwardness of me technically being your boss? How we talked about establishing boundaries and engaging in a professional relationship? And now you're knocking on my door at midnight, asking me to walk your dogs tomorrow. Does that sound like something a building manager – one who isn't my brother, I mean – would be comfortable asking his boss?"

"No, it doesn't. And seriously, if there was anyone else I could ask, I would."

"What about Sluggo?"

"You think I'd ever ask Sluggo to take responsibility for someone's pets?"

"Fair point," I say, nodding. "No."

"No, I shouldn't ask Sluggo…" Bill says hopefully.

"No, I will not walk your dogs. This is a slippery slope, Bill. I understand that you consider me idle rich, but I earned that privilege on my own. You, on the other hand, are not rich. You walk dogs for pot money and subsidize your rent by working as my building manager. If I were to say yes and do your…" air quote, "work," end air quote, "it would open a can of worms that would, I'm afraid, eventually destroy our professional relationship."

"What are you talking about, Dan? I'm a great building manager. When have you ever had any complaints?"

"Bill, your main job requirement is to be physically present in a building where all the tenants, besides Sluggo, me and yourself, work at least ten-to-twelve-hour days. It's a job where I honestly believe that being stoned represents a substantial performance advantage. Sure, you're a good building manager, but is that really the yardstick you want to measure yourself by?"

"That's beside the point," Bill argues limply. "My dog walking side gig has nothing to do with my job as the building manager. So, I'm not asking you as an employee, I'm asking you as a brother," he says, glancing down at the mini tape recorder in his hand and pressing the stop button. "I've got to take Bitsy to the doctor for her two-year-old checkup."

"Can't you reschedule? Or walk the dogs afterwards?"

"This is a reschedule. Betsy made the original appointment two weeks ago. I got stoned and forgot to take her. So, naturally, I lied and told Betsy that I took her to the appointment, no problem, but that the doctor's office told us they were dealing with a huge backlog and Bitsy's blood work might be delayed."

"A clever ruse."

"Thank you. The doctor's office called me earlier today, and a last-minute appointment just opened up. For tomorrow morning. And I've been freaking out that Betsy will eventually get tired of waiting, call the doctor and find out we never showed up for the original appointment."

"I see your dilemma," I say, noticing Bill re-press the record button on the little tape machine. Apparently, he did not want to record anything about missing his daughter's two-year-old check-up.

"Thank you. And when it comes to walking the dogs after we get back, you have no idea how long these doctor appointments might take. The last thing I need is for my dogs doing their business in the tenants' apartments, in case I get held up. That's not fair to the dogs or the tenants."

"True. From a humanitarian perspective, I guess."

"So, I'm asking you as a brother, will you please help me?" Bill looks at me with eyes like a puppy about to be euthanized. You never really stop being a big brother, I guess.

"Bill," I sigh, "I will walk those dogs for you tomorrow."

"You are a saint."

"And you can keep the fifty dollars."

"I don't know how to thank you."

"Just keep being my little brother," I say magnanimously.

"Since I feel like there's so much brotherly love in the room right now, I hope you don't mind if I ask… will you take Bitsy tonight and let me get an hour or two of sleep?"

"No," I say.

Bill turns off the mini tape recorder. I hand over his now-sleeping daughter and escort him out of my apartment.

"Well, thank you, Dan," Bill says, giving me an anxious look.

"What's wrong with you? I said I'd walk the dogs."

"Well, it's just… I spend a lot of time at the dog park, you know?"

"I don't know, but okay."

"And, well, you wouldn't think it, but the dog park is kind of its own social microcosm. And believe it or not, you've got all kinds of weird political relationships and layers of 'these people don't like those people' slants. And, well, spending a lot of time there like I do, I've kind of found a niche where I fit in, see?"

"Ah. You don't want me to screw it up."

"No offence, man. But you're this rich tech hermit and if people find out I'm your brother, then it might upset the balance."

"Bill, nobody at that dog park has any idea who I am."

"You'd be surprised. Anyway, if you could do me a huge favor, please. Just don't engage with them, okay?"

"I don't engage with anyone, anywhere. Why would you think I'd engage with the citizens of your dog park?"

"I know, I know. It's just, you know, my life…" Bill says. I sigh and nod, sympathetic. "For some reason, this whole dog park community is important to me. I mean, I don't have much else," he says silently. I glance at two-year-old Bitsy nestled against his chest and think Bill might want to get some perspective.

"You have nothing to worry about. Hell, I don't even have to go to the dog park. I'll take the dogs for a walk along the waterfront instead."

"Hey, great. Thanks, man. I owe you. Just make sure you bring a lot of bags."

"What's that, now?" I ask.

Bill stops, adjusts Bitsy to a single arm, reaches into his pocket, pulls out the mini tape player and hits the record button.

"You need to take along plenty of little plastic bags when you walk the dogs. You can get them from the owner's apartments, plus I'll drop some off in the morning with the rest of the stuff."

"Why would I need to bring plenty of little plastic bags when I walk the dogs?" Not being a dog owner, the reason doesn't even occur to me.

"To pick up the dog poop," Bill says, a little exasperated.

"I'm not picking up any dog poop," I say, flatly. I have no problem admitting to a childish phobia of all things fecal and/or regurgitated. Blood and urine, not so much. But poop and vomit make me gag. We all have our things.

"It's a New Jersey law that dog walkers, owners and professionals, clean up after their dogs. I'm giving you this information and I will leave you a bunch of little plastic bags tomorrow. If you then decide not to pick up the dog poop on the walk tomorrow, I cannot be held responsible for any consequences that might affect you personally." Bill nods, clicks stop on the recorder. He then turns to walk down the stairs and I shut the door, softly, so as not to wake Bitsy.

Why my brother Bill tape records our late-night conversation is that I have a history of blacking out past eleven p.m. And it's not a drinking thing, even though I was still drunk when he woke me. I've always been like this.

I'm not sure if I'm still asleep or if the part of my brain that tracks memory just doesn't wake up. But ever since I was a kid, if you wake me up at night, there's about a fifty percent chance that I'll dialogue with you like absolutely normal, then go back to sleep and remember none of it.

Bill and I have a history with my disorder, starting one Christmas Eve when I was about twelve, making him about ten. What it was about I'm still not entirely sure, because I don't remember our actual conversation. What I can piece together from Bill's furious ten-year-old accusations is that I hadn't held up my end of some bargain I'd agreed to. So, Bill got in trouble and I, having no recollection of our interaction, ended up being a most unreliable alibi. Since then, especially when a favor is involved, Bill comes prepared. As I have abandoned digital technology, he uses an old-school mini tape player — the kind with a microcassette that I can play on my old-school analog answering machine.

Chapter Eight

I awake the next day with a brutal hangover and absolutely no recollection of a midnight conversation with my brother. As I shuffle towards the Double Layer Waterproof Dome Tunnel Tent I set up to house my bath utilities, I see a microcassette taped to a piece of cardboard that he'd slid under my door. Also taped to the cardboard is a ring of keys, each wearing a little color-coded rubber hoodie. And a list of apartment numbers, each written in a different color Sharpie that matches the color of a key on the ring, each correlated with a name. The names are Oscar and Ginger, Peanut. Tucker, Cooper and Cujo. Only an idiot would be unable to deduce what appears to be expected of me.

I notice one apartment on the list that is not in my building, maybe a block or two away. On top of the list of apartments and names is printed, all caps, "AS DISCUSSED ON TAPE, PLEASE DO NOT ENGAGE AT DOG PARK."

That will be easy, as I have no plans to visit the dog park today. And, having not yet listened to Bill's tape, I have no idea why my brother would have slid his dog walking equipment beneath my door in the first place. And, really, I don't want to know. So, I pick up the cardboard, the colored ring of keys, the color-coded list and the tiny cassette and I toss them all into the trash can outside of the tent I've set up over my open-floor-plan sink, shower and toilet. Hangovers make me dreadful nasty.

After a shower, though feeling only marginally better, I have a bout of conscience and dig the cassette, keys and the list from my trash can. I pop the cassette into my answering machine and hit play. After listening to the prior evening's conversation with Bill, I pop the cassette out of my answering machine and throw it in the garbage can, along with the keys and list. I make myself a cup of coffee and I drink it. Stupid Bill.

I walk to my Ozark Trail Twelve Person Three Room L-Shape Instant Cabin Tent in the northwest corner of my apartment, put on jeans and a t-shirt. Stupid Bill. I pull on a pair of socks. My brother's wonky life is not my problem. I tie my Nike cross trainers. Helping Bill out would only open a can of worms when it comes to our relationship. I actually heard myself tell Bill that on the recording. I grab a Patagonia hoodie from a semi-rigid canvass shelf bin. Even though I clearly agreed to help Bill last night, I think not helping him might actually do Bill a favor in terms of maintaining our relationship boundaries. I walk to the garbage can, retrieve the list and keys. If the bastard had anything at all to offer, I'd be thinking he owes me one. I move towards my front door. Anyway, it's not like I've got anything else to do. And it's a nice day. A walk might not be so bad.

I let myself in to each of the five apartments in my building and collect leashes, dogs and handfuls of little plastic bags. I take the little plastic bags even though there is no way I'm cleaning up after any of these dogs. I negotiate the five dogs through sidewalk traffic. The leashes aren't color coded, so I've already forgotten which name goes with which dog. I realize this might represent a problem when the time comes to return the dogs to their respective apartments, but I let that slide for now.

Reaching the final address on my list, I tie the dogs to a street sign outside of a slummy-looking three-story brownstone. This neighborhood is in transition, not all the buildings updated like mine.

Up the stairs to apartment two-eleven and I'm sticking a key into the lock when I hear a woman's voice, one side of a phone dialogue. I'm not totally sure that the voice is coming from apartment two-eleven, but I knock so as not to intrude. Knock, knock, knock.

"Hang on a second," the voice says, not to me. "Is that you, Dan?"

"Uh… yeah," I say, surprised that she'd know my name.

"Six months ago, you said that raising these funds wouldn't be a problem," says the woman to the phone as she opens the door, leash in hand. "Hold on," she says to the phone. "Who are you?" she asks my face.

Didn't this woman, not three seconds ago, address me by my first name?

"I'm filling in for my brother, uh, Bill," I say to her.

"Well, that's not my problem. Hold on a second," the woman says to the phone. "Sorry. Nice to meet you, Bill. Thanks," she says to my face and hands me a fistful of little plastic bags and a leash attached to some kind of miniature poodle mix.

"Look, we're talking about children, here..." she says to the phone, flashing me a sweet apologetic smile as she shuts the door. Something about her smile makes me feel like I know her, which is weird because I don't know her. I'm pretty sure I've never seen her before. But I have this strange, urgent feeling, like I want to see her again. I shake it off and walk her dog down the stairs.

The six dogs have hit a purposeful stride by the time I reach the waterfront, clearing the sidewalk of non-dog walkers to our left and right, like we're parting the Red Sea. When we reach the waterfront railing, as if they're on the same fecal cycle, they all hunch up and proceed to do their business.

No matter how many little plastic bags I'm carrying, I am not about to start picking up dog poop on this walk. When the last of my charges has given that little shudder-shake to indicate completion, I take a quick glance around and pull the troop to my right, leaving a well-fertilized sidewalk in our wake.

"Uh, you missed a spot," says a voice behind me. Damn it. I just can't cut a break today.

I turn around to see a very tall, very thin, very scraggly man in a very shabby ten-gallon Stetson hat and an equally shabby neon-lime spandex bodysuit, which, judging by the fit of the crotch, is several sizes too small for his frame. If this spandex cowboy is going to call me out for not cleaning up after my dogs, I figure I can call him out for indecent exposure. He's toting leashes attached to what must be at least ten dogs of various shape and size.

Or I could try another angle.

"Thank god," I say, exhaling. "I was hoping someone would show up."

"Your prayers have been answered," the spandex cowboy says.

"Look, I hate to ask this of a brother dog-walker, but I'm in kind of a jam."

"Do tell," the spandex cowboy says kindly, his accent not quite Jersey.

"It's my back. Slipped disc, just went out a few minutes ago. Uh, I'm fine when I'm standing upright, but if I try to bend over and touch the sidewalk, I'm worried I won't be able to straighten up at all," I say, grimacing.

"Not a problem," the spandex cowboy says with a smile, walking behind me. "I can crack your back."

"No, hey. That's not necessary, man." I rotate to remain facing him, my eyes on his bulging neon-lime spandex crotch, which I don't want pressed against my body. "I was just wondering if you could do me a solid and pick up this dog poop."

"Oh, okay," the spandex cowboy says, and with remarkable efficiency gathers all six piles of poop into a single plastic bag. By the time he's finished, the plastic bag is full enough to smear his hand, which, although it doesn't seem to bother him in the least, causes me to dry heave. Twice.

"Ow, dude. You're in some pain, huh? You sure you don't want me to crack your back?" the spandex cowboy asks, trying to circle behind me again, still holding the plastic bag that is oozing fresh dog poop.

"Really, it's okay," I say, pivoting to stay in front of him and simultaneously tangling myself up in the six dog leashes I'm holding. "It comes and goes. Feels fine now. As long as I don't bend over too far, I mean."

"Cool," the spandex cowboy says and stops circling me. Then he looks at the bag and I'm thinking he will finally wipe the smear of poop off his hand. But instead, he just looks at it. Like, studying it. "Looks like Hillary's feeding Ginger that rice meal again."

"You know these dogs?" I ask, amazed at his scatological abilities. I'm pretty sure Ginger is one of the names on my list. "I'm kind of subbing this route today."

"Sure, I know the dogs. And I know the regular walker, Dan."

Now how the hell would he know my name?

"But who are you?" the spandex cowboy asks, extending his poop-smeared hand. I ignore his hand. This is the second time today that someone has addressed me by name and then asked who I am. Surreal. Maybe I'm still asleep and dreaming this whole thing?

"I'm Dan. My brother is the regular dog walker."

"And your name is Dan? Just like Dan?"

"Yeah, just like, uh, Dan. Short for Daniel."

"No, no," the spandex cowboy laughs. "I mean, your parents named you both Dan? That's classic, man. I love it. It's like George Foreman."

"Like George Foreman," I repeat.

"Yeah, you know, the heavyweight champ. The George Foreman Grill guy?"

"I know who George Foreman is."

"Like, how he named all his kids George." I knew that too. What I don't understand is how it has anything to do with me. "Ha! Anyway, is Dan sick or something?" the spandex cowboy asks, suddenly concerned.

And then it clicks. The spandex cowboy thinks my brother's name is Dan. Now why would he think that? And the chick on the phone, my last dog pickup, it has to be the same with her, too.

Please don't engage with the dog park people, Bill had pleaded.

"How well do you know my brother?" I ask the spandex cowboy.

"As well as anyone knows him around here, I guess. I mean, he's friendly with the dog park gang. Not what you'd expect for a rich tech hermit. Then again, I guess you wouldn't expect a rich tech hermit to totally give up technology, would you? I mean, even I've got a cell phone." The spandex cowboy has somehow produced a small, black Motorola flip phone, circa nineteen-ninety, which he is holding in his poop-smeared hand as if to prove his point. I look at his way-too-tight spandex bodysuit and honestly wonder where he could have been hiding the phone.

Oh... also. It's more than a little strange to find out that my brother has been telling people at the dog park that he's me.

Chapter Nine

"Okay, that's fine. But you come down tomorrow and tell these kids they're starting school without the clothes, backpacks, and supplies that you promised. I want to see you say that to their faces…"

Through the door of apartment two-eleven, I hear the phone-voice of the woman who owns the miniature poodle mix. The one that called me Bill and gave me a sweet apologetic smile because she was on the phone when I picked up her dog. I wonder why I'm feeling kind of nervous right now. I don't even know this woman.

"… well, you're the one that made the commitment, so you can be the one to tell the kids." I wonder if she's been talking into the phone since I left her. "They're not my kids either, but they're still kids and they were counting on you."

I'm standing in the hallway like an eavesdropper, hesitant to interrupt, when the dog scratches her door. I hear her footsteps approach so I go ahead and knock.

"Okay, then make the calls and get back to me. Bye." She hangs up the phone and opens the door, wide. "Bastards," she says, not to the phone or to me. "Hi," she says to me. "Bill, right?"

"Bill," I confirm. "Hi."

I've decided that the easiest thing for me to do right now is to pretend I'm Bill so as not to upset my brother's weird applecart. This decision had come to me in a flash, while the spandex cowboy was being fascinated by how both myself and my brother were named Dan, just like the George Foreman family. To realign the spandex cowboy's perception, I simply said, "No, you've misunderstood. My name is Bill and I'm Dan's brother."

To which, the spandex cowboy responded, "Oh, okay. Groovy." And the spandex cowboy did not speak of it again.

"I'm Sarah. Sorry about before," says the woman in the door of apartment two-eleven, looking at the phone in her hand and then at me. I think she has a pretty face, but it's hard to tell behind thick-framed hipster eyeglasses. I've never understood why women wear those. She's not nearly as hot as Clancy is, but there's definitely something pretty about her.

This girl Sarah, she's dressed like, what I'd call homeless chic. Loose cotton layers draped over tight cotton layers, all of the sweatpants and sweatshirt variety. Other than her height, which is maybe a shade under five-foot-four, there is no way to get any kind of read on Sarah's body, aside from the fact that she's got a gimp leg. This I know because she's wearing a giant plastic boot, the sport-medicine type, which would have maybe been a plaster cast twenty years ago.

"Oh, yeah," Sarah says, noticing me noticing the boot. "It comes off on Monday, thank God. Then I can go back to walking Cujo myself."

"Cujo," I say with a smirk, though not unkindly.

"I know, I know. I thought it would be funny – ironic, because of how small he is. But now it just seems kind of stupid and obvious."

"So why don't you change it?"

"He's three years old."

"Oh," I say, not sure why that would matter. I mean, it's just a dog.

"You're Bitsy's father, right?" I suppose, in this context, a nod would be the appropriate response. So, I nod. It's possible she's expecting me to gush about my two-year-old daughter the way parents sometimes do, but I can only carry this charade so far. "Where is she today?"

"Who?"

"Bitsy."

"Oh, she has a doctor's appointment."

"Did Betsy take off work?" So, Sarah's familiar with some details of my life. Bill's life, I mean.

"Ah, no."

"So, who's taking her to the doctor's?"

"Uh… Dan?" I should have just said that Betsy took the day off. Stupid.

"Your brother is taking your daughter to her doctor's appointment? And you're walking his dogs?" Sarah asks, incredulously.

"He likes his afternoon time with her," I say and change the subject. "So, how well do you know Dan?"

"Pretty well, I guess. We met at the dog park. Your brother is a complicated guy, if you don't mind me saying." Sarah, you have no idea.

"I don't mind. How so?"

"You know, a rich tech guy who totally gives up technology, lives like a hermit. Walks neighborhood dogs just because it gives him a sense of peace."

"Yeah," I nod. I guess the pot Bill buys with his dog walking money also gives him a sense of peace. As well as the confidence to lie to everyone in the neighborhood about who he is. Bill's always been a fantastic liar, I recall.

"And the whole IRS audit thing, how they froze all of his accounts." *What's that, now?*

"Come again?" I blurt, staring at Sarah in a complete state of shock.

"You know, how he has all this money and he can't get to any of it because the IRS has frozen his accounts while they investigate the sale of his business?"

I stare at Sarah in a complete state of shock.

"You knew about that, right?" she asks, a bit anxious.

I stare at Sarah in a complete state of shock.

"Tell me you knew about that," she says, pleading. "He wasn't keeping it from you and your parents, was he? Was he? Oh, my God, he was!"

I stare at Sarah in a complete state of shock.

"Aw, man! I can't believe I just did that. I feel like such an idiot! He told me not to tell anyone. I – I assumed you knew!"

I stare at Sarah in a complete state of shock. Why the hell would my brother ever make up something like that? It's bad enough that he's telling these randoms that he's me. Financially ruining me in the process just seems like an unnecessarily cruel thing to do.

"I wasn't aware of that, no." I reply, taking a deep breath.

"Look, I feel terrible about this. He probably didn't want you to worry because you manage his building. Hey, I mean, he told me he's got top lawyers and accountants working on this. I'm sure it will all blow over, you know, real soon. And, like, he told me the building is fine. Apparently, they're not even going after the building."

Sure, why would the IRS go after a recently purchased, mid-seven-figure real estate investment? Like my brother, Sarah obviously knows nothing about how the Internal Revenue Service works. I have to keep reminding myself that none of this is real. My sale was legitimate, and I paid a boat-load of taxes. Literally. I mean, you could probably have filled a boat with the amount of tax money I paid to the government after I sold my company.

"Well, that's good, I guess. About the building, I mean. Sorry, this is all coming as kind of a shock," I mumble.

"It's me that should be sorry. It was so totally not my place to say anything. I mean, just so you know, he really didn't seem worried about it at all. Like, at all. He just acted like it's one of those things that happen when you sell…"

"Hey," I interrupt her, "I don't mean to pry or anything, but how is it that Dan came to share all of this information with you?"

"Well, see, I do pro-bono work for this non-profit called Way-Stop. It helps homeless people get back on their feet. And, well, I don't usually do much fund raising or anything, but Way-Stop kind of lives hand-to-mouth and it sort of overextended itself…"

Ah.

"I mean, Way-Stop is always overextended, but it was in a crunch so I…"

"So, you asked Dan for money."

"Yeah, I mean, not a lot or anything. Way-Stop just had to make rent — which it did, eventually, even though we were a little late. I mean, we lease this old warehouse building on the waterfront and the landlord has been pressing us hard about paying the rent on time. I think he's looking for a loophole to kick us out. Anyway, so I asked Dan for a couple thousand dollars and, yeah, that's how it came up, I guess. Hey, look, I'm really sorry…"

"So, did my brother, like, say he would help you out when all of his tax stuff gets cleaned up? When his accounts are unfrozen, I mean?" I wouldn't put it past the bastard.

"No, no. I mean, it was just a one-time ask. And it's not like I was asking him to make some kind of endowment or anything. I was just looking for a couple thousand bucks to make rent is all…"

"A couple thousand bucks to rent a whole warehouse?" You couldn't get a bathroom in my building for two-thousand bucks.

"We only rent the first two floors, but other than us it's been empty, like, forever. I imagine the owner wants to sell it, but is waiting for the neighborhood to turn around."

"That's happening a lot in Jersey City these days."

"Yeah, I know. But in the meantime, they lease it to us for cheap. The building is perfect for Way-Point – walking distance to the free healthcare clinic, the schools, the food bank and the subways. It's shabby and run-down, but it's well insulated so it holds heat in the winter and doesn't get too hot in the summer."

"How long has Way-Point been there?" I ask.

"Going on three years now."

"Where was it before?"

"Anywhere and everywhere. See, before the warehouse, Way-Stop would rent space at churches or community centers for, like, a month at a time. Sometimes even a week at a time. It was hard on the families, moving around like that. Having a fixed space is such a huge help. But, like you said, the neighborhoods are all upgrading. And our landlord knows it, which is why we're on a month-to-month lease. And, like I said earlier, Way-Point isn't the best tenant when it comes to paying rent on time. I'm just hoping the owner sits on the building for as long as possible. He's had prospective buyers walk through the space a few times, so everyone at Way-Point is kind of holding their breath," Sarah says, sadly.

"I can't imagine that a building filled with homeless people makes for a very attractive sale," I say casually. Sarah looks at me like I'm part of the problem.

"You know nothing about the homeless, do you?"

"Uh, no," I say with a sudden twinge of shame, even though, why would I? I mean, all I know about the homeless is what I see on the street. The leather-skin bag lady arguing with herself, the wild beard guy passed out in a filthy blanket fort, runaway kids in dirty hoodies with vacant drug stares. People so far gone that it's impossible for me to relate to them on a species-level, much less empathize.

"Way-Stop isn't a shelter. It's a second chance. Do you know that over sixty percent of the homeless population in this area is made up of survivors of domestic abuse? We help a lot of moms and their kids who are running away from something terrible, figuring out how to start a new life. Do you know how many people live paycheck-to-paycheck around here? We help dads, too. Guys who lost their jobs through no fault of their own, help them get back on their feet. We give them food and a place to sleep, yeah, but we also have career counseling, job placement services, whatever they need to get a foothold and start to climb their way back to financial independence. Most people don't think about it at all. If they do, they think there's only one category of homeless people. You've got to remember, not everyone is lucky enough to have a rich brother who owns a building…" Sarah puts her hand to her mouth and we stare at each other through a thick awkward pause. "I can't believe I just said that. Sometimes my mouth gets away from me, obviously. I didn't mean to imply…"

"That's okay," I say, impressed by her passion. Wondering if there's anything I'm so passionate about. I wonder this for less than a second because the answer is so clearly, no.

Sarah pulls on a strand of hair that's come loose from her ponytail, sticks the end in her mouth. Nervous habit, I'm guessing. Not something that I would ever have considered cute before. The phone in Sarah's hand rings, she rolls her eyes behind the thick-frame hipster glasses.

"Anyway, it was nice to meet you. And thank you for walking Cujo. And, like, again I'm sorry that you had to find out about your brother's financial problems from me. But don't worry," her phone rings a third time. "Well, uh, bye."

Closing the door to apartment two-eleven, Sarah answers the phone and asks whoever is on the other end, "What have you got for me?"

Chapter Ten

"No, no, honey. Not yet. Don't fall asleep just yet. I know you're tired after those shots, but wait until we get to the bedroom so Bitsy and Daddy can both take a nap together. You still with me there, Bits?"

"Hello, Dan," I say from a shadow on Bill's couch.

"Jesus!" Bill startles. Bitsy starts to cry. "What the hell, man?! I could have dropped… Oh, wait. You just called me Dan, didn't you?" he says over the crying baby. "Give me a second. I need to put her down for a nap."

Bill spends five minutes calming and tucking in an exhausted Bitsy. He spends another five minutes getting high in his bathroom. I sit the dark apartment. I am in no rush.

"Oh. Hey, man. You're still here, huh?" Bill says, walking back into the living room.

"Remember when we discussed you living here?" I ask quietly, "The boundaries? The importance of maintaining a professional relationship despite the fact that we're brothers?"

"Who'd you talk to?" Bill sighs.

"I'd say that you have spectacularly failed to hold up your end of that bargain."

"It was Siobhan, wasn't it? The nanny? The freaking Irish just love to gossip. Can't keep their mouths shut about anything."

"It wasn't Chevron or… whatever name you just said."

"Siobhan. It's spelled S-I-O-B-H-A-N, but you say it like, 'Shev-on.' It's Irish. She's cute, right? But don't trust her. She's obviously a blabbermouth."

"I didn't meet anyone named Siobhan," I say calmly.

"It was Virginia, right? Freaking Virginia Waddle, crazy pet rescue lady. With all the skeletons she's got in her closet, you'd think she'd show just a bit of discretion…"

"It wasn't anyone named Virginia and stop avoiding the subject."

"Just tell me who it was."

"Why?"

"So I can, you know, figure out what scenario I'm dealing with, here," Bill blurts out, and then considers what he just said. "Uh, oops."

"Approximately how many different paths has my life taken on your dog walking adventures, Bill?"

"Not that many," Bill says sheepishly. "Come on, who was it?"

"The spandex cowboy," I say finally, because I doubt this conversation will move forward until I tell him.

"Who?"

"Spandex cowboy," I repeat.

"You mean Rolf?" Bill asks, incredulously.

"Ralph?" I ask his ask.

"Rolf," Bill repeats. "Tall guy, kind of bohemian?"

I shrug, that could be anyone.

"Walks a whole bunch of dogs?"

I shrug again. I saw a lot of walkers with big dog herds.

"Cowboy hat and tight green onesie?" Bill asks.

"You couldn't have gotten that from me calling him the spandex cowboy?"

"Right. That's Rolf. He's from Hamburg." The fact that the spandex cowboy is from Germany somehow makes him a little creepier than I'd originally thought. "Rolf, huh?" Bill continues introspectively. "Now, that's surprising. I mean, what does he even know about me? What did he tell you? Nothing, right?"

"Aside from indirectly letting on that you have been impersonating me, no. Nothing else of substance. He's actually a pretty nice guy when you get past the whole weirdo outfit thing. That and the whole personal hygiene thing, which is obviously a challenge for him. Didn't say much, just followed me around cleaning up after the dogs. I didn't get a German accent."

"You only hear it when he says certain words. Wow... Rolf. Well, it could have been worse," Bill says with a shrug.

"You know, for someone that's been outed in a fairly shameful and humiliating series of lies, you're acting astoundingly glib about all of this."

"Thanks, man," Bill says sincerely. "To tell you the truth, keeping you in the dark about all of it was kind of a drag. Plus, I'm a bit stoned so that helps."

"And..." I say.

"And?" Bill asks.

"So..."

"So?"

"Christ, man. It's not like I'm making some kind of righteous demand for an explanation, but I am a little curious."

"Oh, why I did it, you mean?"

"Yeah."

"Come on, Dan. You don't have to be a genius to figure that one out, do you?" Bill says, rolling his eyes. "Look at my life, man. I'm an unemployed twenty-seven-year-old dad – from an unplanned pregnancy, I might add – who's married to a fat, ball-busting harpy and living in the crummy basement apartment of my successful brother's building."

"Hey, man, this apartment is just as nice as all the others," I say, mildly offended.

"Whatever. Jesus, it would be weird if I didn't lie about my life in the one ecosystem where people don't know what a loser I am."

"You make a valid point," I say. "But why me? Why didn't you just make up a name and a life?"

"I don't know. It's not like I planned any of this. I was walking the dogs and met Siobhan at the park a few months ago and it just came out. I guess

I needed a solid frame of reference for it to be believable – subconsciously, I mean. Anyway, what with you dropping technology and living like a hermit in that shanty town you built on the top floor, I figured, who would ever find out?"

"Right," I say. "Sensible."

"And it's not like I'm doing any real harm, huh? I mean, it's a victimless crime, isn't it? When are you ever going to cross paths with these people?"

"Oh, I don't know. Maybe, like, when you ask me to walk your dogs? I mean, really, Bill. What were you thinking?"

"I was in a bind, Dan. And the chance of you finding out wasn't even in the same risk-assessment ballpark as what would have happened if Betsy found out I'd forgotten about Bitsy's two-year-old checkup. Plus, I don't know… maybe a part of me wanted you to find out. It's a drag trying to keep track of who thinks what. I mean, this whole dog park soap opera I've created has gotten kind of complicated," Bill says, collapsing into a full body sigh.

"How complicated?"

"I don't know, man," Bill says, sheepish. "Once I crossed the line and pretended I was you, I just kind of ran with it. You know, different stories for different people. It really got my creative juices flowing. And the people at the dog park, like, they aren't too bright. So that helped."

"Example."

"Okay, so, for example, you know Siobhan?"

"No, I don't."

"Right, but I mentioned her. Well, Siobhan, she might have gotten the idea that I am actually Bitsy's biological father."

"She might have?"

"Well, she did. I told her I am Bitsy's biological father."

"Okay. So, like, you essentially just told her the truth."

"I guess you could look at it that way."

"How might one look at it otherwise?" I ask.

"Well, she thinks I'm you, right? So, I told her that your brother, who is really me… Actually, maybe it's easier if I just use our first names?"

"If that would help."

"Okay, so I'm Dan, and I tell Siobhan that my brother, Bill, had been dating this nun in training…"

"A nun."

"Siobhan's Irish."

"Ah."

"Anyway, this apprentice nun, she decides to leave the convent before taking her final vows to pursue her relationship with Bill. And the very same day she leaves the convent, Bill gets in a car crash. Hit by a drunk driver."

"Huh. Was it bad?"

"Terrible. Bill was in a coma. So, yeah. And this newly minted ex-nun, she was in a tailspin. She can't go back to the convent. Her fiancé is in a coma…"

"Oh, they'd gotten engaged?"

"Well, yeah. She wasn't dropping her final vows for some fling. This was the real thing."

"Lovely," I say. "Go on."

"So, Bill's brother, Dan, shows up at the hospital and he's just as distraught as the ex-nun because Bill is the only family he has left…"

"What about Mom and Dad?"

"They died of influenza when the boys were teenagers. It was tragic. So, both Dan and this ex-nun are a total wreck. Neither can leave Bill's bedside. So, you know, they start to comfort each other. Then after a few days, one thing leads to another and though it was nobody's fault, the two end up having sex. Right there in the same hospital room where Bill is out cold in a coma."

"Harsh."

"It was sweet, really. They both loved Bill so much that they couldn't contain it. The love they had for Bill, kind of, spilled over onto, into, each other."

"You ever think about writing some of this stuff down? Instead of, like, creating a web of lies in real life?"

"Real people are more exciting. I like to think on my feet."

"Okay, whatever. And then?" I ask.

"Well, then, miraculously Bill comes out of his coma."

"While Dan and the ex-nun were having sex?"

"No, it was like the next day or something. But anyway, Bill ends up marrying the girl, never knowing that his bride had sex with his brother, Dan. And nine months later, a baby. That's why Dan asked Bill – begged him really – to move into his building. That's why Dan spends time with Bitsy whenever he can, like at the dog park, where he dotes on his illicit daughter and dreams about the only woman he ever felt connected to…"

"Betsy."

"What about her?" Dan asks, pulled from his reverie.

"Betsy, your wife. That would be the ex-nun, no?"

"Hell, no. Bill's first bride died in childbirth. He married Betsy on the rebound. Regrets it every day. And no matter how much money Dan has, no matter how many women are available to him – women like Siobhan, if you know what I mean – Dan just can't seem to let go of that one true someone, even though she was his for only the briefest, fleeting moment."

"Well, that *is* a beautiful story," I say.

"Thank you. It means a lot for you to say so."

"And Siobhan, she bought all of this?" I ask, bringing us back to the real world.

"Sure. I mean, why would anyone make up a story like that?"

"That's an excellent question," I say. "Did Siobhan find it odd that you decided to spill your guts to some random stranger at a dog park?"

"Not really. We'd said hi a few times before and one day she asked if something was bothering me because I looked glum. And that's when Dan spilled everything to her. He'd never told another soul about any of this before his breakdown with Siobhan. She's really a special girl. Which is why I was so worked up when I thought she'd, you know, let the cat out of the bag to you."

"Which she didn't."

"I know. I never should have doubted her. She's got connections with the IRA, you know?"

"The IRA?"

"Yeah, she lives in this apartment building that's, like, eighty percent Irish. Big time IRA supporters. Those people know how to keep a secret."

"And yet she told you about her connections to the IRA. Shouldn't that have been a secret?"

"Huh. I didn't think of that. Maybe she is kind of a blabbermouth. Go figure."

"Well, you're rich. I'm rich, I mean. Maybe she was just trying to open a door that might lead to financial support of some kind, for the IRA, that is."

"Maybe. Yeah, that's probably it."

"Yeah," I say. "So, how about you tell me about the IRS freezing all of Dan's accounts?"

"Aw, man," Bill slumps backwards on the couch. "You talked to Sarah, too?"

Chapter Eleven

Why I really decided to totally unplug from technology and live a tent-hermit life in a giant brick-and-concrete box is, it was kind of like a suicide. I know that sounds morbid, but what else would you call it? That guy who had over two-hundred thousand people following his snarky one-liners on Twitter, he's gone now. Might as well have been hit by a bus. No more pictures going up on his Instagram account. You can't Snapchat him or follow the *Coming Attractions* reel of his life on Facebook. That guy no longer contributes to the surplus content problem. Your e-mails, texts and voice mails will go unanswered.

That guy is dead. Technical homicide. Digital suicide. Whatever.

You have to be financially independent if you're really going to unplug. You can't have a job and not have a smart phone, an e-mail address, a LinkedIn account. Who would hire you? How would they get hold of you?

Now, I'm the guy sitting in Starbucks, drinking a Venti black half-caf, all alone among herds of people hopping from platform to platform in the Cloud. I'm the guy who isn't looking at his phone. I'm the guy people-watching in the old school physical world. I'm the guy counting sheep.

I don't hold any grudge against digital technology. I don't think I'm any better than all of those people with eyes and thumbs glued to their phones. I just don't think I'm going to find anything meaningful out where digital technology seems to be leading people. And I'm not one to keep walking down a road when I know it's a dead end.

Not that I know what I'll find in the unplugged world, either. I just think, maybe, if I disconnect I'll be able to actually connect with... something, anything. Either way, for me, being unplugged is better than running out my life on the back of one distraction after another. Although there are times in life when a distraction would be very welcome.

"Put it away, Mom. Dan doesn't do smart phones," Clancy says, rolling her eyes like I'm the vegan killjoy at a great steak place.

"I just want to show him Jenny's new house," call-me-Mandy says, her phone thrust in front of my face at an angle that makes it impossible for me to avoid looking at her exposed right breast. I don't even know who this Jenny is.

"I'm just taking a break from technology," I say, trying to avoid eye-contact with call-me-Mandy's nipple. Every time I've ever been with Clancy's mom, her breasts have made an impromptu appearance.

"And, Jesus, cover yourself up, Mom!" Clancy whines. Call-me-Mandy pantomimes mortification and adjusts her collar. I've seen her breasts so many times that I could sketch them from memory. When she's with her mom, it's the only time that Clancy seems able to avoid accidentally flashing her own body parts. Go figure.

"Anyway, Jenny just closed on this *gi*-normous place outside of Greenwich. What'd it cost her, Ben? Two point four or something? And what she's going to do with all that space is beyond me. So, why are we eating dinner at two p.m.? And why are we at Applebee's?"

Call-me-Mandy is a rather erratic conversationalist.

"It's the Early Bird Special. And I wanted to treat you guys to an authentic Jersey experience," I say, wide smile as our waitress approaches the table. "Plus, this neighborhood gets a little sketchy after dark."

Call-me-Mandy's eyes widen. She is so not comfortable here, with the other ninety-nine-point-nine percent.

"Welcome to Applebee's. My name is Mandy and I'll be taking care of you today."

"Well, then. My name is Mandy, too," call-me-Mandy says to the waitress. Not like it's a happy coincidence. More like she's expecting some kind of explanation. Waitress Mandy stares at the exposed breast that has, once again, freed itself from call-me-Mandy's shirt and then averts her eyes.

"Johnny Walker Black, double, neat." I have a feeling these will be the only words coming out of Ben's mouth this afternoon.

"Do you have wine, dear?" Call-me-Mandy asks waitress Mandy. Her breast has somehow found its way back into her shirt.

"Yes."

"Oh, goody. Is there a wine list, then?"

"It's on the back of the menu," waitress Mandy replies.

"Oh, how quaint," call-me-Mandy says, flipping the menu. Then she frowns and tells the waitress, this won't do.

"Just get a drink, Mom," Clancy says, turning to waitress Mandy. "She'll have a Moscow Mule, Tito's vodka, extra lime. Same for me."

"Just bring me whatever light beer you have on tap, a big one," I say.

"Twenty-ounces."

"Unless they come any bigger." A few months ago, I switched from small-batch craft beers to trashy domestic lights, recognizing that, when it comes to beer, I appreciate volume more than I do taste. Kind of trailer park, sure, but I'm getting older and need to start making some compromises in the interest of my health. Plus, with the low alcohol content, I can drink, like, six giant beers and still drive. Not that I ever take my car out these days, but it's good to know.

"I'll get your drinks and give you a minute to look at the menu."

"Oh, I won't be needing this, dear," call-me-Mandy says to waitress Mandy, handing her the menu. "I brought my own."

"You brought your own menu?" waitress Mandy asks, confused.

"I brought my own food," call-me-Mandy clarifies.

"Mom!" Clancy whisper-shouts. "Sorry," she says to waitress Mandy, who shrugs and heads to the bar to grab our drinks.

"What?" Call-me-Mandy looks at Clancy, like, what'd I do? "You don't expect me to eat the food here, do you?"

"You could be a little more discreet," Clancy says, another eye roll.

"I'm drinking their booze. That should be sufficient. You don't think it's watered down, do you? I'll bet it's not really Tito's, the vodka we get."

"It will be fine, Mom."

"In places like this, we need to be worried about the bartender putting Rohypnol in our drinks. Two attractive women like us. So, do we have a date, or what?" Call-me-Mandy has suddenly shifted topics to our wedding date. Not only are Clancy and I still dating, apparently, we are still engaged.

"Mom, we're not in any kind of rush. Back off, huh?"

"And when are we going to see your place?" Call-me-Mandy asks me directly. "Though I still don't understand why anyone would buy a building on this side of the river, in the suburbs."

"Well, I grew up in New Jersey, so I like it here. And the Jersey City waterfront isn't really considered a suburb. I'd be happy to show it to you anytime," I say.

"We'll just wait until it's finished," Clancy adds quickly.

"It's been almost a year since you bought the building, hasn't it?" Call-me-Mandy asks me.

"More than, actually," I reply.

"And it still isn't finished?"

"Back off, Mom," Clancy says, as waitress Mandy sets down our drinks.

"You can bring me another one of these," Ben says to waitress Mandy.

"Ben, it's the middle of the afternoon," call-me-Mandy says.

"Keep'em coming," Ben says to waitress Mandy, ignoring his wife. You have to admire a man who has so thoroughly given up on life.

"So, do we want to get started with any appetizers? Or are you all set to order?" waitress Mandy asks sweetly.

"I'll just have the Caesar salad, no dressing, no croutons, no cheese," Clancy says, not looking at the menu.

"Do you want the soup and salad combo? It's just three dollars extra."

"What's the soup?" Clancy asks.

"Cheeseburger."

"Cheeseburger soup?"

"It's actually pretty good," waitress Mandy says. "Want to give it a try?"

"What do you think?" Clancy asks, staring down waitress Mandy.

"Okay, just the lettuce, then." Waitress Mandy looks at call-me-Mandy, who waves her off with a turned head and show of palm.

"Ribs, full rack. Extra cornbread," Ben says to waitress Mandy.

"Ben, your cholesterol!" Call-me-Mandy says.

"Extra barbeque sauce, too," Ben says to waitress Mandy, who jots a note, looks at me.

"I'll have the cheeseburger soup," I say, causing both Clancy and call-me-Mandy to gasp. "And a full rack of ribs, same style as his," I tilt my head towards Ben, "and you can bring me one more of these, too," I hold up my twenty-ounce beer mug, already two-thirds empty in the time it took for waitress Mandy to take our orders.

"I have to use the restroom," Clancy says, getting up from the table. Call-me-Mandy follows automatically. I empty my beer. Ben takes a long, slow pull of his Johnny Walker Black.

"If I were you," Ben whispers, as if to himself, "I would walk out of this restaurant, go very far away, and never look back." Good ol' Ben. I say nothing in response and we sit in silence until Clancy and her mom come back.

"What were you two talking about?" Call-me-Mandy asks playfully.

"Life," I say. As in, Ben's apparent life sentence with call-me-Mandy. I wonder why he doesn't just divorce her, maybe have her killed. Then again, here I am pretending to be engaged to my ex-girlfriend in front of her parents. The women in Clancy's family seem to have a way of getting what they want from the men in their lives.

Waitress Mandy brings my soup and I dig in. I usually eat fairly healthy, but have decided to run with this whole Applebee's experience – if only to gross out Clancy and her mom. I'm usually not passive aggressive, either. But with Clancy, I give myself a pass.

"That is, quite possibly, the most disgusting thing I have ever seen," Clancy says as I slurp a chunk of ground beef from broth the color and consistency of Cheese-Wiz.

Call-me-Mandy daintily removes a small, black lacquer box from her Ferragamo bag. She opens the box, takes out a smooth grey stone and sets it on the table. I continue to slurp my soup as she slides two long, thin black lacquer rods from beneath the box. Chopsticks, I realize, as she fits them into her hand and makes a practice pinching motion, then sets them down on the table, ends resting on the grey stone.

From the lacquer box, call-me-Mandy then removes a small, rectangular plate holding two thin pieces of maguro sushi. Fresh basil and fleshy ginger on the side. Next to the plate, she places a small square dish, which she fills with soy sauce from a tiny bottle. Then she takes a deep, cleansing breath. I considerately place an oversized plastic bottle of Heinz

Ketchup on the edge of her placemat. Call-me-Mandy looks at the Ketchup, closes her eyes and takes another cleansing breath.

Ben waves at the waitress, holds up his empty rocks glass. I scoop the dregs of my Cheeseburger soup from the bottom of the crock.

Clancy sits, her chin resting on her palm, looking at her mother, who is doing breathing exercises in front of her miniature sushi garden amidst the clamor of an Applebee's lunch hour. Clancy looks at her mother with what I think is admiration. Respect for someone who, despite all the harsh evidence of reality, can fuel complete fantasy by an overwhelming power of will. I place a large plastic canister of Heinz Yellow Mustard at the edge of call-me-Mandy's placemat.

"Stop it, Dan," Clancy says, spell broken.

This is another reason that I unplugged. The magic of digital technology makes it too easy to live a fantasy on these hundreds of planets in the Cloud. Makes it too easy for everyday people to escape reality. Not to mention the fact that it takes something away from a top-tier elite pro fantasist like call-me-Mandy, who had spent a lifetime perfecting her talents before the advent of everyday technology.

"Go ahead, Mom," Clancy says, meaning go ahead and eat.

"Don't be silly, dear," call-me-Mandy replies, eyes closed. "I'll wait for you."

Chapter Twelve

So it turns out that Clancy, Ben and call-me-Mandy are meeting Gwen for Happy Hour at the Soho House, to which I am, thankfully, not invited. Clancy gives me a lingering kiss on the lips – "For show," she whispers – and they all get into an UBER. I head into the late day sunshine, walking through the meat of Jersey City until I hit the waterfront and turn north towards my building.

"Hey, mister! Little help!" A tennis ball bounces from a wide courtyard at my right, straight into the traffic on my left. The tennis ball hits a moving car, bounces back to the gutter on my side of the street. The car doesn't stop.

"You have to get it yourself, Alex! Other people can't do your fielding for you!"

"They can if it was foul!"

"It wasn't foul. It was straight up the middle!"

"It hit a car – that's a foul ball! Look it up!" The kid who is Alex shouts, as if, somewhere, there's a rule book for stick ball that can settle this dispute. I jog over to the gutter, pick up the ball.

"Don't get too close!" One kid who isn't Alex shouts. "He's probably a pedophile!"

"I'm not a pedophile," I say, tossing Alex the ball, impressed with the vocabulary of his friend, warped though it might be.

"How do we know you're not a pedophile," Alex says, doesn't ask.

"Because I'm not dressed up like a clown or a priest," I reply flatly.

"That's just in movies," Alex says, and I wonder what movies these kids have been watching. "Pedophiles can look like anyone. The policeman talked to us about it just last week."

"Well, maybe, but you can't just go around calling random people pedophiles. It's not nice. So why don't you just come over here and we can hug it out." I open my arms and Alex gives me a double-take. Then we both laugh. This kid Alex is probably only eight or nine years old, but I always give kids the benefit of the doubt when it comes to inappropriate humor.

"You're all right, dude," Alex says smiling, turns and jogs towards the other kids, shouts backwards at me, "... for a pedophile!"

Something about a pre-tween city kid making light of a serious issue like pedophilia makes me go all mushy inside, like maybe the world isn't so screwed up after all. I continue to head North. When I reach the end of the block, I see what looks like a person being devoured by a giant cluster of knapsacks. Really, it's like... picture how a big bunch of multi-colored helium balloons looks when someone is holding them by the strings. Then, change the balloons into knapsacks and drop the bunch down so it's covering the holder's everything from the knees up. That's what's walking towards me. And what's even weirder, one leg underneath the bunch of knapsacks is wearing this giant plastic boot, the sport-medicine type, which I recognize from walking Bill's dogs just yesterday. Sarah, the woman in apartment two-eleven. What are the chances?

I approach the knapsack cluster as it continues walking towards me. I move in gingerly and try to juggle a few of the backpacks away from Sarah's face – without breaking her stride – when a little fist shoots out from the cluster and punches me right in the throat. I drop to a knee, gasping, white lights flashing behind my eyes, and some part of me seriously wondering how she could possibly have had a free arm while holding all of those backpacks.

The cluster of backpacks lowers itself, en masse, to the sidewalk and out of this intact cave climbs Sarah. Oh, I see. She's got some kind of rigging in there that she's hooked with the backpacks. Clever. I haven't taken a breath for what seems like forever and my throat apparently doesn't want to cooperate in reversing that trend. My eyes are full of water, which is, frankly, embarrassing. But I'm not crying or anything, Sarah just messed up all the tubes in my head with that throat punch.

"Oh, my God!"

"Hello, Sarah," I finally wheeze. "Do you need some help with those?"

"Oh, my God, Bill! Oh, my God," Sarah gasps, addressing me as my brother, naturally. "I… I thought you were trying to steal them…"

"Yeah, I got that," I rasp, massaging my throat.

"You should have said something!"

"Hindsight."

"Oh, my God, Bill. Are you okay? Are you okay? Seriously, are you okay?" And even though my nose is running and my eyes tearing and I still can hardly breathe, it's starting to piss me off that this five-foot-four, one-hundred-twenty-pound little lady is asking if she hurt me too badly. Still, I reason, size doesn't have much to do with any kind of throat punch – much less the Krav Magna blast she just laid on me. I'm lucky she wasn't carrying her keys. So I try to contain my machismo indignation, which would be a lot easier if Sarah would stop asking me if I'm okay. She's like a broken record.

"I'm fine. I'm fine," I gasp. "Women hit me in the throat all the time." Sarah stops asking if I'm okay and raises her eyebrow. "Not really," I say. "I was making a joke."

Sarah smiles, tender, and looks past me. I turn my head to see maybe ten of the stickball kids charging the sidewalk towards us.

That's just great, I think. I get beat up by a girl and then have to face attempted rescue by a cavalry of eight-year-olds. I struggle to rise from bent knee, walk towards the kids with my palms up, trying to gesture that all of this was just a misunderstanding. The cavalry continues its charge and I'm waving my hands, showing that everything is okay. As they continue to run towards us I'm a little worried that they will tear Sarah to shreds, but a part of me is totally digging the fact that I made such an impression on the kids. That's the thing about kids, I think. You treat them like peers with a little inappropriate humor and, like, they imprint on you.

As the kids close in, I pat the air with a crooked, patronizing smile – a smile that says I really don't need a bunch of little kids to rescue me, but thanks for the thought – and then they run right past me. They run, whooping and hollering, to the cave of backpacks that Sarah left on the sidewalk.

And now, my humiliation is complete.

"You got 'em, Miss Sarah! I knew you would!"

"You came through, Miss Sarah!"

"Can we pick our own colors, Miss Sarah?!"

"Hey, Miss Sarah," says a small voice behind me. "Why'd you punch out the pedophile?"

"Alex! Bill's not a pedophile!" Sarah shouts admonishingly. "Wait, I mean, you're not, like, a registered sex offender or anything, right?"

"No, I am not," I say weakly.

"No, he is not," Sarah says to Alex, who shrugs and walks over to the backpacks. "Careful, guys — they're full of school clothes and supplies. Don't open them until we're back in the building."

Within seconds, the kids have stripped Sarah's makeshift rigging and are carrying all the knapsacks back down the street. I walk over, pick up Sarah's rig, and follow her.

"I'm sorry for punching you," she says over her shoulder.

"Can we maybe let that go?" I ask. "Anyway, you carried that rig full of backpacks all the way from your apartment? It must weigh a hundred pounds."

"Not that much, actually. The clothes and school supplies aren't heavy."

"And on a bad foot?"

"It wasn't like I was going to fit all that in an UBER, right? Anyway, this boot thingy comes off on Monday so it's probably a good start to my physical therapy." Sarah keeps walking, turns into the large courtyard where the kids had been playing stickball.

"Where'd you learn to make this kind of a rig?" I ask, holding up what looks like a frame of bamboo.

"Ecuador. I used to volunteer there."

"Of course you did," I say, my embarrassment about getting beat up by a girl being eclipsed by a new embarrassment associated with my wasted life.

"Well, we're here," Sarah says, stopping in front of a decrepit-looking brick warehouse on the far rear of the black asphalt courtyard. The warehouse is maybe five or six stories high, looks like it backs up all the way to the waterfront, and is tightly flanked by two larger buildings on its left and right, which extend all the way to the sidewalk. We're only about six blocks from my place, but I'd never noticed the courtyard or warehouse before. It looks like it was built with great care about a hundred years ago, and not at all maintained since.

"This place is kind of a hole, isn't it?"

"Hey!" Sarah says, punching my arm. "Yeah, it's a little run down, I guess. But it's what Way-Point can afford. And like I said the other day, having a permanent spot is so much better than moving around to different churches and community centers every week. And the location couldn't be more perfect. Plus, the courtyard makes for a great playground for the younger kids."

"Wait," I say. "Those kids – they're all homeless?" I'd been so focused on my own series of unfortunate events that it didn't even occur to me what I'd walked into.

"Yeah. I mean, we don't really like to label them like that. But they're all staying at Way-Point for now. Hopefully, we'll be able to help their parents get back on their feet."

"*Those* kids are homeless," I repeat. A statement, not a question. Those kids can't be homeless. They all seem so… well, normal.

"You know nothing about the homeless problem," Sarah says, not unkindly.

"I know nothing about the homeless problem," I agree, shaking my head.

"So, come on in. Maybe you'll learn something."

Chapter Thirteen

"Hey, Miss Sarah," a cute, kind of chubby, high school kid chirps, walking out the door of the warehouse just as we are walking in. She's wearing a Yogurt Land t-shirt, khaki pants.

"How'd you do on the English test, Annie?" Sarah asks.

"B minus," the girl shouts, walking away, "not too bad."

"She's homeless?" I ask.

"She's a guest. We call them guests, here. But yeah, she has nowhere else to live."

"But she's got a job."

"Minimum wage. It would take about twenty people earning minimum wage to afford a two-bedroom apartment in this city."

We walk past a large common room where eight or nine kids are drawing and coloring at a beat-up wooden conference table. Not the same kids who were playing stickball, these kids are even younger.

"What the hell is with all the kids?" The only kids I ever thought of as homeless were runaways on the street, the kind always begging or trying to scam you. The kind you avert your eyes from as you walk by.

"Fifty-eight percent of the homeless in this country are children."

"You've got to be kidding."

"I'm not," Sarah says.

"Why? I mean, I'm just so not familiar with this problem."

"Lots of reasons. Domestic violence, for one. Abused women get backed into a corner. Not just with the violence. There's sexual abuse, too, of women or their children. Or both," Sarah says matter-of-factly, "so they either stay at home and take it, or they take the kids and go… where?"

"I don't know," I reply quietly. "There wasn't a lot of domestic violence or sexual abuse in my family."

"Well, consider yourself lucky. Because that's all it is – luck. None of these kids had any control of the factors that landed their moms or dads on the street."

"So, they're all, like, victims of some kind of abuse? The kids or the moms?"

"Not all, but some. A lot are veterans – a nice 'thank you for your service' there. And a lot are just regular people with regular jobs who got tripped up. When you're living paycheck-to-paycheck, any kind of bump in the road can cause things to spiral."

"Like what?"

"Like you or your wife gets sick and you have to pay medical bills instead of the rent. Like companies downsize, lay off workers and you can't find a job in the three weeks 'til the rent is due. Jesus, forty percent of Americans can't cover an emergency over four hundred bucks without a major life change. Most of the people in this world don't have a safety net, you know."

"What's that supposed to mean?"

"Asks the stay-at-home-dad living in his brother's building."

Oh, right. I almost forgot that she thinks I'm Bill.

We walk past a room with a few desktop computers arranged around the top of another shabby conference table. A normal-looking guy, maybe forty years old, is hacking away at one of the keyboards. Sarah continues to walk in front of me.

"Hey," I say, "I'm getting a kind of judgy vibe from you right now. I mean, if I said anything offensive, you know, I'm sorry, but…"

"No," Sarah says, softening, "it's not you. Not you specifically, I mean. It's more what you represent that pisses me off so much."

"Can you explain what you mean so I can, like, figure out how to be offended by that?" Sarah stops, turns to face me.

"Look at your face. Ever since we walked in here, you've been dazed and confused because these people don't fit into the stigma of homelessness you had safely tucked them… far away from anything you'd ever need to care about. But don't feel bad," Sarah continues, turns and keeps walking. "You're, like, typical. I mean, yeah, bad things can happen to good people, but it just amazes me how everybody can so easily create a reality where these people simply don't exist."

"Hey, Miss Sarah?" Out of nowhere, a tough-looking boy, maybe twelve-years-old, steps in front us. He looks pretty normal, just – well, tough. Like he's seen some stuff a twelve-year-old probably shouldn't have seen.

"Hey, Trev," Sarah says brightly.

"Can I hold on to this one?" He holds up a cotton-candy pink backpack, faux fur trim. This Trev kid doesn't look like he's struggling with pre-teen gender issues. Maybe he's just such a bad ass that he wants to carry a sparkly pink backpack at school, like some kind of challenge to the rest of the kids. Or maybe he thinks it would be funny, like sarcastic or something. Who knows what kids do these days to maintain their image?

"It's for my sister," Trev continues. "Gabby's at the clinic getting her shots and I want to make sure no one else takes it. She starts first grade next week."

Or maybe I misread the situation entirely.

"Sure, sweetheart," Sarah says, "but what about you?"

"I thought we were only supposed to take one."

"Go back and get yourself a backpack, too. Okay?"

"Really? Awesome. Thanks!" Trevor's face looks like Christmas morning. For a backpack and school supplies. Wow. He spontaneously hugs Sarah, tight, then darts back to wherever he came from.

I lick something wet from my lip and realize that my eyes are, like, dripping tears. I'm not an emotional person. I don't think I've cried since I was a kid. Certainly not since selling my company, unplugging from technology and effectively dropping out of society. Not that I'm bawling or anything, but these tears are of the emotional variety. This is all too weird.

"It can get to you," Sarah says, looking at my tear-streaked face.

"Does that kind of thing happen a lot?" I ask, wiping my face.

"All the time. You wouldn't believe how tight these families become, when they stay together and don't give up."

"Look, I really had no idea…"

"Sorry, Bill. You can't use ignorance as an excuse. You don't know because you don't want to know… just like everyone else. All the stigmas, the categorizations people use to convince themselves that helping each other isn't, like, the lowest priority in our society. I wish everyone could just wake up, you know, live in the world that's actually going on around us."

What Sarah's saying to me, I'm not feeling at all offended. It's more like I'm having something like a Satori moment. A spiritual awakening. Which, I'm a little ashamed to say, has not much to do with the homeless. Not directly, at least. It's more about me.

Because here I've been, feeling all Zen master about the way I abandoned technology and my relationship with Clancy and, like, rooms and furniture and stuff. Here I've been, feeling all superior about not spending my days staring at a smart phone or hopping from platform to platform in the Cloud. Here I've been, congratulating myself for walking away from all the digital-distraction. When really, at least in this case, I was doing the same thing as everybody else, ignoring the reality all around me. My eyes were totally closed. That is so unlike the me I'd been thinking I am. Wow.

"Uh, you with me here, Bill?"

Oh, right. Sarah is still standing in front of me.

"Sorry," I say, shaking my head. "You sort of touched a nerve."

"Good," Sarah says.

She removes the thick hipster eyewear from her face. I notice that her eyes are green. Clancy's eyes are pale blue, like a China doll. Sarah's eyes are this kind of deep green and hazel, like a feral cat or some other living thing. Without backpedaling on anything she said, she's now talking about how she feels bad, spilling all of her frustrations with the world onto me, yada, yada, yada.

She's rubbing the lenses of her glasses clean with the front of her t-shirt, innocent of the fact that I can see her belly button in the taut swipe of flesh above the waistband of her sweatpants. She looks at her glasses, then looks at me. Jesus, her eyes are so green. Aside from her belly button and tight stomach – a lovely surprise – her baggy clothes give me no clue as to what kind of a figure she has. I mean, she dresses worse than a lot of the guests walking around Way-Point. And her dirty blonde hair – dirty blonde as in darkish blonde, not as in unwashed – is piled on top of her head in a way that is totally cute but could never be confused with sexy. So why do I feel like I'm imprinting on her or something?

"So, anyway," Sarah continues, "how about you cut me some slack for getting all soapbox on you, and I'll cut you some slack for being, well, just like everyone else."

I don't think I've ever seen eyes that are so green.

"What?" Sarah asks.

"What?" Damn, I must have said that last bit out loud. Jesus, is she blushing? I have an overwhelming desire to kiss her right now. What the hell is happening to me? Before right now, if you looked up "not my type" in the dictionary, you'd find a picture of Sarah.

"So, we can be friends then?" Sarah asks, turning to stroll down the hallway again. "Maybe I can walk Cujo with you and Bitsy at the park sometime. Betsy can come along, too."

She's not so subtly redirecting our conversation towards her knowledge of the fact that I have a wife and kid. Wait, is Sarah the one who thinks Bitsy is Dan's illicit love child? No, that's the Irish girl, Chevron or something. Sarah's the one who thinks all of Dan's accounts have been frozen by the IRS. I wonder how Bill keeps this stuff straight.

"Betsy works, like, all the time." I say perfunctorily.

"That must be hard." Sarah has clearly never met Betsy.

"Sometimes," I say, as we stop in front of a closed door. "What's in here?"

"It's where we keep the guests' stuff," she replies and opens the door.

"You don't keep it locked?"

"We kind of have an honor system around here. Everyone watches out for each other."

Behind Sarah is a room lined with cheap metal shelving. It's maybe three-quarters full of duffel bags, boxes and a few knickknacks like ornamental lamps, vases, some cooking utensils. Small stacks of framed photographs, that kind of stuff. There are also two litter boxes.

"You keep cats in here?" I can tolerate dogs, though I would never own one. Cats, on the other hand, I cannot tolerate.

"Some guests have pets."

"Oh," I say, "so this is everything these people own?"

"Everything they could take with them when they left or got evicted, yeah. Why?"

"It doesn't look like much. I mean, considering all the guests you've got here."

"It isn't much," Sarah says. "Like I said, we used to have to move regularly to different churches and community centers that offered us short-term space. Our guests have learned to travel light. The second floor is where people sleep."

"How about the other floors?" From the outside it looked like this warehouse was about five or six stories.

"We only rent the first two floors. The others are vacant. We've sometimes used the third floor for overflow sleeping arrangements, but rarely. Like I said, Way-Point isn't a traditional shelter where people come in and out on a short-term basis. We're really about helping families who want a safe place to regroup and get their lives back on track."

"You keep saying 'we,'" I mention. "Do you have, like, a set job here?"

"No, I volunteer at the site a lot, but mostly I just do pro-bono legal work for the group. When I say 'we,' I guess I'm not talking about Way-Point specifically."

"So, what, then?"

"I guess, the 'we' I'm talking about is, we people who give a damn."

Chapter Fourteen

"Finally," Sluggo sighs, startling me as he rises from a folding lawn chair in my dark apartment. "Come on. We've got to go."

I need to start locking my door.

"Not tonight, Sluggo." My head is still swimming from the chance encounter with Sarah, what I saw at the Way-Point facility. The homeless kids. How I thought my new, unplugged, hermit lifestyle was bringing me closer to reality, when it wasn't reality at all. Not like Sarah's reality.

"Definitely tonight," Sluggo replies, pulling on his coat as I take mine off. "Keep that on. We have to move."

"I've got a lot on my mind right now, Sluggo."

"Good. You're in some kind of transition. That helps. All the more reason for you to join me. Come on, we've got to go."

"Seriously, man. I'm not in the mood to go out tonight."

"Don't think of it as going out," Sluggo pauses, contemplates. "Think of it more like an intervention."

"Right. I'm definitely not going."

"It's not, like, an active intervention, dude. I just want you to meet some people so you can, like, observe them. I talked to Clancy about your lunch with her parents."

"So?"

"They're starting to suspect that there is something wrong with you. Clancy's parents are worried about her."

"I assume you're referring specifically to Clancy's mother, given her dad's consistent tendency to warn me away from repeating the hell that is his life?"

"I don't know which of Clancy's parents is having trouble with you. I only know it's time for you to meet these people."

"And you're going to stay here, bothering me, until I join you?" I sigh.

"You know I will. So how about you spare yourself some pain and just come along quietly?"

Sluggo's UBER takes me deep into western Jersey City for the second time that day. Drops us at this hideaway bar across the street from the same Mike's Place where I got just a little too drunk, just a little two nights ago. We walk through a door with no signage and into a bar that, as far as I can tell, has no name. It's nine p.m. on Friday night and the place is practically empty. Sluggo reads my mind and tells me that the place doesn't fill up until after two a.m. on weekends.

"I thought all bars close at two a.m. in Jersey?"

"They do. That's why this place fills up."

"So, what makes this bar so special?"

"This bar doesn't care."

"Ah."

"Anyway, I think one owner is a cop, so they kind of turn a blind eye, you know?"

"Okay. So, what are we doing here now?"

"Them," Sluggo motions his chin toward the one, two, three… eight old men who are stooled in elbow sequence at the dark corner of the bar. Sluggo walks towards them and I follow.

"O'Shaughnessy!" roars one of the old men, raising a glass.

"O'Shaughnessy!" echo the other seven, glasses raised in response.

"Ah, O'Shaughnessy," groans the old man who's made the toast. "Sure, he knew how'ta do it right."

"Aye," hisses the old man to his left. "The daft genius, didn't he ruin it for the rest of us?" He lifts his pint and shouts, "O'Shaughnessy!" The other old men at the elbow of the bar respond with boisterous shouts of "O'Shaughnessy!"

"Is this an Irish wake?" I whisper to Sluggo.

"In a manner," Sluggo responds. "These here are O'Shaughnessy's boys."

"Which one's O'Shaughnessy?"

"None of them."

Sluggo steps behind the old man who'd made the first toast, puts a hand on his shoulder. The old man looks backwards with a brown tooth grin.

"O'Shaughnessy!" Sluggo shouts, raising a pint of Guinness that he picked up, I don't know from where.

"O'Shaughnessy!" the old men, all of them, respond.

"Ah, 'tis himself! How are ye, Sluggo?" the old man says, wiping his mouth.

"Cleary, I'm glad you guys are here tonight," Sluggo says to the old man. He hands me a pint of Guinness, which, like his own, has somehow magically appeared on the bar. I don't like Guinness.

"And where else would ye expec' us ta be?" mumbles Cleary.

"Cleary. Boys. This here is my good friend, Dan." The old men glance my way. Sluggo elbows me in the ribs.

"Ow! What?" I flinch.

"Come on, dude. You're embarrassing me," Sluggo juts his chin towards the old men, makes a furtive toasting gesture with his right hand. This is so stupid. Anyway, I raise my glass.

"O'Shaughnessy!" I lackluster shout.

"O'Shaughnessy!" the old men respond heartily, go back to their grumbling conversation. I firmly place my arm around Sluggo's shoulders and step him back a few paces from the bar.

"Seriously, man. Why?"

"You unplugged from the digital world, right? Well, that's twenty-first century suicide as far as I'm concerned. And that there… that is an honest-to-god suicide club."

"O'Shaughnessy's boys."

"Yup," Sluggo nods.

"Explain."

"They're philosophers," Sluggo replies in perfect non sequitur.

"I don't know what you mean."

"What I mean is, they've all got advanced degrees in philosophy."

"Oh," I nod. "Still not getting it."

"Okay, here's the backstory. They all majored in philosophy as undergraduates. And after they graduated, they all got advanced degrees in philosophy. It's, like, they make this undergraduate decision to rack up huge amounts of debt while simultaneously aborting any chance of getting the type of job that would allow them to possibly pay that debt down. And then, postgraduate, they all double down on that bet."

"So, when you say 'suicide club,' you're actually just talking about career suicide?" I have an undergraduate degree in literature, which is roughly the same thing as a degree in philosophy in terms of, you know, practical value. Dabbling in tech was always just a hobby when I was a student. You'd think it would have been the other way around.

"No, no. I mean suicide of the bodily variety. The end-your-life kind of suicide," Sluggo replies.

"Well, they obviously aren't very good at it."

"Good at what?"

"Suicide."

"Why would you say that?"

"Because they're sitting right here in front of us," I say, and grandly extend my Guinness towards the elbow of old men at the bar.

"I'm not going to explain it to you if you're going to be all overcritical."

"Sorry. Please continue," I say demurely.

"So, this lot is coming up on their graduation – all of them about to become Doctors of Philosophy – when they decide that they've seen the best that life has to offer them."

"When was this?" I ask, thinking circa nineteen fifty.

"A year ago. Maybe two years, tops. Why?"

"What are you talking about?"

"What are you talking about?" Sluggo answers my question with a question.

"Dude, they're, like, old."

"Dude, they're, like, younger than us," Sluggo responds with a disdainful shake of his head.

No. Way. There is no way. I walk to the bar and lean my head over, study the hunched shoulders and yellow-skin faces. No way.

"Quit staring, ye gobshite. Not a one of us has seen thirty yet," the one who is Cleary says in a low tone.

Impossible. I look closer at Cleary, his nicotine-stained skin like a deflated, mustard-color balloon. Eyes glassy with drink, yellow where they should be white. I look at the rest of them. In the dim light of the bar, I recognize what I'm actually looking at. It isn't age, but rather the most extreme effects of an unhealthy lifestyle. No way! Wow. I realize that I'm ogling the group of them in a way that's hard to be considered anything but offensive, so I smile, nod and take a few steps back to Sluggo.

"All set, then?" Sluggo asks, referring to my detective work.

"Unbelievable."

"Shall I go on?"

"Please do."

"Where was I?"

"One or two years ago these guys were about to graduate with advanced degrees in philosophy..." I repeat.

"Right, and they all decide that they'd peaked."

"Peaked in college?"

"College and post-grad, yeah. See, all they'd been doing for, what, seven years, all they'd been doing in that time was drinking, playing video games, shagging chicks and amassing epic amounts of debt. And it was all coming to an end. Life would never be as good. I mean, a lot of graduates have these types of discussions. But these guys have advanced degrees in philosophy, so you can see how they might, kind of, turn the volume up to eleven on the conversation."

"But what's the deal with them all being Irish?"

"What?"

"Was it just the Irish students who decided to bail on life?"

"What do you mean?"

"What do you mean, what do I mean?"

"They're not Irish," Sluggo says flatly.

"What do you mean they're not Irish?" I ask, incredulous. Who else talks like that? Maybe they're Scottish or some weird cockney variation.

"No, they're all East Coast guys. Far as I know, at least. But sure, I can see how you might be confused, what with the brogue and vocabulary and all. I mean, I'm sure some of them are second or third generation Irish, but they're all Americans, practically speaking."

"So, what the hell is with the brogue, then?"

"Well, the way I understand it is, *Boondock Saints* – you know the movie?"

"I know the movie. Nothing special, cool to see that actor from *The Walking Dead* when he was just a young guy, though."

"Yeah, sure. I agree. But anyway, *Boondock Saints* apparently got stuck in their DVD player way back when they were undergraduates. And, being philosophy guys, no one could figure out how to fix it. So, between liking the sound of the brogue banter between the two main characters, and having it on in the background all the time, they just kind of adopted it."

"They speak in an Irish brogue because of a movie? You can't be serious."

"I can and I am."

"How did you find out about all of this?"

"Cleary and the guys told me one night, here at the bar."

"They just... told you about it? Like, they weren't the least bit embarrassed at how idiotic that sounds?"

"You got to remember, Dan. These are guys who willingly chose to study philosophy at the undergraduate *and* graduate levels, racking up insane debt to do so. They're not likely to be embarrassed about any of their life decisions."

"Fair point. Okay, go on."

"Where was I?"

"Life peaked in college, they were drowning in debt and they started a suicide club, which obviously didn't take."

"Who said it didn't take?"

"Sorry, just an assumption on my part, considering all of them are still sitting at the bar over there. Or did they decide to drink and smoke themselves to death?"

"In answer to your second question, no they did not decide to drink and smoke themselves to death. They drink and smoke to pass the time. And, in answer to your first question, what makes you think all of them are sitting at the bar right now?"

"What do you mean? So, some of them went through with it? And these are just the guys who, what, chickened out? So, they just sit around, drink and smoke because they can't deal with the shame?"

"You're asking too many questions in rapid succession, Dan. It makes it difficult to have this conversation with you. But yes, two people actually went through with it. And no, these guys did not chicken out. Believe me, they were all in. And, yes, they do drink and smoke from shame. But their shame has nothing to do with cowardice. It's the honorable shame of beaten men – men who respect a hero who gave them a purpose, even though it was that same hero who took it away from them."

"O'Shaughnessy!" toast the old-young men at the bar.

"Okay, so tell me," I say to Sluggo, who's wordlessly raising his pint to O'Shaughnessy.

"No."

"No?"

"No. I just wanted to give you the back story. The front story, you get that right from the horse's mouth," Sluggo says, walks up to the bar and grabs another pint of Guinness. I'm wondering if the bartender just leaves a bunch of pints on the bar for anyone to take, like peanuts or a snack mix. I follow Sluggo to the group, set my elbows on the stained dark-wood bar.

"Sluggo here," the one called Cleary says, not looking at me, "he tells me ye be wan'tan ta know the tale of O'Shaughnessy."

"O'Shaughnessy!" toast the old-young men at the bar. I nod.

"Well, I'd be happy ta enlighten ye, young friend," Cleary says in his fake Irish brogue, "if ya got the guts for it."

Chapter Fifteen

A jaundiced twenty-something scooches his skinny legs off the bar stool next to Cleary, holds his beer gut like a third-term pregnant woman as he makes his way to another bar stool at the end of the line. I get the impression that I'm supposed to take this guy's place next to Cleary, primarily because Sluggo grabs the back of my collar roughly and leads me to the open stool.

"Give the man a fresh one," Cleary says, not to the bartender, but to one of his crew.

"Actually, I'm not a big fan of Guinness," I say and draw icy stares from the full line of O'Shaughnessy's boys, like I just said I'm not a big fan of the Virgin Mary. Seriously? They're not even really Irish. Whatever. "What I mean is, I'm not a big fan of Guinness without a Jameson's sidecar."

"Aye, aye," mumble the young-old men, nodding to each other approvingly. I drop a fifty on their bar kitty, make a finger swirling gesture to the bartender, indicating Jameson's all around.

"And do ya know who could put away the Jameson's? That brilliant, bloody prick O'Shaughnessy," Cleary hisses, then raises his pint and shouts, "O'Shaughnessy!"

"O'Shaughnessy!" the crew shouts, pints raised, in well-practiced unison.

"Ah, t'wasn't much O'Shaughnessy couldn't put away, sure," chimes a gnarled figure to Cleary's left.

"Aye, Patrick. He certainly put us away, didn't he now?" Cleary answers.

"Sure, tis the truth," Patrick says, pauses, raises his pint. "O'Shaughnessy!"

"O'Shaughnessy!" the crew roars.

"Agh, O'Shaughnessy, the clever feckin maggot, sure he knew how ta do it right," Cleary sighs.

"So, anyway," I say.

"So, sure. Did Sluggo tell ye that we're all Doctors of Philosophy, then?"

"He did. Congratulations," I say, lifting my pint to the crew, "to all the doctors at the bar."

"Ta, boyo," Patrick sighs, "we get hardly a bit of recognition these days." The crew nods and mumbles, silently raises their pints.

"So, sure, didn't we all graduate with them esteemed, bollox degrees? After having spent, what, seven years? Yeah, seven years shaggin' an playin' video games an gettin' wasted in every way known to man. And havin' philosophical discussions all the while. And weren't it the best craic of our young lives?" Cleary says the last part more to the bar than to me.

"Aye, twas a dream, that." Patrick nods and the crew mumbles and nods among themselves. I'm getting the impression that the only stools allowed a voice are to the left, right and center of Cleary.

"So, then, we're all olagonin' bout the graduation an the crushin' debt an the end of the glorious life as we did know it, wit out a place for us to go on as such in the bastard real world. Truly we had bottomed-out an t'was all tatters. And at our most miserable low, didn't that bloody genius O'Shaughnessy climb right up on this very bar and give us the hope? Gave us a rasion d'etre at our very darkest hour, the very day before our graduation." Cleary raises his pint.

"O'Shaughnessy!" the crew roars.

"So, he convinced everyone to kill themselves rather than face the real world," I say, a statement rather than a question. This is such a ridiculous conversation I'm having.

"Ye'll be minding yer tone, ye gobshite," Cleary growls, then softens, "And t'wasn't like that. T'was a philosophical conclusion he led us to, and aren't we all Doctors of Philosophy? O'Shaughnessy gave us perspective. Made us realize tha we could either view the past seven years as a hole to be dug out of or rather as a mountain we'd summited – where we could sound our barbaric yawp over the roofs of the world."

"Whitman," I say.

"*Dead Poet's Society*." Cleary replies.

"Good movie."

"It holds up," Cleary nods.

"And killing yourselves, that would be the yawp, then?"

"Well, if yer jest tryin to sum it up, sure. But the key aspect of the message 's that we all off ourselves in the most *spectacular* fashion. Tink 'bout it. Bad decisions, followed by a seven-year stretch of debaucherous introspection, capped by a spectacular statement suicide. A glorious means to end a life gone pear-shaped. Far better than the alternative, no?"

"I'll have to think on that one."

"Well, then ye ain't someone that's knotted up your own life, sure."

"I'll have to think on that one, too."

"Aye, so anyways, the idea appealed to this crew here. I mean, a light at the end o' the tunnel is still a light at the end o' the tunnel, even if tis a train. Though not everyone understood O'Shaughnessy's meaning at first, if ya git me."

"I don't get you, no."

"Seamus McNally," says Patrick at Cleary's right.

"Is it ye tellin' the story, Patrick?" Cleary hisses. "Shut yer gob."

"Was his name really Seamus McNally?" I ask, thinking it weirdly coincidental, given the whole fake brogue thing.

"Nah, his real name was Doug Nelson, but sure, he looked like a Seamus McNally," Patrick answers.

"I'll not be tellin' ye again, Patrick," Cleary growls, then continues. "So I'd be lyin' to say we weren't thoroughly pumped up by O'Shaughnessy's plan. But, in the case of poor Seamus McNally, happens a bit too pumped up, if ya git me."

"I don't get you, no."

"Well, didn't poor Seamus shout his barbaric yawp and charge through that front door right there? And straight into traffic he went. Blammo! Immediately dispatched by a bus, if ye'll excuse the pun."

"So, your friend Seamus, he actually died?"

"Oh, aye. Dee-oh-friggin-ai, as the paramedics say. Though they din't bother to send an ambulance, did they Patrick?" Patrick shakes his head and smiles. "No, just a street sweeper was necessary, the state Seamus was in."

"Jesus," I say. Of course, Cleary's exaggerating for effect. I'm not sure if this Seamus-slash-Doug character actually died, but if he did, they would have obviously sent an ambulance, if only as a matter of protocol. It's not like they would have really picked up his body with a street-sweeper.

"Jay-sus is right, and all the saints in heaven."

"So that's when you put the kybosh on your suicide club?" I'm figuring that, having recognized a twisted plan gone too far, now they drink away the guilt and shame of Seamus-slash-Doug's death. Though that doesn't explain the endlessly repetitive toasts to O'Shaughnessy, who appears responsible for instigating all of this in the first place.

"Hell, no!" Cleary says. "For a brief, confused moment, wee Seamus was our hero. Standin' in the doorway, Seamus's crushed skull and brains poolin' on the road, didn't we give him our finest cheers?"

"Whoa. Hold on. So, you're telling me that your friend runs into traffic, dies instantly, and your reaction is to cheer."

"We were a bit confused at the time," Cleary admits.

"You guys were that serious about O'Shaughnessy's plan?"

"Serious as a heroin overdose."

"And you're telling me you were happy about Seamus's death."

"At first, sure. We were ecstatic."

"And then, what? The LSD wore off, and you felt normal human grief?"

"I'll tell you then what, boyo. Didn't I turn around to see himself, the only one of us not cheering?"

"Himself?"

"O'Shaughnessy, ye eejit."

"O'Shaughnessy!" the crew roars.

"O'Shaughnessy wasn't cheering?"

"O'Shaughnessy was furious, man! Here was Seamus, a friend of seven years, about to become a Doctor of Philosophy no less, and the most creative he can get offin' hisself is to run in front of a bus? A disgrace, O'Shaughnessy spoke. And weren't the rest of us cheerin' wee Seamus on, O'Shaughnessy spoke. The shame, it haunts us all, still today."

Cleary and the boys all shake their heads in shame.

"So, O'Shaughnessy was upset about *how* Seamus killed himself?" These people are psychopaths.

"Right, yeah. Lack of creativity, like I says."

"Okay. And then?"

"So, O'Shaughnessy, he gives us what-for like you would not believe. Really tears inta us. Sure, not just Seamus but all of us, as it was the rest of us that let O'Shaughnessy down with the cheering. And once he finished cursing us out, O'Shaughnessy, he walks out of this bar and it's the last we'd ever hear his voice."

"I assume that's not the end of the story? I mean, you guys have toasted O'Shaughnessy over two dozen times since I've been here. He had to have done something more heroic than cursing you out and then walking out of the bar in a snit."

"Course t'aint the end o' the story, ye gobshite! O'Shaughnessy, he weren't no man o' words. O'Shaughnessy, he was a man of action! The daft brilliant feckin gobshite, didn't he know how ta do it right," Cleary says sadly, raising his glass. "O'Shaughnessy!"

"O'Shaughnessy!" roars the bar.

"O'Shaughnessy, the daft genius, sure he knew how'ta do it right," Cleary repeats, pauses, stares straight ahead. For, like, an entire minute. As we all stare in silence, I wonder if something is expected of me at this juncture.

"And?" I ask, eventually.

"And, I'm getting ta' *and*, ya feckin maggot. Don't be rushin me."

"Sorry," I say. We all continue staring straight ahead for another minute or two.

"So, it was our graduation day, come along the next morning, and all of us were there, ceptin' poor wee Shamus course, who'd flattened himself the day before. But sure, we didn't see O'Shaughnessy among us. Not until that gobshite Patrick looks to the sky and points him out."

"He was on top of the Gilbert Hall, standing there on the roof. Ten stories that building is," Patrick sighs from his stool beside Cleary.

"Standing like a god in the still sunlight, O'Shaughnessy was. Like a mighty god. And he didn't wave to us or nuttin. But once we'd all gotten a look at him, he raises his arms. And he's holding a couple of straight razors."

"They were gleaming in the sunlight, like they was made ah gold," Patrick adds, "like they were made ah gold and fire."

"I'll be telling this story, Patrick!"

"How'd you know they were straight razors?" I ask. "I mean, from ten stories down."

"How'd we know they were straight razors, he asks! Well, didn't O'Shaughnessy cross his bare arms and drag them bloody straight razors right up both his wrists!"

"We felt the drops of blood from where we were, all the way down on the ground."

"Shut yer gob, Patrick!"

"So, he slit his wrists, then," I say flatly to Cleary.

"Aye, he slit his wrists, and he sprayed the crowd below wit his own blood. But that weren't what did him in! O'Shaughnessy had more in store for us. Didn't he then reach one of those bleedin' arms down towards his feet, wobbly with loss of blood, and grab a gallon jug of Clorox bleach?"

"So, what? He poured bleach on you guys from the roof?"

"Ha! O'Shaughnessy din't pour the bleach on us. He drank it!"

"O'Shaughnessy, he could eat more Tide Pods than anyone in our cohort," Patrick says sadly.

"I'll not be telling you again, Patrick! Aye, O'Shaughnessy tipped that gallon jug of Clorox back and glugged it like mother's milk, he did. Brilliant bloody bastard. And then he swoons, maybe cause of the bleach or maybe cause of the blood or maybe twas a combination of the two, but then he swoons and drops straight off the roof."

"Whoa," I say open-mouthed, nodding, not sure how much of this to actually believe. "That's quite a story."

"And who said it was finished?"

"There's more?"

"Aye, there's more," Cleary replies, "for O'Shaughnessy doesn't fall more than ten feet from the rooftop when a noose pulls taut on his neck and stops him short."

"He'd secured a hanging rope to the roof, ya see. We didn't even notice the noose around his neck in all the excitement," Patrick asides.

"Sure, I tink that was implied, Patrick. Now shut yer gob."

"So, he hung himself," I say. "I mean, he slit his wrists and chugged some bleach and fell off the roof and hung himself. Wow."

"You'd tink that's how t'would end now, would'ncha?"

"There's more?"

"Aye, there's more. For O'Shaughnessy didn't stay hung for more than a coupla ticks before the rope snapped clean, dropping his body like a sack of meat."

"So, he fell," I say.

"Aye, he fell. Like a wingless angel from the heavens, he fell. And he'd about halfway reached the ground..."

"More like a third of the way, I think," Patrick interjects. "It was around the seventh floor."

"Fine, whatever. Quit yer interruptin'. So, around the seventh floor, then," and Patrick gives him a satisfied nod, "that's when he burst into flames."

"We think he soaked his clothes in gasoline. And he obviously had some sort of incendiary device," Patrick says. "But the timing was remarkable."

"Patrick, Lord help me, I'm not gonna ask you again. So, yeah, dear O'Shaughnessy, his body just, like, ignites in mid-air. It was spectacular!"

"Jesus," I gasp. "And then what?"

"And then what? And then the burning bloody piece of meat falls splat on the concrete. What'ja tink was gonna happen? But the brilliant bit is, no one will ever know how he died. Sure, that mad genius certainly knew how ta do it right. O'Shaughnessy!"

"O'Shaughnessy!" roars the crew.

"So, but, what did you guys do then?" I ask.

"Sure, we gave him a sincere round of applause, waited for the medical units to do their work, continued on wit our graduation and then came here for a drink. What else were we to do?"

"And that was the end of your suicide pact?"

"It wasn't so much of a pact as it was a club. And anyways, we didn't really see the point anymore. I mean, who wants to follow that act? T'would be like followin' the Beatles with a ukulele. No, that mad, brilliant gobshite ruined it for us all, God bless him."

"It's a shame he could only do it once," Patrick reflects quietly.

"Aye, Patrick. Tis that," Cleary raises his pint. "O'Shaughnessy!"

"O'Shaughnessy!" roars the crew.

"That's quite a story," I say, introspectively. "And now you guys just smoke and drink all the time?"

"Aye. We discussed it and thought that to be the best course of action. Until we can come up with a redemption plan, that is."

"So you, kind of, took charge, then?"

"Aye, wasn't I O'Shaughnessy's right hand? Though, truth, I betrayed him. Like Peter in Gethsemane." That seems a little extreme. I mean, all he did was cheer Seamus-slash-Doug for a cosmetically botched suicide. Maybe this crew just needs a push in another direction.

"Cleary!" I shout, pint raised. And you could hear a pin drop.

"Show a little respect, ya gobshite. We only raise our glasses to one man in this place," Cleary whispers.

"O'Shaughnessy!" I shout, not wanting to offend my new friends. They're obviously insane and I don't know how much of the story I really believe, but something about their desperation is oddly appealing to me.

"O'Shaughnessy!" roars the crew.

I glance around for Sluggo and find him hitting on the only woman in the bar. Because Sluggo is Sluggo, and a woman is a woman. Even though this particular woman must be pushing eighty-years-old. Cleary is done with his story. His head is back with his boys. I tell Sluggo to get us an UBER. Sluggo looks at the old woman, looks back at me, then rolls his eyes.

"You're a total blocker, you know that?" Sluggo says as we drive back to my building.

"She was older than my grandmother, dude."

"That's the point, man. It would have checked a box."

"There's always a next time."

"So, are you ready to plug back in," Sluggo changes the subject, "having seen a more extreme version of this antisocial suicide thing you've got going on?"

"I don't know. I kind of liked those guys."

"You kind of liked those guys," Sluggo says flatly, "that is, like, the opposite of the reaction I was hoping to inspire."

Chapter Sixteen

"Come in!"

I hate coming down here on a Saturday. I knock again.

"It's open! Come in!!"

Betsy said the same thing last month, and I walked into my brother's basement apartment to find her breastfeeding Bitsy while simultaneously eating a pint of *Ben and Jerry's* on their *Bob's Discount Furniture* wraparound pleather couch. The memory truly haunts me. I mean, she wasn't even wearing one of those wrap things to cover up. She was just pale and topless, her belly and love-handles tumbling over the ultra-wide elastic waistband of her pregnancy jeans, which, by the way, she continues to wear even though Bitsy is over two-years-old. And the fact that Betsy still breast-feeds her toddler, I don't even want to get into that.

"I'm just looking for Bill!" I shout through the door.

"He's in the bathroom!" Betsy shouts back. "He's been in there for the past half hour!"

I get the impression that Betsy is shouting this not only for my benefit.

"Can't a guy get any alone time in this place?!" I hear Bill shout at Betsy. From the bathroom, I assume.

"I can wait!" I shout through the door.

"Don't make me get up, Dan! Just let yourself in!"

So, I let myself in. And there is Betsy. Wrapped in a tan Snuggie, on the same couch where I saw her topless, with a pint of Haagen Dazs resting on one thigh and her laptop on the other.

"Don't get up," I say quickly. Please, for the love of God, don't get up. I'm not sure if she's wearing sweatpants under that Snuggie and I'd rather not find out.

"You know the water pressure in this building is garbage, right?" Betsy says without looking up from her laptop.

"It's fine at my place."

"It's not fine down here. I can barely wash my hair, the way it dribbles out." Betsy wears her mousy brown hair in a "mom cut" – that short bob do that signals to the world that she has abandoned any interest in personal sex appeal in lieu of her new identity as a mom.

"You'll have to talk to the building manager about that." I just own the place.

"Ha! Your building manager can hardly tie his own shoes. I won't hold my breath."

"Still…" I say and let the statement hang. The funny thing about Betsy is there was once a time when she was actually attractive. Not, like, Clancy attractive. But she made the best of what she had. Now, sixty pounds of baby weight and a mom-haircut later, Bill must be counting the days until his own death. Makes it difficult to blame him for smoking so much pot and making up stories about being someone else for the dog park people. Even if that someone else is me.

The toilet flushes and, speak of the devil, Bill walks into the living room.

"Where do you think you're going, buster?"

"What? I'm just coming out of the bathroom to say hi to Dan."

"Is that what it takes to get you out of the bathroom? I should have Dan on speed dial."

"Hey, man," Bill says to me, ignoring his miserable wife. "What's up?"

"Hey. You got a sec?"

"Don't even think about going out, Bill," Betsy snaps, like a prison matron. "This is the first Saturday I haven't had to work in a month, and I will not spend the day taking care of Bitsy. That's your job."

"I'm not going out," Bill says to Betsy. "Wait, are you here to take me somewhere?" he asides to me with a glimmer of hope.

"No."

"I'm not going out," Bill repeats to Betsy, who is pretending not to listen as she shops online. "Can you give me a few minutes with Dan?"

"Like, what? I'm supposed to get up?"

"Fine, we'll go into the kitchen."

"Don't be loud. You'll wake Bitsy. And don't eat my ice cream!"

"Would you just back off for one minute?" Bill says, a rare moment of exasperation for which he will later pay dearly, I'm sure.

"Someone woke up in a bitchy mood," Betsy says to nobody in particular.

"Did she just call you a bitch?" I ask Dan when we get to the kitchen.

"She said I was being bitchy."

"Same diff."

"Is there something you want, Dan?"

"I guess, what I really want is for you to walk back in there and punch that gross fishwife of yours right in her fat mouth. Figuratively speaking, of course." I would never advocate physical violence, even with someone as awful as Betsy.

"Is there something else you want, Dan?" Bill asks, patiently.

"Yeah, uh. Look, I was wondering if I could walk the dogs again today?"

"Wait a second. You *want* to walk the dogs?"

"I do, yes. I'd like that very much."

"Why?"

"It's a beautiful Saturday morning, Bill. I'm just down for a walk in the park." And Sarah's air-cast boot thing doesn't come off until Monday, which gives me an excuse to stop by her apartment.

"I don't think it's a good idea."

"How come?"

"How come? Let's start with the fact that everyone in the dog park thinks I'm you. And I'd prefer to keep it that way."

"So, I'll be you. No big deal."

"I don't think so. Things are complicated enough as it is."

"Not to take anything away from your hideous home life, little brother, but I believe I'm being extraordinarily generous in allowing you to use my identity for your own warped pleasures. The least you can do is let me take the dogs today."

"Yeah, that's fair," Bill sighs. "But I don't walk the dogs on Saturday. The owners aren't at work so they walk the dogs themselves."

Damn, that should have occurred to me.

"The only dog I'm walking today is Cujo, unless Sarah's foot is better and she can walk him herself. I'll give her a call," Bill says, pulling out his cell phone. Sarah, just yesterday, toted a hundred pounds of school supplies several blocks from her apartment to the Way-Point building. I'm fairly certain she'd be able to walk her own dog today.

"No, don't call her!" I say too quickly, and suddenly a wide smile spreads across Bill's face. "I mean, I'll just stop by and see if she wants me to walk Cujo. No big deal."

Bill continues to smile. He's on to me.

"Sarah, huh?"

"It's nothing."

"You're not acting like it's nothing. Oh, my God, are you blushing right now?"

"Stop it."

"Look, no offence to Sarah, but she's not really your usual type, right? I mean, she's cute and all, but my masturbatory fantasies would be much better served with a sister-in-law like Clancy."

"I'm not… there's nothing… look, I accidentally bumped into Sarah yesterday at the place where she helps homeless families and we got to talking. I just want to talk to her about the charity is all."

"I'm picking up a little more than that from your vibe, big brother."

"Bill, there is absolutely no way that anything would ever happen between me and Sarah."

"Really, why's that?"

"Because she thinks I'm you."

"Ouch. That's cold, man."

"Don't take it personally. She just thinks I'm married with a kid. She knows nothing about the deep, deep misery that is actually your life. Speaking of which, are you ever going to do anything to better your situation with Betsy?"

"Like what, switch from pot to heroin?"

"Seriously. You need to man up. Stick Bitsy in daycare and go try to make something of your life."

"Says the hundred-million-dollar hermit who gave up technology and dropped out of society to live in a pillow fort."

"I'm worried about you, little brother. That beast in there sucks the joy out of everything within a hundred-yard radius of her rotten stink. And, by the way, she does treat you like a bitch. Your dog park fantasies and self-medicating bong-hits aren't a long-term solution. You need to get a life, man. What you've got here, it's not healthy."

"Physician, heal thyself," Bill says, waving me off. "That's from the Bible, you know."

"I'm working on myself," I reply. "Just think about it, okay?"

"I will think about what you said," Bill replies. We bro-hug and I walk out of the basement apartment without exchanging words with Betsy, who doesn't even look up from her laptop. What a miserable human being she is.

CHAPTER SEVENTEEN

"I meant to call you, Dan! I can take Cujo today!" Sarah cracks the door. "Oh, it's you."

"It's me. Helping out my big brother again." I notice that Sarah isn't wearing her glasses. I also notice that she's wearing yoga pants. The loose t-shirt doesn't give away much upstairs, but she definitely has a set of legs on her.

"Come on in," Sarah says, opening the door. "Like I was just saying, my foot is fine. It's no problem for me to take Cujo on his walk today."

"Well, I'm already here, so…"

"It's okay. I'm not doing anything, anyway."

"I mean, neither am I."

"So, how 'bout you join me?"

Score! What is it about this girl that has me so rapt?

"Sure. Yeah. That would be great," I say, nonchalant.

"Cool. It's actually hard for me to bend down and bag Cujo's poop when I'm wearing this boot thing."

I briefly consider making up an excuse to get the hell out of Dodge. As I may have mentioned, I'm not a fan of things fecal. But I glance at Sarah's green eyes – no glasses! – and decide to power through it.

"So, anything new with Dan's situation – the IRS thing, I mean?" Sarah asks as we follow Cujo to the dog park. Her shoulder keeps touching mine as we walk side-by-side.

"Since the day before yesterday?"

"Oh, yeah. Right."

"Anyway, Dan isn't aware that I even know about his problems with the IRS."

"Oh, good. You didn't tell him. That's good. I still feel bad about how that all went down. I mean, I shouldn't have let the cat out of the bag like that."

"Dan's a creative guy. I have no doubt that he'll come up with a storyline that gets him out of trouble with the tax people. In the meantime, if he wants to keep his financial woes a secret, that's fine with me."

"So, where's Bitsy today?"

"Taking a nap. Her mom's at home."

"Cool. Oh, would you mind getting that?" Sarah hands me a little plastic bag.

"Ah," I say hesitantly, staring at a pile of poop ahead of us on the sidewalk, "that's not Cujo's."

"Yeah, but people can't just let dogs do their business on the sidewalk like that."

For some reason, I find the prospect of picking up the poop of a dog I don't know even more revolting than picking up the poop of dogs I know. This may not be a moral dilemma, but it's in the same ballpark.

"But if we pick it up, then people are just going to keep doing it, right? I mean, we don't want to enable that type of behavior." Not my best knee-jerk argument, but I have to try.

"You're kidding, right?"

"Of course," I sigh.

I don't even know how to do this. I mean, the spandex cowboy could pick up dog poop with one hand the other day, but the specific mechanics are eluding me. I reach down with both hands, holding the edges of the plastic bag over someone else's dog's poop, and try to kind of shimmy it in.

"Did you just gag?" Sarah asks, giggles.

"Yeah, uh, something I ate earlier didn't agree with me." How exactly do you get the poop into the bag?

"You don't know what you're doing, do you?"

"What makes you say that?" Oh, my God, I think the poop just touched my finger! Another involuntary gag.

"Seriously?" Sarah pulls out another plastic bag, sticks her hand into the bottom, and turns the bag inside out. She wiggles her fingers in the bag, like a glove. Oh, I get it! I do the same thing with my bag, grab the poop, pull the plastic edges over my fist and knot the top. That was remarkably easy. I actually want to do it again.

"Got it!" I say, with way too much enthusiasm.

"How is it you walked all those dogs the other day and don't know how to pick up their poop?" This girl is always asking the hard questions. I scan my mind for reasonable responses, find none, decide to come clean.

"I had a helper."

"Who?"

"The spandex cowboy."

"Rolf?" Sarah knew exactly who I was talking about. Bill's an idiot.

"Yeah, Rolf. He helped me out. I have, kind of, this thing about feces."

"Yeah, the gagging sort of gave it away. But, I mean, you must be used to it, right?"

"Because…?" Why must I be used to trafficking in feces, I wonder?

"I mean, aren't you Bitsy's primary caregiver?"

Ah, that would be why.

"You must change diapers five or six times a day."

"That's different," I say. "Bitsy's my daughter. I've got the whole love thing going on with her." In no universe would I ever change Bitsy's dirty diaper.

"It must be nice, having a kid," Sarah says, thankfully tilting the subject away from poop, "even given your circumstances."

"My circumstances?"

"Oh, sorry. I mean, Dan told me about you and Betsy." I'm not even going to try to rift along with this topic. There's absolutely no telling what kind of story Bill weaved for Sarah about Bitsy's parentage. Prison baby? Exiled European royalty? Best to just keep my input to a minimum.

"Right," I say, nodding.

"But you're making it work, right?"

"Define 'work'," I say, impressed by my own clever response.

"Sorry, I don't want to get too personal. It's just a thing I do."

"No, please. I don't mind."

"Well, I know it can't be easy when you weren't planning to have a kid. Especially with someone who's so staunchly pro-life," Sarah says haltingly.

So, Bill actually told her the truth about himself and Betsy?

"No judgments, I mean. It's just a kind of rough way to get into a marriage."

Huh, Bill did tell her the truth.

"And it must have been doubly hard for you, being pulled out of the workforce to take care of a child."

"Doubly hard because…?"

"Oh, don't be modest. Dan told me how you came up with the whole idea for his app."

"Did he, now?" And there's the lying sumbitch of a brother I know and love.

"Yeah, and how you couldn't live the shoestring life of an entrepreneur while supporting a child, so you had to rely on Betsy's legal career to be the breadwinner. But having to sit on the sidelines and watch someone else make a fortune off of your idea, that must have been tough."

"Well, ideas kind of grow on trees. Dan took all the risks, managed all the execution," I say, giving my true self a modicum of credit. I think about mentioning the fact that my app had been on the market for an entire year before Bill got Betsy pregnant, but decide to keep that bit of information to myself.

"Still, it must have been difficult."

"I manage," I say coolly. "So how about you?"

"How about me, what?"

"How'd you get involved with Way-Point?"

"I told you yesterday, I'm just someone who gives a damn about the people around me."

"Yeah, I know you said that. Are you going to get all judgy on me again?"

"Maybe," Sarah laughs. "I just get so frustrated all the time. I mean, why am I the exception, here? Some really bad things can happen to really good people. I just don't get why so few of us feel like it's our responsibility to help them."

"I don't know," I reply, thinking as I talk. "Maybe people don't know how to help. Or maybe they don't know who to help. I mean, think of all the people who do everything they can to scam the systems out there. The world is full of con artists, especially in the populations you're talking about." At least I would figure as much.

"Yeah, there's a percentage of homeless people you can't trust. And there's a percentage of homeless people with mental and emotional problems that you can't just throw money at. But there's also a big percentage of homeless who did their best to make it, and still got dragged under by circumstances they couldn't control, you know? Whether they lost their jobs or were victims of domestic abuse, it doesn't matter. They're real families. With real children – who definitely don't deserve to be in the situation they're in. And it would take so little money and effort to help them if we all worked together. But, no, it's so much easier for people to dump everything into one big 'homeless' category, identify it with the bad parts of the population, and use that as an excuse to just forget the whole thing. That whole 'ignorance defense' just makes me sick."

"Okay, I get it. And I'm guilty of it," I admit, "but why aren't you?"

"Why aren't I what?"

"Why aren't you like every other delusional, self-centered bastard who makes up the majority of society?"

"I don't know. Probably because of how I was raised. I grew up in a tiny farming town in the Midwest. We had to help each other out. Sometimes my family gave help, and sometimes we got help. That's just the way it was. Makes it difficult to move out to the cities and ignore the people around you when they need a helping-hand. I mean, coming from a small town where everyone was hand-to-mouth, season-to-season… everything was so… so real, you know? What I can't get over is how people can just delude themselves – or distract themselves – from the world around us. We didn't have that luxury, where I grew up."

"Sounds like quite a place."

"It was Podunk. I spent my whole childhood wanting to get out into the real world. I read and I studied. I got scholarships – the town helped a lot with that. And finally, I made it out into civilized society."

"I wouldn't exactly call Jersey City civilized society."

"You know what I mean. I work for a law firm in Manhattan, the greatest city in the world. It's what I dreamed about as a kid. And now that I'm here, I just dream about living in a place where people care about each other, you know – exactly what I had when I was a kid trying to kick off the dust of my hometown."

"So why don't you go back?" I ask.

"What kind of solution is that?"

"Well, I guess you might be happier?"

"You can't just turn your back on a problem to make it go away. I mean, that's what everyone does, isn't it? I'd rather keep my eyes open and do what I can."

The way she says it, I want to open my eyes, too. This whole conversation is making me want to be a different person, actually. And then I realize, what's stopping me?

"Okay, so what do you need?" I ask.

"What do I need?"

"If you had money, I mean. What would you do right now? Don't think about it, just answer." I say. Sarah looks at me and decides to play along.

"First thing that comes to mind? Okay, we had a trip planned for the families tomorrow, to an apple orchard about forty-five minutes away in Northwest Jersey. We try to do it every year. We had to cancel because I used the money for backpacks and school supplies."

"Okay, great. So, we un-cancel it."

"I just said, I used the money for backpacks and school supplies. We were still short on what we needed to make the trip, anyway," Sarah sighs.

"How much?"

"How much were we short?"

"How much do you need?"

"Like, a thousand dollars or so."

"I can get it." I might have more than a thousand dollars in cash on me right now. When I unplugged from technology, I also stopped using credit cards.

"*You* can get it," Sarah says, a statement, not a question. "No offense, Bill, but you live in your brother's basement apartment."

"I can get it from Dan."

"Dan's accounts have been frozen by the IRS."

"But Dan's got rich friends. Some of them owe me favors. Let me do a little fund raising. I guarantee I can get the money."

"You're serious."

"Deadly."

"Look, I already canceled the trip. I can't get the kids' hopes up again if you don't come through. Maybe we should just let it slide."

"Give me a chance, Sarah."

"Seriously?" she asks again. I'm tempted to pull the cash from my wallet right now and drop this whole charade, but that would open another can of worms. "I'll need the money tonight. Are you sure you can get it?"

"I'll have it to you in an hour or two."

"I'll wait to tell the kids, just in case."

"Okay."

"You're going to love the orchard!" Sarah says, clasping her hands near her heart like a child would.

Wait, *I'm* going to love the orchard?

"There are a bunch of orchards up in the Chester area, but Riamede Farm, the one we go to, it's huge and so not commercial…" Sarah pauses, catching the quizzical expression on my face. "You are coming, right?"

"I, uh," I wasn't expecting an invitation. But I mean, I am picking up poop at a dog park just to spend some time with this girl. Why wouldn't I want a whole Sunday at an apple orchard with her? It's just, this type of thing is so unlike me. The old me, I mean. But I think again, there's nothing really stopping me from becoming somebody different. So, what the hell. "Sure, of course I'm coming. It'll be fun."

"Yeah," Sarah says. Am I detecting a hint of shyness in her? "Good boy, Cujo! Can you get that for me, Bill?"

I pick up Cujo's poop like a champion.

Chapter Eighteen

Clancy is wearing a tiny pink thong. Victoria's Secret, some kind of metallic satin fabric if I'm remembering correctly.

I'm not the type of guy that gets all pervy about women's underwear, but I do remember this thong as a statement piece in Clancy's collection. Back when we were in a relationship. Back when I was in a relationship with her, I mean. Since she's so clearly still in a relationship with me. I know that she's wearing the statement thong because, when I get back to my apartment after walking Cujo with Sarah, Clancy is standing in front of my huge front windows, bathed in bright sunlight, which has the effect of making her thin, white sundress virtually disappear. She has to know, right? I mean, how can she not know how naked she looks right now?

"There he is!" Clancy says, turning slowly as I shut the apartment door. "Hey, baby!"

"How'd you get in here?"

"The door was unlocked."

"But you don't know how to work the handle." A toilet flushes and Sluggo emerges from the Double Layer Waterproof Dome Tunnel Tent that is my bathroom.

"Sorry," Sluggo says, unabashedly looking Clancy up and down. "I just needed to crank one out. I mean, look at that dress, dude. She is a vision." Did Sluggo just say he needed to crank one out? Clancy must think he's joking, though I'm pretty convinced otherwise. Christ, the things he can get away with, being his best friend's girlfriend's best guy friend.

"Oh, Sluggo! You're such a rascal!" Clancy giggles, twirling in her transparent sundress. She has to know what she's doing right now. There's no possible way she couldn't know what she's doing. Anyway.

"What's up, Clancy?" I ask, trying to keep my eyes level with hers. I wonder if Sluggo's eyes have ever been level with Clancy's.

"I was in the neighborhood. Where've you been?"

"You were in the neighborhood? In Jersey City?"

"Yes, that's correct."

"Why?"

"Gwen is working on a new project, not far from here. I thought I'd stop by and say hello."

"Hello," I say.

"Hello," Clancy says.

"You two," Sluggo says with a romantic twinkle. "You want I should give you some private time?" Clancy looks at me, shrugs.

"No, I don't want private time, thanks." What I want is to get back to Sarah with a thousand dollars. But I should probably kill another half-hour or so, whatever reasonable amount of time it might take someone like Bill to round up a thousand dollars. "Clancy, listen. We talked about you just stopping by unannounced, right?" Sluggo gives me a dagger stare.

"I am announced. See!" Clancy points at the blinking red light on my analog answering machine. I walk over, press the play button. It's Clancy, telling me she will be in the neighborhood and plans to stop by.

"Thank you for that," I say, rewinding and erasing the message.

"Anyway, it's not just a social call. Do you feel like taking a walk with me?"

"I just came from a walk. So, no."

"Well, let me put it this way, do you feel like taking a walk with me to check out the project that Gwen is so excited about, because you might want to get involved? Financially, I mean."

"Oh, that's so much worse," I say. "No, thanks."

"Come on, Dan. They're looking for more investors and if you put money in, it would go a long way towards making it all up with Gwen."

"What makes you think I want to mend fences with Gwen?" I lift my face into the same light that is making Clancy's sundress totally see-through, flash her the scars on my face. "*She* attacked *me*, remember?"

"Pointing fingers will not help the situation."

"There is no situation. I'd be happy if I never saw Gwen again in my life."

"She's my best friend!"

"She's a psycho."

"Let's just cool down here, lovers," Sluggo steps between us, patting the air. "What's the project, Clancy?"

"It's a re-gentrification project. They're renovating a whole city block, right on the waterfront. It's top secret. They're still buying up the properties. But it will be, like, this amazing, high-tech, self-contained community. Shared work spaces, shopping and restaurants, condos, the works! Why, do you think you might be able to get your father to invest?"

"Ha!" Sluggo bleats. "Sorry, cutie-pie, my dad doesn't hold my investment advice in very high esteem."

"Well, how about you invest personally?" Clancy asks.

"I'd have to murder my parents, my older brother and my younger sister to make that happen. There are a few layers between me and control of the family trust. I hope this doesn't make you love me any less."

"Of course not, Sluggo!" Clancy flashes Sluggo a smile he doesn't notice because he's very openly staring through her sundress, and she turns back to me. "Come on, Dan. Please? I told Gwen you'd come by!"

"Clancy, try to read me, here. First, I don't do arms-length real estate investments. They're not my thing. Second, your concerns about Gwen and my relationship mean absolutely nothing to me. Because, third, we broke up. We are broken up and you can't keep coming around here acting like we aren't." I take a deep breath, notice Sluggo silently fuming at me. For a few seconds, no one speaks.

"I'll tell Gwen you need to take a rain check," Clancy says with a big smile. "She'll understand."

"Great," I sigh. "Glad we got that straightened out." And it occurs to me that criticizing Bill about his relationship with Betsy is kind of hypocritical of me since I'm doing a variation on the same type of behavior with Clancy right now.

"Do you want me to stop by when I'm done with Gwen? Since I'm already over here and everything?"

"Yes," Sluggo says, "definitely."

"No," I say. "I've got plans tonight."

"That's crap," Sluggo replies. "You don't have any plans."

"Dan, if you don't want me to stop by later, just say so."

"I don't want you to stop by later, Clancy."

"Let's play it by ear then," she says, another big smile. "You'll be around if Dan is out, right Sluggo?"

"I will not leave this building tonight," Sluggo replies, fully committed.

"Great!" Clancy sashays to my front door with minimal impact because the indoor lighting has made her sundress relatively opaque again. And then she is gone from my apartment. If only it were forever that she'd be gone.

"You're going to ruin this for us," Sluggo says, dead serious, "and then I will have to kill you."

"Sluggo, as much as I admire your dreams of forever remaining your best friend's girlfriend's best guy friend, it might be time you start to reach a little higher."

"My father gives me a substantial living allowance in exchange for me agreeing to remain disconnected from his entire social network, and I honestly consider myself to be the luckiest man in the world. How much traction do you think you're going to get with that 'reach higher' routine?"

"Fair point," I say reaching for my door, hopefully giving myself enough space and time so as not to confuse Clancy that I'm trying to catch up with her. "Let yourself out, okay?"

It's been maybe forty-five minutes since I left Sarah at the dog park. I'm hoping this is a reasonably convincing amount of time for Bill to have acquired the thousand bucks. Jesus, it's just a thousand bucks. I wonder why Sarah didn't cover the spread herself? Maybe I don't know enough about what civil rights lawyers make in a year, which apparently is not a lot.

I knock on her door.

"Hey," Sarah says wary of my efforts.

"Hey," I reply, handing her twelve crisp one-hundred-dollar bills.

"You got it?" Obviously.

"I said I would. Oh, and our benefactor prefers to remain anonymous."

"Whatever," she says, opening the door with a huge smile. "Come on in."

"Thank you," I reply, happy to enter her apartment, which smells like, I don't know, something good. It smells like a home should smell.

"I can make you out a receipt."

"A receipt?"

"Yeah, a receipt - so whoever gave it to you can deduct it from their taxes."

"This is tax deductible?"

"Sure, Way-Point is a legitimate 501(c)(3) nonprofit. What'd you think?"

"I didn't, actually. Anyway, don't worry about it."

"Don't worry about it? That's like throwing money away."

"Yeah, but capital gains are, like, twenty percent. Add another nine percent for New Jersey State and you're still only looking at a net gain of around three-hundred dollars after the deduction." After my nine-digit cash-out, I can pretty much calculate the net tax benefit of any earnings or deduction in the State of New Jersey.

"So, who doesn't want three hundred dollars?"

"Not really worth the effort of holding onto a receipt. Uh, for the guy who donated the money, I mean. He's that kind of rich."

"You're familiar with the tax system, huh?" Sarah raises an eyebrow.

"As much as the next guy, I guess."

"Well, anyway, this is so great. Thanks. And thank your brother's friend for me, too."

"He was happy to help."

Sarah counts the bills, not in a suspicious way, but in the way anyone who was just handed a bunch of hundred-dollar bills naturally would.

"There's twelve here. You gave me twelve hundred dollars."

"Yeah, he threw in a little extra just in case you went over budget."

"We're not going over budget. Here," she says, handing back two hundred dollars.

"What are you doing?"

"I've got this thing about honesty. Your brother's friend donated to the field trip. It won't cost more than a thousand bucks, so give this back."

"You are kind of a crazy person. Do you know that?"

"What I know is this. Once people start being dishonest, no matter how innocent, it becomes a very slippery slope. Especially for organizations like Way-Point. So, I've got this rigid honesty thing going on. Get used to it."

"Admirable," I reply. "But my brother's friend donated to Way-Point, not the field trip. So just put the rest towards next month's rent or whatever else you need."

"Are you sure?"

"I am so sure."

"Okay," Sarah sighs, glances at the stack of bills in her hands. "You have no idea what this means to the families."

"You're right, I don't. But at least I can get a better idea tomorrow."

Chapter Nineteen

I'm sitting on the bar stool next to Cleary.

"When I was nineteen," I say, "I went to a staff Christmas party at this strip mall pub called O'Neil's down in South Jersey. See, a friend of mine, his brother was a bartender at O'Neil's, and the staff was allowed to bring guests to their Christmas party. This is more than ten years ago, remember, when those prefab franchise pub chains were still all the rage. O'Neil's went bankrupt right afterwards, I think, just like most of those places. Anyway, that's beside the point. It was an open bar, so me and my friend, we were totally jacked. So, I've got this Pennsylvania driver's license – probably stolen, my friend gave it to me – and it says I'm this guy named Frank Glass, who's like, twenty-two. And aside from the fact that we both have brown hair, I look nothing like the picture of Frank Glass. So, the ID worked to get me into the Christmas party because it was private – just staff and guests – so the bouncers didn't really care. But I'm pretty sure this license wouldn't get me into any real bars that actually gave a damn about underage drinking. So, anyway, that night I'm twenty-two-year-old Frank Glass and this party is, like, off the hook. We're kids and we're at O'Neil's so we're drinking, like, Long Island Iced Teas in pint glasses and that kind of childish nonsense. Anyway, one thing leads to another and I meet this girl. Cutest little thing you've ever seen, and that's not the booze talking. She had this awesome black hair, kind of big – as was the fashion of day – and she was wearing this little green minidress with green stockings and green pumps. She looked like Snow White would look if you dressed her up as a new millennium contemporary Christmas elf. So, we dance a little and then we sidle up to the bar and we talk. And I'm, like, thoroughly buzzed and I've introduced myself as twenty-two-year-old Frank Glass, so I've got pretty much no inhibitions at this point, right? And me and this girl, we just talked about life, you know? She didn't go to college, worked as a secretary for some business outside of Philly. And there was something so genuine about her. It was maybe the most genuine conversation that I'd ever had. Which is funny, because she's thinking I'm this guy Frank Glass. So, we talk all the way through last call and then she gives me her phone number — her land line, because not everyone had cell phones back then — and then we kiss. And it's, like, a really great kiss. And I tell her I'm going to call her, and she's expecting me to call, but of course I'm not going to call because I'm only nineteen and if she wants to meet at a bar somewhere and they bust me for not being Frank Glass, then I'll be, like, outed as a kid and humiliated in front of her. So, before she leaves I kiss her one more time and I can tell she thinks the kiss is the beginning of something, but I know it's a kiss goodbye, right? And still, to this day, I feel like that was one of the most genuine connections I've ever had. And I don't even remember the girl's name."

"Might ye be findin' yer way to the point of this story sometime soon, boyo?" Cleary asks gently.

"My point is, I've only felt a genuine connection with a girl twice in my life, and both times the girls thought I was someone else."

"Aye, well ye certainly took the long way around ta explain that, then."

How I ended up at the no-name bar across the street from Mike's Place is that I didn't want to go back to my building and see Clancy again, knowing full well that she would be there. Why I unloaded all my truth to Cleary, Patrick, and the rest of the O'Shaughnessy boys is… why not? I mean, this crew is clearly stuck at the end of their own collective rope, so what could be the harm? Plus, they're all Doctors of Philosophy. Who better to provide insights into a mixed-up life?

So, I'm maybe seven pints of Guinness in and I've told them all about me unplugging, not just from technology but from Clancy and everything else that had been part of that life before I sold my company. And I tell them about Bill and the dog park. And I tell them about Sarah and Way-Point and my clandestine funding of tomorrow's excursion to the apple orchard. And then, for some reason I can't completely understand, I tell them about the O'Neil's Christmas party more than a decade ago.

"Ye know who would have the right words for ye, lad?" Patrick whispers.

"O'Shaughnessy." I say flatly, for the third time tonight.

"O'Shaughnessy!" toasts the crew.

"Sure, O'Shaughnessy would ken how'ta slice through all tha muck ye made o 'yer life an put ye on the right track," Cleary sighs, takes another pull from his Guinness. "And wha I tink he would tell ye – O'Shaughnessy, that is – what I tink he would say is that this old life of yours with Clancy and all the distractions o' modern technology, that be the life o' ye head. An these new feelin's yer tryin' to describe – quite poorly, I might add – these feelin's would be the life of yer heart. An if there be one ting O'Shaughnessy knew well enough, it's that ye got to live from the heart."

"Aye, livin' from the head is why we got wars an poverty an all the world's evils. Ye got to live from the heart, whatever the cost, is what O'Shaughnessy would tell ye," adds Connor, whose real name is Stan.

"Look, guys," I say, "I'm trying to live from the heart, aren't I? The problem is I've messed it up already. Sarah thinks I'm Bill."

"I wouldn't be worrying ye self about that aspect," Conner replies. "Just be Bill if ye need ta be Bill and let it work itself out. No harm will come as long as ye live from the heart. Sometimes folks need to wear a mask in order ta be who they really are. Certainly, seems to be the case wit you then, does it not?"

"Says the guy using another name and putting on an Irish brogue."

"Well, sure. We would know, now, wouldn't we?"

CHAPTER TWENTY

"Okay, remember now," Sarah is mostly addressing the kids, but she's speaking to garner support from the parents as well, "we're guests here and we want to be invited back. So, you can taste the apples when we're picking them, but no throwing. And no shouting or wild stuff either, okay?"

The busload of kids and parents nod and murmur assent, agreeing to this pact with Sarah before turning their eyes back to the windows. Outside, a blinding sun smiles all over the best part of New Jersey. This is the reason it's called the Garden State, I think to myself.

And somehow, sitting up front with Sarah, I'm feeling just like a little kid on a field trip, too. Everything so new and exciting and overwhelmingly… innocent. I'm thinking about how good it feels, to just feel good about where I am right now.

The bus has trouble making it up the steep paved driveway of Riamede Farm and even more trouble inching along the pocked and unpaved dirt road that loops into a huge grass parking lot at the front of the orchard. We stop and everyone scrambles out of the bus, excited but showing more patience than I might have expected. We do a head count, twenty-eight kids and twenty-three adults, including Sarah and myself. The kids range in age from two to maybe fourteen, the bulk probably around eight to ten years old.

To look at them, nothing suggests homelessness – or what I'd always thought of as homelessness. There's nothing wrong with them, I mean.

They're just happy families, some with one parent and some with two, all of them fully embracing the gift of traveling forty-five minutes outside Jersey City and finding themselves in legit farmland. I'm a little ashamed at the fact that this continues to surprise me. And I could come here every day if I wanted to. I could buy a house or even a farm out this way, no problem. But as much as I am loving every part of this scene, I know that I could never appreciate it with the same depth that these people do.

"Hey, Mr. P!" Alex shouts. "Mr. P, you can stick with me today, okay? I was here last year so I know my way around."

Mr. P is short for Mister Pedophile. It's an abbreviation that we compromised upon prior to the trip when I was able to convince Alex that the inside joke from our first meeting might possibly be taken the wrong way by the adults among us, not the least of whom, his mother.

"I'll catch up, Alex," I say, hanging back so I can walk with Sarah.

"Isn't this, like, the most beautiful place you've ever seen?" Sarah asks as we stride alongside each other towards the entrance gate. "Wait till you check out the actual orchards. They're so huge you could get lost."

Linda Park, the executive director of Way-Point, coordinates our group's entrance with the front gate staff. Linda is a large, dark-skinned woman who had, at one time, been homeless herself. When I met her this morning, it made an impact. She's got this air of being a genuinely good and selfless person, while simultaneously putting out a vibe that she might literally tear you into pieces if you even thought about messing with her families or her organization. I get the impression that the families both adore and fear Linda to an extreme degree and are very happy to have her on their side.

Linda exchanges money for heavy-duty plastic bags at the gate, then hands a single bag to each of the families as they pass through. Sarah and I each get our own and I'm kind of disappointed that Linda didn't give us a single bag to share.

En masse, we follow a beaten path about two hundred yards into the front orchard. All the trees to the left and right of the path are cordoned off with yellow rope on which hang signs indicating "not ripe" or "all picked out." This takes nothing away from the fact that in every direction you look, there is nothing but grass, sky and apple trees. It's hard to believe we're only forty-five minutes from the Way-Point facility where these families are trying to turn their lives around. It feels like a different world entirely.

"It's early in the season so there are only a few varieties with enough apples for picking," Sarah explains. "The Galas and Macintoshes are the best right now, I think."

"Where are they?"

"End of this path, left another two hundred yards and there are a few rows on the right."

"Is your foot going to be okay with all this walking?"

"My foot's fine. I should have had them take this thing off last week," Sarah replies, looking down at the giant air-filled boot as it shuffles through the grass.

"You know this place pretty well. How many times have you been here?"

"I've only been twice with the Way-Point group, but I try to come myself two or three times a season. I love this place. It reminds me of home."

"If that's the case, I'd love to visit your hometown some time."

Sarah blushes.

"It's nice being friends with you, Bill."

"It's nice being friends with you, too."

"And, look, I don't want to make anything awkward between us, and maybe it's all in my head and I'm thinking too much, but I have to say… I mean, you know that I'm not the type of person who would ever get involved with a married man, right?"

A chill runs down my spine.

"Sure, yeah. I'm not the type of person who would ever get involved with a married man, either."

"Seriously," Sarah says, stopping and turning to face me. "I like you a lot. And I feel a strange sort of connection to you. And I want to be friends as long as you understand that's all we can ever be. I just need to be clear about that, up front. You know how brutal honesty is my thing, right?"

"Right, totally clear," I say, wondering why I don't just tell her everything right now. "We can be friends, and that will be the extent of it. Just don't push me away, okay?"

"Okay, deal," Sarah says, and we turn and continue walking until we reach the spot where the path T's to the left and right.

"Hey, Mr. P!" Alex shouts from about two hundred yards to our right. "Come on! Right here's the good stuff!"

Sarah puts a finger to her lips and pats the air in front of her, signaling Alex to not shout across the orchard. Alex quickly puts a hand to his mouth, ducks his shoulders, signaling to Sarah, "Oops!" Then he darts back into the row of trees.

"Go on ahead," Sarah says to me. "I'll catch up."

I come to realize that Alex wants not so much my company, but someone who can lift him up to reach the high apples in the trees. His mother, Rita, a mid-thirties survivor of domestic abuse, is far too frail for the job.

"You're touching my butt, Mr. P," Alex says as he sits on my palms, my arms extended above my head to put him in reach of a particularly shiny red Gala apple.

"How else am I supposed to lift you this high?" I huff, fully exerted.

"Just saying," Alex says, patting the side of my head to inform me he has, indeed, picked the apple. "But this is the only time it's okay for you to touch my butt, all right?"

"I'm fine with that, Alex. In fact, I'd be willing to stop touching your butt altogether, right now."

"Nope," Alex replies. "The best apples are up high. We're just going to have to power through it."

I set him down and Alex darts off to find another high-hanging apple.

"He's a great kid," I say to Rita.

"He's a smart aleck," Rita smiles, "but I love him. Hey, listen, Miss Sarah told me how you found the money to get this trip back on. I know it's an extravagance and we should be spending any money we get on rent and school supplies and that kind of stuff, but this really is so important. To see Alex like this, outside the city, running around like normal kids do. There was a time when I never thought I'd see anything like this again. I just want to say, well, thank you so much."

Rita's eyes fill up and mine start to sting, too. I'm awkwardly trying to think of something to say when Alex shouts that he needs another lift.

Two hours later all the kids have distended bellies from tasting too many apples and are struggling to carry their over-full plastic bags as we make our way to the front of the orchard.

"I'm never eating another apple again, Mr. P." Trevor, the kid who got his sister the pink backpack with faux fur, says to me.

"That's a shame. It looks like you've got about twenty pounds of them in that bag," I reply, not thrilled that all the kids are now addressing me as Mr. P, though I doubt many of them know that it's short for Mister Pedophile.

"I'm betting on the fact that I might not feel the same later," Trevor replies as his seven-year-old sister, Gabby, who might be the cutest little girl I have ever seen in my life, pulls an apple out of her brother's bag and hands it to me as a gift. I thank her and she runs away, giggling.

"It looks like someone has a crush," Sarah smiles.

"You know, this whole pedophilia joke is getting a little old."

"I'm talking about Gabby, you idiot."

"Oh," I say. "Cute."

By the time Sarah and I make it to the little barn where customers check out and pay, Linda Park is managing a minor crisis.

"Everybody, just take three or four apples out of your bag and put them in the barrels there. I am so sorry about this," Linda says to the cashier, who does not seem very pleased with the situation.

"What's up?" I ask Linda.

"We're short," she replies, holding up two hundred-dollar bills. "Either we picked a lot more apples or they've raised the price per pound from last year."

"How much are you short?" I ask, reaching into my pocket.

"About sixty dollars," Linda replies, grimacing.

"Not a problem." I hand the cashier another hundred-dollar bill.

"Can we get the donuts, Mr. P?" Gabby asks, pulling on the end of my t-shirt.

"Gabby!" Linda shouts.

"It's okay," I say to Linda, squat down to cup Gabby's chubby cheeks. "How can anyone say no to a face like that? Let's get five dozen of the donuts and, uh, yeah, three gallons of the cider, too. Do you have cups?" I ask the cashier.

"Sure, right over there," the lady behind the counter says to me, smiling as she takes another hundred-dollar bill from my hand.

"You're a Godsend, Mr. P – the kids love those cinnamon-apple donuts they got here," Linda says, grabbing my hands. I'm not sure how I feel about the fact that Linda Park now calls me Mr. P. too, but I'm definitely feeling good about the cheers from the kids. And then I look to my left and see Sarah staring at me, mouth agape.

Aw, hell.

"Look, before you say anything, it's not what you think," I say, approaching Sarah.

"What? You mean you didn't take a *little commission* on the money you raised yesterday?"

Huh? Apparently, it's not what I think, either. And I was afraid that the jig was up, that Sarah would think I was paying the overage out of my own pocket. Which would not be a bad thing. Why don't I just tell her now and get it over with? Nah, it's way too complicated to address at an apple orchard, surrounded by a bunch of kids.

"What are you talking about? I just put a couple hundred dollars aside in case we went over budget – which, we did – thank you very much. I was going to give you the balance after the trip, anyway."

"What made you think we'd go over budget?"

"I've never been involved with anything in my life that hasn't gone over budget. That's the truth," I say. "And anyway, you weren't even going to take the extra two hundred dollars I offered you yesterday. You wanted to give it back."

"Well, I…"

"And if I was scamming some commission on the money I raised, why would I use it to cover the apples, and then buy everyone cider and donuts, too?"

"I just, when I saw the hundred-dollar bills, I…"

"You thought the worst. And I thought we were friends." I might be pouring it on a little thick here. Sure, I'm offended, but it's not like I've been totally honest with Sarah, either. Standing on the moral high ground seems like something more than likely to bite me in the ass later on. "Look, just forget about it."

"Forget about being friends?!"

"No, no, no, no." I have to admit, I'm so totally digging the hint of panic that I hear in Sarah's voice. "Forget that you accused me of pocketing some commission on my little fundraising initiative yesterday. I get how it looked."

"So, you forgive me?"

"Yeah. I mean, it was offensive, but whatever."

"So, you forgive me," Sarah says, this time not a question.

"Sure."

"Thanks. I owe you one."

"You owe me one what?"

"One pass to act like a jerk, embarrass yourself and hurt your friend's feelings," Sarah says shyly. And this is very cool. Because I suspect this pass will prove useful in the not too distant future.

"I'll hold you to that," I say, smiling. I totally want to grab her hand as we walk back to the bus together, but don't want to blow my one pass so soon.

Chapter Twenty-One

"Where've you been all day, bro'?"

"Is Betsy here?"

"No, she's at her mom's."

"With Bitsy?"

"No, actually. Bitsy's in her room. And how weird is that, anyway? You'd think a maternal grandmother would welcome the opportunity to…"

"I'm going to tell Sarah."

"Tell Sarah what?"

"Tell Sarah everything. I like her." I say and wait as Bill processes this information.

I don't want Bill to feel embarrassed or ashamed – that's not what I'm after here. But he never should have started this whole "escape from reality" thing in the first place. And he certainly shouldn't have involved me, albeit indirectly. So, this is totally not my fault. Still, I'm worried about my little brother. His life is awful. Do I really want to pull a single ace from the house of cards he's built?

"Whatever," Bill says, finally.

"Whatever?"

"Yeah, whatever. It's fine. Go ahead and tell her."

"You're okay with it?"

"Yeah, I mean... hey, can you ask if she'd be willing to keep her mouth shut vis-à-vis the rest of the dog park people, though? She's a friend of yours, right? Maybe she could do you a solid," Bill says calmly.

"How is it you're not more upset about this?"

"I don't know. I mean, the dog park people were going to find out eventually, right?"

"Yeah, but the humiliation of being caught in a web of lies like this..."

"Bah. It's nothing compared to what I live with on a daily basis. Anyway, when people find out, I think they'll understand."

"You think they'll understand that you lied to their faces?"

"Eventually. I mean, you understood, didn't you? I just have to give them a little insight into my actual domestic situation. After hearing about my home life, anyone who doesn't sympathize into forgiving me, I wouldn't want to be friends with them, anyway."

"You've thought about this, obviously."

"Played it out a few times after I told my first round of lies, yeah."

"Okay. Fine. So, you're okay that I'm going to tell Sarah, then?"

"Sure. Except, you're not going to tell Sarah, are you?"

"Sorry?"

"You're not going to tell Sarah anything, are you?"

"Is this some kind of Jedi mind thing? Because that only works in the *Star Wars* movies."

"It's not a Jedi mind trick. It's the truth," Bill says, cracking a smile.

"Really? And why would that be?"

"Because you like her. You just said it. And anyway, I can tell. It's written all over your face. You really like her."

"That's exactly why I'm going to tell her... because I like her."

"No. That's exactly why you're not going to tell her."

"How stoned are you?"

"A little. But that has nothing to do with what I'm saying. Now I'm about to lay the truth on you, big brother. So, prepare yourself."

"Okay, I'm prepared. Shoot."

"You're not going to tell Sarah the truth, even though you like her, because you're not ready."

"I'm not ready?"

"Correct. You're not ready to leave the limbo that you've been living in for more than a year now. That's the only reason you haven't told Sarah the truth already. It has nothing to do with me."

"Please explain."

"On the one hand, you're not ready to let go of your old life. You can't let go of Clancy."

"I broke up with Clancy."

"Come on. She's over here all the time. And didn't you have dinner with her parents two nights ago?"

"Lunch. At Applebee's."

"Right. It could have been Burger King, doesn't matter. You still had lunch with her parents, right?"

"Yeah."

"That doesn't sound like something a broken-up couple would do."

"She's… She's really freaking difficult, Bill. She won't accept…"

"Listen to yourself. God, you sound like me – which is pathetic. If you want to end it, then end it. This whole breaking up but still allowing her to be in your life thing, that's garbage. Wake up, man. You don't want to let her go because you're not confident in your new life choices. Same as this whole tech abandonment thing. You could afford to buy a thousand acres and go all Walden Pond for real, but instead you live in that Hooverville you built on the top floor. Face it, Dan. You can't commit."

"Easy, Bill."

"Easy, nothing. And now you like Sarah. Who, if you don't mind my saying, is definitely no Clancy. And maybe that's what you like about her. But your whole life, you've been conditioned to think Clancy is the perfect wife. You would be the envy of, like, everyone if you married Clancy. She might drive you crazy, but you're not ready to give that up. So, it's easy for you to like Sarah when you're pretending to be me, but it's a whole different story when you try to like Sarah and you're actually you."

"You're crazy."

"Crazy like a fox!"

"Not the correct use of that expression."

"Whatever. You know I'm right."

"You're an idiot," I say.

Bill's right, of course. As much as I like my Hooverville, I'm not ready to go live on a compound in the woods somewhere. And as much as I can't stand Clancy, something in me isn't ready to give her up.

"So, you'll let me know if you ever do decide to tell Sarah? So, I can, like, get my house in order?" Bill asks.

"I'm going to tell her," I reply, weakly.

"Yeah, whatever. But if that ever does, you know, make its way from idea to action, you'll let me know first, right?"

"Sure," I say. "Fine. I'll let you know."

"Fine," Bill says.

I walk out of Bill's apartment, head up the stairs to my place. Then I stop, turn around and walk out the front door of my building. I walk towards Sarah's brownstone, thinking about my conversation with Bill, how aside from the part about giving up technology, everything he said was pretty much spot on. But giving up technology – even though I didn't go all Walden Pond – I think that was necessary for me to take the first steps away from my old life. It's like I gave up digital technology in the same way that some people give up alcohol in order to finally address whatever's really bothering them, without the booze haze reinforcing the idea that everything is fine as it is.

I make it to Sarah's stairway, take two steps up... then turn around and walk away. Instead of going to Sarah's, I walk into the meat of Jersey City.

"I was on my way to Sarah's place."

"But ye ended up here, did ye?"

"Aye, but I was on my way to Sarah's place. Truly I was."

"Is that a hint of brogue I hear, then?!" Connor shouts.

"Aye, it's contagious, in'it, laddie?" That's Patrick.

"I didn't speak with a brogue just then."

"Sure, and I'm not speaking wit' a brogue now, am I?" That's Connor again.

"Augh, for Chrissakes, leave the lad alone for a moment," Cleary says and turns to me. "And who's this Sarah yer goin' on about?"

"Oh, come on, man! Sarah. The girl I was telling you about last night."

"Ah, that's right. And what were it ye was tellin' us about her, then?"

It's my fault for choosing a group of suicidal drunks to populate my group therapy session.

"You said to live by my heart, right? Well, I'm trying to live by my heart, but I can't seem to let go of my head. Does that make any sense?" I ask desperately.

"Aye, tis a problem that has plagued many a man."

"And what did many a plagued man do about this particular problem?"

"When the time is right, time will tell," Cleary says philosophically.

"What the hell is that supposed to mean?"

"It means there will come a time when ye hav'ta make a decision. And at tha time, you will either move forward or you will fall backward."

"That's helpful. Thanks."

"Ye will know what I mean when the time comes, boyo. Believe ye, me."

CHAPTER TWENTY-TWO

"Hey."

"Hey, what are you doing here?" Sarah doesn't seem very warm right now. I wonder if it's something I did.

"You're home."

"I'm home, yeah. I only go into the city, maybe one or two days a week. Most of my work is on the phone. They call it a perk to work at home. But it's really just a way for them to save on the square footage of their office space."

More cynical than yesterday, for sure.

"Right. Hey, so I wanted to talk to you about something," I say.

"Talk away," Sarah says, "but I've got a conference call in, like, eight minutes. So, keep that in play from a time budget perspective."

"Okay," I say. It's Monday morning. Part of me hoped that Sarah wouldn't be home. It's time for me to tell Sarah everything. It's time for me to really let go of Clancy. It's time for me to get out of limbo and start living again. It's time. It's…

"So, I wanted to talk to you about Way-Point." Bad Dan! Weak, stupid, bad Dan!

"What about it? Oh, I mean, thanks again for yesterday. It meant the world to everyone, you know. And, well, I'm sorry again for accusing you of, well, you know…"

"Yeah, no, it's in the past, as they say. No need to speak of it again. So, what I wanted to ask is, well, I think I can raise some more money, see? So what else does Way-Point need, exactly?"

"What else does Way-Point need, *exactly*?" Sarah repeats my question in a nasty tone. "Lots of stuff. Tons. A universe of stuff." Sarah is definitely not herself this morning. Maybe she's not a Monday person?

"Could you be a little more specific? I mean, so I can focus my fundraising efforts, well, accordingly?"

"You want specific? Let's start with a broad-brush answer. First, we need a functional space with working utilities and appliances. That goes without saying. Second, we need people – we've got people to spend time with the families, but we need professionals for job-skills training, psychological counseling for both parents and children, tutors to help kids catch up because of missed school. We need a janitor and a handyman, a cook would be nice, and probably dozens of other people I can't think of off the top of my head. Third, we need technology – computers, they don't have to be new, they just have to work. We need a consistent broadband Internet connection for job searches and online interviews. We need cell phones and a basic plan because who's going to hire someone that doesn't have a cell phone. Shall I go on?"

"What about food?"

"The New Jersey Food Banks have us pretty well covered."

"Medical?"

"We've got the clinic I mentioned. It's right down the block, so we're okay there, too. For now, at least."

"Good. So, why do I feel like you're talking to your worst enemy when I just stopped by to ask about raising some money for Way-Point?" I ask pointedly.

Sarah deflates in front of my eyes. "God, I'm sorry. I'm so sorry. If you can raise more money, that's so great. Thank you."

"Hold on a second," I interrupt. "Talk to me. Why the outburst?"

"Look, it's nothing."

"It's not nothing," I say. "Talk to me."

"It's because you had a moment."

"I'm not following you," I say, honestly.

"You had a moment. You had a moment with the kids and the families. It happens. And right now, you're basking in the glow. And right now, I should be all over you for as much money as you can raise from all your brother's rich friends in as short a timeframe as possible. I should be dumping promotional sob stories on your ass. Because... you know why they call it a moment? They call it a moment because it's temporary. It doesn't last long."

Sarah looks like she's close to hyperventilating. Still, all of this seems way out of line as a response to me offering to help her raise money for Way-Point.

"Yeah, again, I was only stopping by to see if I could help." Actually, I was stopping by to end this whole charade with Sarah, but of course, I chickened out. "By raising more money, I mean. I definitely didn't mean to offend you."

"I've got three minutes until my conference call."

"Jesus, I don't get it, Sarah! What did I do that makes you not happy about me wanting to raise money for Way-Point? You're not making any kind of sense here!"

"We're getting kicked out of the building," Sarah says, collapsing in a sob. "The owners are in negotiations to sell the building, and we'll probably be out by the end of the month. Just in time for winter." She's full-on crying now. "These people will have nowhere to go. Do you understand that? These same people who you had your moment with at Riamede Farm, they're gonna be out on the streets at the end of the month. And there's nothing I can do about it."

Here she crumbles, physically I mean, right into my arms. She's hysterical now, tears and snot and saliva soaking the front of my sweatshirt, Sarah shaking and shuddering while I hold on tight.

And all I can think is, thank God. I thought she was mad at me for some reason.

A few minutes later, Sarah has missed her conference call, still sobbing and shaking and severely muddled with her face jammed hard against the front of my sweatshirt. Part of me is thinking, don't mess with the physical contact, while another part of me recognizes that she's clutching me around the arms, pinning my hands straight down at my sides, so I'm really not hugging her even though she's hugging me. And, truth be told, she's a freaking mess at the moment, so I'm not in the frame of mind to try to parlay this outburst into anything romantic.

Therefore, gentleman that I am, I gently hook her chin and pull her face from my chest. My sweatshirt looks like the Shroud of Turin. She heaves, hiccups, heaves, hiccups, heaves, hiccups.

"It's okay, Sarah. Let it out," I say compassionately.

"Shut up!" she shouts at me, without much compassion.

"It's not your fault," I say, thinking it's the right thing to say.

"I know it's not my fault, you freaking jackass. But that doesn't help the families, does it? That I tried my best, it doesn't give them a place to stay, does it? Look, I'm sorry you had your *moment* right before these people are going to freeze to death!"

"Sarah, I know I'm the only one here. But you've got to stop being mad at me, you know? I had nothing to do with it."

Sarah looks up at me, nods slightly, a modicum of comprehension. And then she takes a few deep yoga breaths, calming herself. Then, out of nowhere, she unleashes this unbelievably loud banshee howl and roundhouse punches the wall of her apartment.

Sarah's tight little fist goes straight through the drywall, the tough little mudder. Unfortunately, her tight little fist literally implodes when it hits the support beam just behind the drywall. Most unfortunate. Probably a one in twenty chance that she'd hit a support beam behind the drywall, judging by the square footage of the apartment.

"Whaaa-ah-ug-ah-ah-mother-whaaa-nguaaaah!"

"Honey, we will need to get you to a hospital," I say. Remaining calm is key in situations of high stress. She's flailing around her living room and at this point I'm not sure if it's from the pain of her liquefied hand or her frustration about Way-Point getting kicked out of the building. Regardless, here is where something amazing happens.

I pick up her iPhone. It's unlocked because she was waiting for her teleconference, and I call an UBER. It's her account, sure, but I used the smart phone to call an UBER. This is the first time I've used digital technology in over a year.

"Sarah! I called an UBER! I used your phone, but I'm the one who called it! It should be here in," I look at her phone. "Three minutes!"

Sarah stops her flailing and just stares at me. Stares at me like I'm a retard. Not twenty-first century special needs, no, like I'm a nineteen-nineties retard. And then I remember that she still thinks I'm Bill. How embarrassing.

In the UBER, I'm holding Sarah's smushed hand, wrapped in ice and dishtowels. She is clearly in a world of pain, so I do my best to say supportive things that don't require any response. I think she blacks out a few times on the way to the emergency room, which is probably best for her, as well as for me and the UBER driver, because in her more lucid moments she can't seem to help shouting the most horrible curse words imaginable.

I mean, she really seems like a sweet girl and I know she's in a lot of pain, but I have no idea where this degree of profanity could be coming from. Our UBER driver, a young dude from India or Pakistan or somewhere, looks like he's learned a lot of new American words today, and probably has a whole different opinion of this country where his family has likely struggled to emigrate.

When we get to the hospital, I hand the appalled UBER driver a hundred-dollar bill – more than five times the cost of the ride that will be charged to Sarah's iPhone – and try to justify my friend's sporadic abuse of all things holy by playing the Tourette's card. The well-paid driver graciously helps me with the car door, and I carry a now unconscious Sarah into the emergency room. Because Sarah is unconscious and everything below her exposed right wrist looks like white chocolate chips swimming in smashed tomatoes, the ER nurses quickly attend. Within seconds, she is in a wheelchair and whisked away from me.

I know I should seem less nonchalant about Sarah's spaghetti hand debacle, but I also know that she will live. She may not play the piano like she used to – if she ever played the piano in the first place – but she will be fine. She punched a wall. It happens. People survive those types of things. And anyway, I am so freaking happy right now I could just about bust open and spray confetti all around the ER waiting room. Because I know why Sarah lost it, like, totally and completely lost it. She found out the building that Way-Point leases is being sold!

That's perfect!

I run the halls until I find a pay phone. I call my lawyer and tell him to offer twenty-five percent above asking for a guaranteed close tonight. And before Sarah even goes into surgery, I've bought the building – right out from under whoever was trying to buy it before I stepped in. Offering a twenty-five percent premium allows you to do that kind of thing.

Hells, yeah!

Chapter Twenty-Three

"Hey, baby! Oh my God, what's wrong! You look a mess!"

"Hello, Clancy," I say flatly. I mean, you have got to be kidding me. It's nine-thirty p.m. on a Monday and here she is, in my apartment, like where else would she be? This has got to stop.

"Where were you? I've been worried!" Clancy adjusts herself on the fold-out camper couch beneath my huge waterfront windows.

"Where I've been is at the hospital," I say wearily. "A friend of mine crushed her hand like an accordion and I needed to take care of her."

"*Her*?" Clancy asks pointedly.

"Yeah. She helps out with a nonprofit I donated some money to," I yawn. "I was at her place when she hurt her hand."

"And how old is this *her*?"

"I don't know. Mid-to-late twenties, I suppose. Something like that."

"Mid-to-late twenties. So, you were with another woman?"

"Well, yeah. I mean, she'd still be a woman no matter what her age, right? And she hurt herself so I had to help her."

Here Clancy gets up from my fold-out camper couch and walks into the light beneath my doorway. She's wearing pale yellow lululemon yoga pants and a matching top. And that's it. She is oh so obviously wearing nothing underneath the skin-tight fabric that's stretched north and south of her exposed belly-button. The outfit was clearly sized for a ten-year-old, and I imagine it's from a lululemon collection circa two-thousand-twelve because both the top and bottom are stretched totally see-through, even from the front.

I mean, seriously. Clancy has got to know what she looks like when she wears this kind of stuff in public. The frequency alone rules out any possibility of simple carelessness. God, she does have a killer body, though.

"... and even though we might be taking a break, you will not disrespect me in what is soon to be our own home!"

Man, I didn't even notice that Clancy's been talking this whole time. That stuff with Sarah really wore me out. I hope she's okay. Sarah, I mean. I'll get up early and check on her first thing in the morning. The nurse said she'd be out for at least another ten hours, what with the sedatives they gave her. No use checking back until after seven a.m.

"... and if you think I'm going to wait around worrying about if you're alive or dead – with no word – just to find out you've been out with another woman? Mister, you have another think coming!"

Right. Clancy's still here.

"So, what do you have to say for yourself, buster?"

"What I have to say is, please go home, Clancy."

"Excuse me?"

"You heard me. Please go home. I've had a hard day, and we broke up almost a year ago so I'd appreciate it if you would respect my personal space and please go home."

"Danny?" Christ, I hate it when people call me Danny. Or baby, for that matter.

"Clancy, you've got to get this through your skull, okay? I'm not an infant, so I don't like it when you call me baby. And I'm not a tween, so Danny doesn't work, either. Dan or Daniel would be fine. Now, please, go home."

"Baby?"

Really? Now it seems like she's just doing this to piss me off. I don't offer a response.

"Come on, baby! I need you. You're not the only one who's had a hard day. Gwen's project ran into a major roadblock. It might be kaput!"

"Cry me a river."

"Don't be like that, baby. I promised Gwen we'd help. I don't care if you had to take care of some nonprofit hag all day. I was just being jealous is all. You used to like it when I got all jealous when other women were attracted to you."

"Yeah well, we used to be engaged. We're not anymore."

"You're being awful to me, Danny Johnson!"

"And yet, you're still here."

At this, Clancy storms out of my apartment. I hear her feet stomp down the fourth-floor stairwell. Unfortunately, I hear her stomp down only the fourth-floor stairway. I walk over to my phone, wait a few seconds until it rings.

"Hey, Sluggo."

"Dude, first. I got to thank you."

"You're welcome. Like the outfit?"

"Holy cow. It's like she's read my diary of masturbation fantasies."

"You keep a diary of masturbation fantasies." Statement, not a question.

"A spank bank. Of course, I do. You get an idea in your head that turns you on, you don't want to forget it. Save it for a rainy day, right? That said, Clancy has checked-off at least a dozen of these fantasies without even trying."

"How many Clancy fantasies have you jotted down in total?"

"A few hundred, I'm sure."

"So she hasn't checked off so much… in terms of percentages, I mean."

"What? It's not like you expect any of them to come true. Clancy has been an all-around champion when it comes to my fantasy work. I don't want to hear you putting her down."

"Understood. What do you need from me, Sluggo?"

"Okay, let me start by repeating the same old thing. If you mess up my indirect relationship as Clancy's best friend's girlfriend's best guy friend then I'm afraid I will have to murder you outright, that clear?"

"Crystal, as always."

"Good. Anyway, it looks like Clancy is pretty upset and will be down here talking for a while, right? So, you don't happen to have a red wig, do you? Like the kind that would make a girl's hair look like Ariel, from *The Little Mermaid*? There's something about the yellow lululemon outfit that's just screaming for a *Little Mermaid* wig."

"Can't help you with that one, pal."

"Christ, I've got nine out of the fifteen Disney Princess wigs and she comes down in yellow spandex."

"Of all the gin joints in all the world…" I'm wondering how Sluggo thinks he'd be able to get Clancy to put on a princess wig in the first place, but I'm in no mood to discuss it right now.

"Whatever, man. Just find a way to make up with her when we're done here."

Sluggo hangs up. I place the receiver back on my landline phone, then pick it up again. I dial the hospital just to see how Sarah's doing. To my surprise, the desk nurse puts me through to her room.

"Hello?" Sarah says in a drug-hazed voice.

"Hey, Rocky. You know there are three more walls in your living room that are itching to take on the champ."

"Ugh, I'm so embarrassed."

It's cute how Sarah is embarrassed despite all the drugs that must be in her system right now.

"Don't be embarrassed. I'm totally impressed with the power of your right hook."

"Listen, it doesn't matter. I've got news," she says anxiously.

"Tell me."

"Someone else bought Way-Point's building."

"Really?"

"Yeah."

"Who?" I ask, poker-faced, which doesn't really matter because I'm on the phone.

"I don't know. But I don't think it was one of those big private equity consortiums that have been trying to upgrade the neighborhood. I think an individual purchased it. He or she just swooped in and bought it. I've got a call tomorrow with the buyer's attorney, to talk about Way-Point's lease."

"What do you expect to happen?"

"I expect they will kick us out," Sarah says. "But at least the new owner didn't make Way-Point's removal a condition of the sale. That's a little encouraging."

"Who knows? If it's an individual, maybe they're just buying it as real estate they can sit on while the surrounding neighborhood appreciates. Maybe they'll let you stay."

"Doubtful, but at least we're not out for sure – like I thought we were earlier today."

"One step at a time."

"You don't sound very worried. I mean, you connected with the Way-Point people yesterday, right?"

"Of course, I connected with them. Like you pointed out earlier, I had a moment. And that moment is still happening – so it's more than just a moment, by the way. It's just that, well, I called to see how you are. Like, your hand and all."

"My hand is fine. I mean, I broke eleven out of twenty-seven bones, so I'll be wearing a cast for a while – right when I get the boot off my foot, if you can believe it. But no permanent damage. Still, is anything wrong? You thound funny," she slurs. Whatever pills they've got her on seem to be kicking into a higher gear.

"Funny ha-ha or funny weird?" I ask.

"Maybe it's the medication. I'm stoned to the gills."

"Okay. See if you can pocket some meds for me. In the meantime, do you need me to do anything for you while you're laid up?"

"You can walk Cujo for me, 'morrow morning? I'm not getting out of here until noon at least."

"Sure, I'll get the key from Dan."

"Great. Also, Bill?"

"Yeah?"

"Thanks for coming by my apartment earlier, even though I was in a super foul mood."

"Sure."

"And Bill?"

"Yeah?"

"Thanks for taking me to the hospital when I busted up my hand."

"Would you expect anything less?"

"No," Sarah yawns huge, the sedatives continuing to kick in. "And Bill?"

"Still here."

"Thanks for calling to check in on me."

"Sure thing, peanut. Get some sleep, huh?"

"Did you just call me peanut? That's so funny. My dad used to call me peanut. He died last year. What made you call me that?"

"Uh… you look like a peanut." Why am I suddenly sad that I'll never get the chance to meet Sarah's father? "Anyway, get some sleep, okay?"

"Okay. Love you, Dad."

"I love you, too, peanut," I say, my heart breaking just a little.

Chapter Twenty-Four

"Outstanding business acumen, son."

"Thanks, Leonard."

"Did you have any idea that the Rejewski's were in the process of buying out that entire city block?"

"I had an inkling."

"Well, the owners at the nine-two-seven warehouse didn't. The Rejewski people made sure of that. Thought they'd drag their feet and get it for a bargain. And then you come in and buy it right out from under their noses. Your take-it-or-leave it offer might have been high relative to the rest of the properties in the neighborhood, but the building is right in the middle of the block they're planning to develop. I can't believe the Rejewski's dropped the ball like that. I guess that's what you get for being so greedy."

"I suppose."

"So, what do you want to do with it?"

"Sit on it."

"Naturally. The Rejewski's have already put out well over fifty mil for the more expensive properties on the block. You hold out and they'll buy it for three or four times what you paid."

"Let's hope," I say.

"Hope is for suckers, Dan. You've got yourself a sure thing."

"Yeah. Hey, in the meantime, I want to do some improvements on the building."

"You want to put money into it? What the hell, Dan? It's a tear-down."

"It's a tear-down for the Rejewski's. If I upgrade the space, they'll have no choice but to pay more. I want top-tier utilities and appliances throughout the building. And I want a tech upgrade, fiber optic to the modems, pervasive wi-fi. Also, we need to hire a janitorial service and a handyman… to make sure the place doesn't slip."

"You're going way overboard, Dan. No one's even renting space in the building. Just sit on it and you can squeeze the Rejewski's for huge multiples."

"The building isn't empty."

"It's as good as empty. The only tenant is a cut-rate non-profit that's on a month-to-month lease. I've got a call with their lawyer tomorrow. They're out as soon as you say 'boo.' I mean, I can appreciate the fact that you want to bolster your negotiating position, but what you're talking about is just throwing away money. No offense, of course."

"None taken. Can you contract people to make the changes I just outlined?"

"Your building, your money," Leonard sighs. "Not a problem."

"I'd like to get moving on this in the next twenty-four hours."

"That might cost you more."

"Regardless of the cost."

"I'll get on it as soon as we hang up."

"Great. One more thing. I want to set up a cellular account for the building."

"What do you mean?"

"I mean I want to set up an account with a cellular provider in the building's name."

"Okay, but why?"

"Don't worry about why. Can you do it for me?"

"If you say so."

"Also, that cut-rate non-profit tenant?"

"You want me to evict them? They'll be out legally in forty-five days."

"No, I want to change their lease. Same terms, but make it annual."

"Annual?"

"You heard me."

"I can't see any reason for that. You're not making any sense, Dan."

"Just do it for me, okay? And don't let the tenants know who I am. I want to keep my ownership of the building on the down-low for the time being."

"What's up your sleeve, Dan? You've got to be working something."

"Possibly. Can you make it happen ASAP?"

"Sure. I can get them the paperwork today."

"Great. Last thing, can you get the tenants a dozen new computers, too? Laptops. Apple would probably be best, I think. Just put them all on my account."

"As your lawyer, it is my duty to inform you that you have entirely lost your mind."

"Maybe. How soon can you get it done?"

Chapter Twenty-Five

Getting hugged by a woman like Linda Park is like going to a bad chiropractor. And she has no idea that I've got anything to do with what's happening to the building. Just imagine if she did.

"I just wanna hug everyone!" Linda screams when she greets me, excited enough to forget that big city accent she's developed over the years, reverting instead to the good old deep South.

"You're hurting my vertebrae," I croak, squirming in her embrace.

"It's a good day, Mr. P. We don't get many, but we got a huge one today!" The big lady finally releases me and I take a deep breath.

"What's up?"

"What's up is we're getting new HVAC and new plumbing on every floor! All the bathrooms are getting fixed and we're getting a whole new kitchen… like, the industrial restaurant kind! We're getting fiber optic lines and free WIFI for the whole building! And we're getting computers, too! And a handy-man service on call twenty-four seven! And a janitorial service every single day! I swear, I woke up yesterday thinking we were gonna be moving out next month and then today all the treasures of heaven are showering down upon us." Linda lists the building upgrades with the enthusiasm of a tent-revival preacher.

"Wow, that's amazing."

"No, what's amazing is that they're giving us all this stuff, and at the same time they're changing our lease so we don't have to worry about getting kicked out for a whole year. And they're not even raising our rent!"

I haven't known her for very long, but I'm pretty sure I've never heard Linda raise her voice or speak with a Southern drawl. The last time I talked to this woman, she sounded like a school principal from Boston. Accents are funny things.

"Well, it's about time someone treated you how you treat everyone else, don't you think?" I ask.

"I don' know what to think, Mr. P. All I know is that I's happy. We been turning away almost half of the families that reach out to us. Now we can take twice more than we have now!"

"I'm really happy for you, Linda. You deserve it," I say. "Have you seen Sarah?"

"She's upstairs somewhere. Go on up and find her yourself!"

I take the stairs two at a time and then settle myself when I reach the second floor. I take a breath. I am way too into this girl. I take another breath, deeper this time. I'm going to tell her the truth – the truth about pretending to be Bill, the truth about the building. Screw my old life. This one's better. Sarah will be a little freaked out, but really, I didn't do anything so wrong. She just thought I was Bill for a while, that's all. Everything I've felt for Sarah and the people at Way-Point, that's all been totally genuine. She'll understand. And, I mean, after what I did for Way-Point with the building, that's got to add a bunch of points in my favor.

The hospital released Sarah on Tuesday morning. I know this because I drove her back to her brownstone – in Dan's car, I explained, when she wondered what I was doing in a convertible Jaguar F-Type V8 S. Truth is, I rarely take the car out on the road and probably should just sell it, save the garage expenses.

I planned to tell Sarah the truth on the car ride, right after lying to her about the car being Dan's – even though I guess that's technically not a lie. But she was super quiet on the way back to her brownstone and I assume she was in a lot of pain, despite the obvious drug haze. She had done sufficient damage to her hand that it required elevation. She was wearing a cast, and a rig attached to her whole arm so that her hand remained parallel to, like, her ear. I have to admit; it was hysterical to look at. Sadly, she didn't find it quite as funny and wanted nothing to do with me after I dropped her off. But that was yesterday, and she was still pretty sedated as well as worried about her call with my lawyer, Leonard. Though I expect that call went much better than she could possibly have hoped it would.

Now, twenty-four hours later, I'm bouncing off the walls, waiting to see her. I'm actually looking forward to telling her the truth about this whole stupid charade. This is so not like me.

"Are you going to make fun of me again?" Sarah asks when I poke my head into the office where I've found her.

"Would that be a problem?" I reply sincerely. "I'm not sure if I can help myself."

"No, it's fine. I deserve it for being such an idiot."

"Does it hurt?"

"Only when I breathe."

"I hear there are some changes afoot?"

"Yeah," Sarah says glumly.

"I'm sorry, what?"

"I said, yeah."

"I heard you, I'm just not following. I thought you'd be over the moon about all this stuff going on with the building."

"You're joking, right?"

"I don't think so, no. What's the problem?"

"It's too much, Bill. It's everything we need. There's something going on here. I don't trust it. We don't even know the name of the person who bought the building."

"What do you mean? Linda told me they changed the lease from monthly to annual, without changing the rent. Regardless of what's going on, we've got a whole year here."

"You realize that you just said 'we,' right?" Sarah asks.

I didn't realize that, no.

"Sure," I shrug. "I mean, if I'm allowed to be someone that gives a damn, that is."

"You're allowed. I just don't buy it. Not you, I mean. The building stuff. Something's up."

"You're looking a gift horse in the mouth."

"I've been doing this for ten years, Bill. We don't get gift horses in this field. Something's up."

"What you just said, that's the exact definition of looking a gift horse in the mouth."

"What I just said is realistic."

"So instead of being happy, you'd rather just sit around waiting for the other shoe to drop? That doesn't make any sense."

"You're full of clichés today."

"Come on, Sarah. Talk to me."

"Fine. You know what's worse than having the rug pulled out from under you? Getting your hopes up and then having the rug pulled out from under you. I'm not setting myself up for another heartbreak."

"Another heartbreak," I say flatly. "Exactly what happened to make you so shell-shocked?"

"I got my hopes up, once," Sarah sighs, "and then I let a lot of people down. Because someone let me down."

"Who?"

"My fiancé."

"What? You're engaged?" I ask, totally startled. I mean, what the hell?

"I *was* engaged," Sarah sighs.

"Tell me."

"I met him my last year of law school. He came from money, a real estate family."

"His family sells real estate?"

"Buys and sells. They own, like, a hundred buildings in Manhattan."

"Ah, that kind of real estate family."

"I was stupid. I mean, everything happened so fast. I'd never even had a serious boyfriend before. He came up to me after a class on civil rights, right after I'd gone off on one of my soapbox jags about the homeless problem, and, I don't know, he was just so into everything I was saying. So into everything I was into."

"You cared this much about the homeless, even in law school?"

"I've always cared this much about the homeless. I told you. I came from a poor town in Middle America, where lots of people struggled... where *everyone* needed help sometimes."

"Everyone? What, you mean, like you, too?"

"Yeah, like me, too," Sarah sighs again, exasperated. "When I was ten years old, my father couldn't keep up the payments on our farm. The bank took everything. We had to live in a camper for almost a year until he finally got a factory job."

"I had no idea."

"Why would you? Anyway, our neighbors and the town – people were there for us. They let us use their showers and washing machines, let us park in their driveways, invited us in for dinner, that kind of thing. Without them, we wouldn't ever have gotten back on our feet," Sarah says, then narrows her eyes. "Don't look at me like that."

"Don't look at you like what?"

"Don't look at me like I'm different. Are you going to lump me into your *homeless* category now?"

"Jesus, Sarah, what are you even talking about? We're friends. I'm just sorry you had to go through all that."

"No, I – I'm sorry, it's me," Sarah says, softening. "It's just, when you go through something like that, as a kid, I mean, it's like, the shame never really goes away, you know? No matter how much you know that it's not your fault, and it's not your parents' fault – that it really could happen to anyone, I mean – the shame and humiliation never really goes away. That's why I worry so much about these kids."

"But these kids, they seem pretty happy."

"You'd be amazed how many cry themselves to sleep at night."

"Christ, do they really?" Sarah talking about the kids, being one of those kids, it's like a kick in the gut.

"Of course, they do. They're kids. I mean, they don't feel like that every waking hour. But a lot of the time, what you see is just a brave face. At night, sleeping in a bed that isn't yours, not knowing where you'll sleep tomorrow or next week or next month, of course they cry themselves to sleep. Believe me, I know."

I say nothing, because… how can I? Instead I just nod. As bad as I feel, I can't empathize. I never went through anything like she's talking about in my life. I don't know what I'd be like now, if I had. I watch as Sarah shakes herself off.

"Anyway, where was I?" Sarah asks, a sadness still in her voice. "That's right. I was engaged to this guy who comes from money, right?"

"Right," I say, wondering if I should tell her she doesn't have to go on. But I feel like I need to hear this.

"Yeah, well, this guy – he tells me he totally connected with everything I said in class – asks to buy me a cup of coffee. So, I say, sure, and we spend, like, six hours at a Starbucks. Me, talking about very specific ways that we can build an organization that can actually help the homeless – him, agreeing to everything I say and talking about how to fund it. Real, practical examples of how we could make everything I was talking about work. It felt like we were puzzle pieces, the way his ideas and mine fit together. I remember thinking that. And I didn't know he was filthy rich at the time, just that he knew about money. I can't believe I'm telling you all this. I haven't talked about it, like, ever."

I nod slowly. I want to touch her, but am afraid to add any additional weirdness to this cathartic release of hers. And I'm feeling ashamed of myself because, for a second, I did feel different about Sarah when she told me she'd been homeless. Because, as much as I've connected with the people at Way-Point, it's obvious that I'm still holding on to some kind of subconscious stigma when it comes to homelessness. I know it's wrong – it's the part of me that's part of the problem – but knowing it's wrong doesn't just make it go away. Not that it makes me feel any differently towards Sarah, or anyone at Way-Point. Instead, it just makes me feel bad about who I am.

"And after that, he and I were connected at the hip," Sarah continues. "For the whole last semester, we went everywhere, did everything together. It was like he didn't have a life before he met me, and I felt like my life was finally, like, complete when I was with him. And the whole time, we're working on a new way to help homeless people reset their lives."

"Wait, wait. What are you telling me here?" I ask. "Did you guys, like, start Way-Point?"

"No, no. Way-Point's been around since the eighties. The project I was working on, that's how I met the people at Way-Point. We were developing a high-tech solution to help coordinate job opportunities, training, subsidized housing on the state and federal level – that kind of thing. We were going to help organizations like Way-Point speed up the process of getting homeless families back into the self-sufficient, working population. They lose so much time with the low-tech training and job search processes, you know? Time is what's so painful for these families. I know this from my experience, when my dad was trying to find a job and we were living in a camper."

"So, this thing you guys were developing, it was an app?" Even though I unplugged from technology a year ago, we're finally hitting on some territory that's familiar to me.

"A software platform, yeah. We had a prototype, a beta system that Max – that's my ex-fiancé – paid for out-of-pocket. We did a case study with Way-Point and their partners, found we could reduce turn time by over seventy percent."

"Turn time?"

"Homeless family in, self-sufficient family out."

"For all homeless families?"

"No. I mean, both the experimental and control groups were made up of people who were already making a serious effort to find work and a place to live. I don't think the results would be as high as seventy percent in the real world, but I bet we could have eventually cut the turn time in half."

"Could have?" I ask.

"Yeah. But like my engagement to Max, the project didn't go anywhere."

"What happened?"

"With the engagement or the project?"

"Both."

"I guess, look, I'd never had a serious boyfriend before Max, okay? And I was, you know, not experienced," Sarah says warily.

"At relationships?"

"At everything. I mean, we were taking things really slow, like, physically. And Max, he said it was okay. He said he didn't mind. We didn't sleep together for, like, three months."

"You dated for three months and never slept with him?" I ask, dumbfounded.

"You've got to understand, ever since my family had to live in that camper, all I did was study and work on getting scholarships. I never had time for dating or boyfriends or any of that teen stuff. It takes me a long time to get comfortable enough to be intimate with a guy."

"But you're… I mean, you're really pretty." I probably shouldn't have said that, for several reasons. But three months in an adult relationship and no sex?

"What does that have to do with anything?" Sarah asks defensively, though she's blushing.

"Sorry. Go on."

"So, we get engaged – and we finally slept together. And that was it."

"That was it?"

"I never saw him again."

"He, like, ghosted you after a three-month relationship? After you got engaged?"

"Not exactly. I mean, we talked on the phone twice and he told me that things were really screwed up with his family, yada, yada, and that we'd need to cool things down for a while. And then he stopped answering my texts and emails. So, I guess, yeah, he pretty much ghosted me."

"What about the project?"

"He walked away from it."

"He just walked away from the project? After all that work and money?"

"He wasn't interested in the project, Bill. He's just a guy who gets off on pursuing hard-to-get girls until he can have sex with them. Once that's done, so is the relationship."

"You're pretty matter-of-fact about all this."

"I got over it when I eventually figured out what a garbage human being he was," Sarah says. Then she seems to steel herself and continues. "I was obviously a mess after we broke up so I called up a friend of his I'd gotten close to when Max and I were together. Eventually, this guy broke down and told me that Max had been engaged three times, twice as an undergraduate and once in law school, all two-to-three-month whirlwind relationships, essentially all the same story as what happened to me. What's weird is, then his friend, this guy I'd been friends with for three months, no attraction or chemistry whatsoever, he tried to hit on me. Catch me on the rebound, I guess."

Max's best friend's girlfriend's best guy friend, I assume.

"Jesus, Sarah."

"But the worst part was my project. I'd already told Way-Point and seven other organizations that we were rolling it out and they'd put together waiting lists of families super excited to use the platform. And then, bang, out of nowhere it just stops. Way-Point and the other groups forgave me, of course, once they heard the whole story. Explaining it to them was maybe the most humiliating thing that ever happened to me, aside from living in a camper when I was ten."

"I... I'm sorry, Sarah. I don't know what to say."

"You don't have to say anything, Bill. Just maybe understand why I'm so gun-shy about miracles... about, like, everything that's happening with the building right now. I can't get my hopes up just to have them shattered again," Sarah says, and for the first time in our conversation she lets out a huge sob. She'd been holding it together like a clinician until this point. I want to give her a hug, but she's got that weird brace thing holding up her arm at a right angle to the ground and I don't think I'd know how to negotiate it, even if it were the right thing to do.

"I get it. I just – I wish there was something I could do, you know."

"You're listening to me. That's something. I mean, I'm not good at opening up to people, but it helps to talk about this stuff. Just..."

"What?"

"Just... can you promise me one thing?"

"Sure," I say. Anything, I think.

"If we're going to be friends, I just need you to be completely honest and up front with me. Like, rigid and brutal honesty, okay? Because I don't think I could take it if someone close to me ever played me for an idiot again. Does that make sense, Bill?"

I nod, say nothing, gently place my hand on top of hers – her good hand, I mean – and it's genuinely a safe, platonic gesture. I nod and I think.

What I think is, now would definitely not be a good moment to tell Sarah that I've been pretending to be Bill ever since we met.

Chapter Twenty-Six

"Sure, it's a pickle yer in there, boyo," Cleary says with uncharacteristic tenderness. "Have ye considered takin' yer own life, then?"

"I'm not going to kill myself, no."

"Well, ye don have'ta be actin' all superior 'bout it," Cleary replies, reminding me that all of these fellows at the bar right now are just waiting around for a right opportunity to off themselves, and that I should probably be a little more considerate.

"I meant ye no offence," I say, then realize how I say it. Damn, that freaking brogue *is* contagious. Or maybe it's the six pints of Guinness that I put away telling the O'Shaughnessy boys about my problems. I don't know.

"So if yer nay after takin' yer own life, then, what is it ye plan ta do?"

"I plan to get unreasonably drunk."

"Aye, yer becomin' one of us, sure."

"Otherwise, I have no idea what to do. I mean, I've got to tell her, right?"

"Aye."

"But I really like this girl. And when I tell her, she won't ever want to see me again."

"Aye."

"So, what would you do?"

"Humph," Cleary clears his throat, rolls his eyes. "T'aint me opinion ye shuld be concernin' yerself wit." He stares at me, waiting.

"Seriously? You're going to make me ask?"

"Ask wha, boyo?" Patrick says innocently, his eyes wandering around the bar.

"Fine. What would O'Shaughnessy do, then?"

"O'Shaughnessy!" cheer the suicidal drunkards.

"Knowin' O'Shaughnessy as I do, rest his soul, I'd tink he'd say you'd be needin' the grand gesture. Something big. Something huge. And ye spring the truth on her at that same time."

"What? You think I should do something good to counterbalance my dishonesty?"

"Nay, yer not listening. Ye do something big – grand and brilliant big – an it'll confuse her. Doesn't matter if tis good or bad, so long tis big. See, the brain can only take so much at once. If ye blow her mind wit something else just when ye tell her the truth, sure, she'd not be able to focus so much on yer lyin'. That, I believe, is what O'Shaughnessy would reckon."

"O'Shaughnessy!" cheers the bar.

"Distraction. That's your advice? Sorry, I don't think some sleight of hand will help my situation with Sarah."

"Tis the grand gesture I'm talkin bout, ya gobshite! The *grand* gesture! None kenned the power of the grand gesture more than our daft feckin genius, O'Shaughnessy!"

"O'Shaughnessy!"

"Sure, ye can boil it down to a distraction," Cleary sighs philosophically, "but what is life really but distraction on top of distractions? Sure, tis far more distraction than anything else, when ye tink about it. So ye must embrace it and make it work *for* ye. The grand gesture, applied correctly, tis the most powerful reorganizer of life in the universe. One great flip of the sheet and all the wrinkles disappear, boyo. Tis the very secret of life, O'Shaughnessy would say."

"O'Shaughnessy!"

"Anyway, this is all abstract talk," I reply. "Have you got any wisdom of a more practical variety to share with me? Like, what do I do, specifically, the next time I see Sarah?"

"Aye, but that's an easy one, boyo."

"Okay, so what?"

"Ye wait."

"I wait," statement, not a question.

"Ye wait. The way this universe works, if ye fully embrace the concept of the grand gesture, it'll come to ye. 'Trust the force,' as they say, and don't do nothin' to muck things up in the meantime."

"So, you're saying that I should not tell Sarah the truth? Not try to unwind this whole debacle the next time I see her?"

"Course that's what I'm sayin', ye eejit."

"And instead I should just embrace the idea that the universe will deliver an opportunity for some kind of grand gesture, which I can act upon to fix all of my problems."

"Now yer gettin' it!" Cleary shouts, straight-faced, and slaps me on the shoulder. This is all so freaking bizarre.

"And you believe this completely?"

"Aye, one-hundred percent. There be an order to the universe, boyo. Everyone has the potential for greatness if they just accept their role in the vast, unknowable plan of tings. Tis why we're all here now, isn't it?" Cleary gestures to the O'Shaughnessy boys, who return nods and raised pints.

"So, okay. All of you are fine just waiting for the universe to deliver an opportunity for your own grand gesture?"

"Sure, sure," Cleary replies calmly. "O'Shaughnessy, he was a prophet of sorts. The universe would na have given us his grand gesture without having a plan fer ourselves. Ye can't rush it."

"And you think sitting in a bar, drinking yourselves to death, is the best way to make yourselves available to the opportunity for this grand gesture of yours?"

"Where we sit don't matter, ye blind eejit. Tis our open hearts that make the only difference. Mind me, the universe, it will deliver. And if we must wait, then why not do so at our leisure? What happens to these bodies in the meantime, it matters not."

"You really believe this."

"Aye."

"And if the opportunity for your grand gesture…"

"When," Cleary interrupts.

"Okay, when. *When* the opportunity for your grand gesture arrives, you will trade your lives to embrace it?"

"In the words of O'Shaughnessy, it will be a spectacular peak to an otherwise sub-par existence."

"O'Shaughnessy!"

These people are truly insane.

"And so, you're telling me I should, in my own way, follow suit."

"We all have different versions o' greatness, but the path to get there is always the same," Cleary says.

"So, you suggest that I put everything on hold – in terms of telling Sarah the truth, I mean – and just let things happen… happen until some totally undefined opportunity for a grand gesture arrives, and that will make everything right."

"If ye seize the opportunity at the time, sure."

"So do nothing."

"Open yer heart," Patrick corrects me.

"Okay, open my heart and do nothing."

"Aye, that's the way."

This is, without a doubt, the worst advice I have ever received from anyone in my entire life. Oddly, I believe it is also the most genuine advice that I have ever received in my entire life. And unfortunately, it is the only advice that I have received about my specific problem with Sarah.

And sure, the O'Shaughnessy boys are clearly insane. But they're obviously all-in. How many people do I know who are all-in to anything?

So, I figure, why not?

Chapter Twenty-Seven

"You would be Bill, then?" asks a pretty, dark-haired girl as she greets my dogs. Behind her is a little boy, maybe four years old, poking at a piece of dog poop on the grass with his finger.

"That would be me, yes," I say, trying to direct the girl's eyes towards the toddler who has, by this time, picked up the dog poop in his bare hand. In his bare hand!

"I've been wondering if I'd ever meet ye," the girl says, either oblivious to or ignoring my facial expressions attempting to guide her eyes back to the toddler, who is now smelling the dog poop, "I'm Siobhan."

"Hey, Siobhan, nice to… Oh, God, no!" What kind of child would even think about raising a piece of dog poop towards his mouth?! The little boy freezes, dog poop less than an inch from his mouth. I gag involuntarily, twice. The toddler gives me a wicked smile.

"Fer Chrissakes, Jamie! How many times do I have to tell ye?!" Siobhan says for – obviously – not the first time. The toddler drops the poop, shrieks maniacally and darts across the lawn. I assume to find another treasure and a bit more privacy.

I gag again and my dogs look back at me with what appears to be concern.

"Where's Dan today, then?" Siobhan asks, as if nothing grossly abnormal just happed with the child in her charge.

"He's not here," I say, absently. "Ah, what the hell is with that kid you're watching? I mean, not to step on toes, but don't you think you should keep a closer eye on him?"

"He's just trying ta git a rise out of you, the evil little bastard. Ignore it." After all the time I've spent listening to the heavy, unnaturally developed brogues of the O'Shaughnessy boys, Siobhan's seems so mild as to hardly exist at all. "And I can see that Dan's not here. I was asking, where is he?"

"He's with Bitsy. She's, uh, got a doctor's appointment."

"You let your brother take Bitsy to the doctor?"

"Why not?" I ask, trying to remember the specific town and county where Siobhan lives in Bill's imaginary world. And... I've got it. Siobhan is the one who thinks Dan is Bitsy's biological father, unbeknownst to his brother Bill, who is me. "I mean, Dan's always very helpful with Bitsy. He takes her on walks, like, all the time."

"I just think it's sweet, is all. How close the two of you are."

"Me and Bitsy?"

"You and Dan," Siobhan says, "and Bitsy, too, of course. Dan's told me about your troubles with her mother."

"With Betsy? Yeah, she's pretty awful."

"No, actually, I mean her biological mother. It was a very sad story and you have my condolences."

Oh, right! The nun who died in childbirth! A wide smile spreads across my face as the pieces of Bill's story fall into place and I stand there, grinning like an idiot. This is obviously not the reaction that Siobhan was expecting, so she is now looking at me like I'm some kind of psychopath. I quickly pull myself together and frown appropriately.

"Things still aren't completely right up here," I say, pointing to the side of my head in a weak attempt to excuse my apparent mirth at the mention of my dead wife. "Since the accident, I mean. Sometimes it takes a minute to remember that... that..." Did Bill give me a name for this fictional deceased ex-nun? Anyway, "... uh, that she's not with us anymore."

"I'd better be going," Siobhan says, a little weirded out. She spots her charge on the lawn of the park, about ten yards behind me. I turn and see a monstrously overweight bulldog furiously humping the little boy, now in full missionary position beneath the dog. "Jamie! Sweet Jesus, what did I tell you about bumping uglies with the dogs!?"

"Bye," I say, and Siobhan hurries away just as Sarah and Cujo walk into the dog park. I wave and they head my way. Sarah's still wearing the cast and medical gizmo that keeps her hand elevated at a right angle to her body. I smile and she blushes.

"You're making a habit of this," Sarah says, nodding at the dogs.

"I wouldn't call it a habit. Actually, I was hoping I'd run into you," I say, having specifically timed this dog walking session with Sarah's lunch break. "I mean, to see how you're doing."

"Bill," Sarah says again, more firmly. "Listen, thank you for yesterday. It made me feel a lot better. To unload like that, I mean. I usually don't have anyone to talk to when something's bothering me, and I'm afraid maybe I unloaded too much."

"Stop," I say. "I'm happy to be there for you. It's nice to have a friend who's, like, a good person. I don't have anyone to talk to, either."

"What about Betsy?"

My face involuntarily contorts into an expression of utter repulsion.

"That bad, huh?"

"I don't even want to talk about Betsy," I reply, truthfully.

"Then talk about you," Sarah says, as we walk side by side with the dogs.

"I don't know what I can tell you," which is true in more ways than one, but I try to thread the needle a bit. "I mean, it's like there was this person I used to be before…"

"Before Betsy got pregnant."

"Okay, sure. That works. Anyway, I realized that I didn't want to be that person anymore. I didn't want to be in that life. So I just, you know, disengaged. It's, like, that old life still exists and is waiting for me to come back to it. And this disengagement, it's like, my whole life now. But that's not much of a life, just being disengaged, is it?"

"You're talking about how you had the idea for Dan's app? How it could have been you who sold the company and made lots of money?"

"Okay, yeah, something like that. My point is I feel like my life now is about not being something, instead of being something. Does that make any sense?"

"Kind of?" Sarah says, in a way that means, not really.

"What I'm saying is, I want to stop trying not to be the person I was and start trying to be the person I want to be."

"That's a little confusing, but okay. So, what kind of person do you really want to be?"

"I don't know. That's the problem. All I know is what I don't want to be. What kind of person do you want to be?"

"I am the kind of person I want to be."

"There's nothing you would change?"

"There's a lot I would change. And I'm trying to change it. But my problems are with the world, not with who I am."

"You're lucky, then."

"Lucky? I know you're not rich, Bill. But you sure have rich people problems."

"What's that supposed to mean."

"You've got a place to live. You've got food to eat. You've got all your basic human needs met. And you're making yourself miserable trying to figure out how to make yourself happy. Just get out of your own head for a second and speak from your heart. What kind of person does your heart want to be?"

Poor people have it so easy. Sarah is maybe not technically poor, but she's definitely in the ballpark. The ballpark where right and wrong is so damn clear because you have nothing. When you're rich, everything is much more confusing. It's like, people with money, they're trying to chase these dream-life goals. Better house, better car, better vacations, better friends, Ivy League kids – everything's about whether you have more or less than someone else. And you can always have more, so the dream-life changes with every new horizon. You never get there. It's a losing game. A wasted life. Maybe that's why rich people are so obsessed with distracting themselves. Maybe that's why I pulled out of everything digital technology. Maybe something inside me knew that it was distracting my head so I wouldn't listen to my gut.

"You still with me, Bill?"

"Yeah, just thinking."

"Well, stop thinking. What kind of person does your heart want to be?"

I don't want to be confused anymore. I don't want to wonder if the decisions I make hurt people somewhere down the line. I want simple. I want clear accountability for my actions, and I want those actions to be good. I don't want to be directly or indirectly responsible for anything bad happening to people who are trying to live a good, simple life.

"Bill, what kind of person does your heart want to be?" Sarah's sounding a little exasperated now. She's so cute.

"I… I just want to be a good person. That's all. Not even a great person. I just want to be a good person, to know that I'm not a bad person."

"Okay, great. Now, what does that mean?" Sarah asks gently.

"It means I want to know that I'm not doing anything that can hurt other people. If I can just know for sure I'm making the world a better place with my life, I'd gladly trade that for whatever traditional dream-life that a wealthy entrepreneur would otherwise live."

"Okay, you went back up into the stratosphere for a second there. But I think I get you. You're ready to stop regretting the life you could have had as a wealthy entrepreneur and to do some good with the life you have."

She's a little off, but still in the ballpark, so I'll give it to her.

"Yeah."

"Great. So, you can start by spending a little more time down at Way-Point."

"Is this a recruiting mission?"

"No. But I think it would help. I mean, I think you need it more than they do."

"Okay. I'm not sure what to do there, you know?"

"Just be with them. Spend some time, help where you can. Be yourself and you'll know what to do."

"Will you be there with me?"

"Sometimes."

"When should I go?"

"You can stop in any time you want."

Chapter Twenty-Eight

Before I open my door, I hear the shower running in my Double Layer Waterproof Dome Tunnel Tent. When I do open the door, I see Sluggo sitting sentry-like on a plastic chair outside the tent's unzipped flap.

"What are you doing here?"

"Clancy's in the shower."

"Why are you here?"

"I let her in. She can't open your door."

"I get that, but why are you still here?"

"Clancy's in the shower."

"Ah."

"I'm not planning to stay long, but don't want to miss that transitional, just-out-of-the-shower time. You never know what you're going to get."

"Why is Clancy in my shower?" I ask him and hear the water shut off.

"Ask her. She just told me she wanted to use your shower and I wasn't about to say no."

"Hey, baby!" Clancy steps through the tent flap. A small towel, pinned under her arm, covers maybe twenty-five percent of her body.

"There are bath towels in there, Clancy."

"Only one. I thought you might be mad if I used it. I didn't know you were still here, Sluggo!" Clancy chirps.

"I wouldn't let you take a shower all alone, in an unlocked Jersey City apartment, my dear."

"Sweet."

"Why, Clancy?"

"Why what?"

"Why are you naked in my apartment at two o'clock in the afternoon?"

"Fundraiser," Clancy replies.

"Fundraiser," I say. "What? Like, Sluggo is donating some money to a charity in exchange for watching you shower?"

"I'd do that, you know," Sluggo says to Clancy, "if you're interested in raising funds for charity."

"Sluggo, you rascal!" Clancy giggles, scooping a breast that has slipped free of the towel. Her entire left nipple remains in full view for at least three stumbling seconds. Seriously?

"Hold a sec. Let me put something on." Clancy slips back through the tent flap and emerges several seconds later wearing an old, well-worn pair of my linen boxers and a t-shirt so small that I assume it could only have come from Baby Gap. "Anyways, like I was saying, I've got a fundraising dinner tonight."

"Since when have you ever been involved with charities, Clancy?" I ask, incredulous.

"I'll have you know that I've done a lot of charity work in my time!" Clancy says, offended. "But, anyways, this isn't a charity fundraiser. It's a dinner for some private equity firms that are investing in the project Gwen's working on. She has to give a PowerPoint presentation about the interior design of public spaces. There will be, like, thirty different presentations on all aspects of the project that would be important to investors. Anyways, do you want to come?" Clancy sets herself down cross-legged on a plastic chair, the billowing hem of my old boxer shorts giving Sluggo a view more typically reserved for practitioners of gynecology. She seems to have dried off her entire body except for her breasts, her pink nipples soaking through the Baby Gap fabric like a Spring Break wet t-shirt contestant. There is no way that this could be simple carelessness. I do wonder if it's conscious or unconscious, though.

"No, Clancy. I do not want to come to your private equity fundraising dinner for Gwen's project."

"Boo!" Sluggo shouts. Clancy gives Sluggo the sweetest smile, uncrossing her legs to give him another look up her boxer shorts.

"That's fine, baby. I'll jot down all the information so you can get a feel for the investment opportunity."

"I'm not looking for an investment opportunity, Clancy."

"You can't know that until you understand the details of the investment opportunity."

"I can, actually. Hear me on this. I'm not looking to make any more money than I already have. In fact, what I'm really looking for is some way to give my money back."

"Give it back? To who, the private equity guys who bought your company?"

"No, not to the private equity guys who bought my company."

"Well, I was going to say, in my opinion, one private equity firm is as good as the next, so if you're looking to give your money to private equity, then the companies supporting Gwen's project would be as good as any." She obviously missed the part where I said that I'm not looking to make any more money than I already have, and everything else I've said to her, like, ever. "And you get the added bonus of putting things right with Gwen! That would be such a help, you know, in the long run."

"You should at least give it a look, Dan," Sluggo says, his eyes alternating between the open crotch of my old boxers and the transparent Baby Gap t-shirt, his jeans tented shamelessly. "I mean, from a societal perspective, it's not right to have that much money just sitting on the sidelines. Putting your money to work helps everyone, you know?"

"He's right, baby," Clancy says. She beams a gracious smile at Sluggo, who misses it because his eyes are otherwise occupied by her lower body parts.

"Thank you, professor," I say to Sluggo, "for your unbiased economic insight. Now, would the both of you mind getting out of my apartment?"

"Don't be silly, baby. I'm hardly dressed. Anyways, the fundraiser thingy doesn't start for another few hours, so I thought we could get some lunch."

"Broken up people don't have lunch together, Clancy."

"Does that mean we weren't broken up on Friday when we had lunch with my parents?"

"She's got a point, Dan," Sluggo asides from the peanut gallery.

"Clancy, I need you to take me seriously, okay? I'm trying to move on with my life. You can't keep showing up at my place. You've got to give me a chance to be broken up with you – really broken up, I mean. Think of it this way. I can never come back to you if you don't let me go." As if.

"What if I don't take you back?" Clancy says, baiting me.

"That's a chance I'm willing to take. If you love something, you've got to set it free, right?"

"And if it comes back, it's yours forever," Clancy says with a kind of dreamy glow. I really think she needs to talk to a mental healthcare professional. Her perception of reality is so distorted.

"I, for one, don't approve of this plan," Sluggo says unhelpfully, briefly flashing me the stink eye before returning his gaze to Clancy's body parts.

"What do you say, Clancy?" I'm doing my best to be earnest, here. It helps that I really do want her out of my life. And, somehow, that whole "if you love something, set it free" schtick seems to have made an impression on her. I should probably have said that to her weeks ago.

"I guess," Clancy sighs. "If you think it will help us in the long run."

"For this to work, we both have to be open to the real possibility that there won't be a long run. Do you understand?" I ask, continuing to press my advantage.

"I understand, baby. If you love something, you've got to set it free. Okay. We can do this. I'll leave you alone. I'll stop showing up at your apartment unannounced."

"Really?" It can't be this easy.

"I will set you free, baby. If that's what you think is best, then I'll do it."

"You're finally going to embrace our break up and move on with your own life?"

"I am. With no expectation that we will ever get back together again," Clancy says, sounding like she really means it. That she's even engaging in a dialogue about our break-up is a small miracle in itself.

"And we're not going to see each other?"

"Nope."

"And we're going to try to meet other people? Like, have other relationships?"

"If you choose to have other relationships, then it's none of my business."

"I'm proud of you, Clancy."

"Thank you," she replies. "I'm glad we're finally doing this."

"Me, too."

"It will be, like, something we can tell our grandkids about," Clancy says, sneaking me a smile.

I will never be rid of this person.

CHAPTER TWENTY-NINE

"This is something new."

"Yeah, what?"

"I've never turned a grown-up into my bitch this quickly before."

"I'm not your bitch," I say. "Just move."

"For sure, you're my bitch," Trevor says, aggressively placing a brown coat-button two squares from my Cheeto. "Checkmate!"

"You can't move the coat-button diagonal."

"Sure I can. That's the queen."

"The quarter's the queen!"

"The quarter's the king."

"This is impossible. There's no way I can play with all of these substitute pieces!"

"Home field advantage, Mr. P."

"I'm getting us a real chess set."

"It's not going to make any difference. In fact, it'll probably just make you feel worse when I beat you."

"I've never really thought chess was a game that lent itself to so much trash talk."

"Then you've never played with the old guys at the park. It's worse than on the basketball court." Trevor holds out his palm, onto which I deposit a five-dollar bill. "Double or nothing?"

"Are you two betting?" Linda Park asks, walking up from behind us.

"Sorry, is that against the rules?" I ask, craning my neck to look her in the eyes.

"I'm willing to look the other way. How much did you take him for, Trev?"

"Fifteen."

"Consider yourself lucky, Mr. P." Linda pulls a vibrating cell phone from her pocket, answers it.

"So, you're a hustler, then?" I ask Trevor.

"I win a few," he replies with a shrug. "Wouldn't necessarily call myself a hustler."

"What are you trying to tell me?!" Linda says into the phone, more than a hint of desperation in her voice. "Well, they can't do that, can they? I mean, how are we supposed to get in and out?"

As Trevor is resetting the chess pieces, I notice that he's swapping a few substitutes on his side — the coat button is now the knight, the quarter is now a rook — making his home field advantage a little more advantageous. But I'm more interested in Linda's phone call than in the clever little cheat.

"But they can't do that! It can't be legal!" Linda hesitates, then continues into the phone, "I'm sorry. I'm not shouting at you. I just don't understand what you're telling me. It doesn't make any sense. How are we supposed to get in and out of the building? Okay, okay. I understand. Call me back when you know more, okay? Okay, thank you."

"What's up?" I ask as Linda disconnects the call.

"That was Sarah. What's up is that the universe is conspiring against us. That's what's up. Good Lord, when are things going to fall our way?" Linda says to no one in particular.

"It's not the building," I say, because it can't be. "What's going on?"

"Oh, no, it's not the building. It's the block."

"The block?"

"The people who own the other buildings on our block. They're shutting off access to the courtyard. Building across it or something, I don't know." Linda lifts her hands to her face, lets out a small sob. "We won't be able to use the courtyard."

"So the kids will find another place to play stickball. There are parks nearby. I don't get why you're so upset," I reply.

"You don't understand. From what Sarah tells me, they're going to cut off access to the courtyard entirely. We won't even be able to walk across it."

"Linda, that doesn't make any sense. How are you supposed to get deliveries? How are people going to get in and out of the building? The courtyard is the only means of entry and egress to the building. They can't just cut it off. That couldn't be legal. And who would want to build onto that space, anyway?"

"It's apparently part of some big gentrification project going on around here. Sarah thinks they're doing it to get rid of us – you know, like, starve us out or something, so we have to move." Linda puts her big hands over her eyes, sobs again.

This is ridiculous.

"I need to make a phone call," I say to Linda, then hesitate. God dammit! "Uh, Linda? Can I borrow your phone? I must have left mine at home."

Linda hands me her cell phone.

"Don't worry, okay? We'll figure it out." I bump fists with Trevor, walk outside the building, and for the second time in a year I use a cell phone. If I wasn't so freaked out about what Linda just told me, I'd probably be congratulating myself for moving on from the whole unplugged thing. But I've got bigger fish to fry.

Fifteen minutes later, my lawyer has brought me up to speed regarding a thoroughly ridiculous gesture on behalf of a private equity consortium – led by the Rejewski family – that is seeking to re-gentrify and upgrade the block on which is centered my newly purchased building.

It appears that the courtyard in front of my new building does not represent a public thoroughfare. Instead, it was built by some manufacturing and warehousing concern that had occupied my building over a hundred years ago, when the entire block was one parcel of land with a single owner. When the block was parceled out and sold as smaller lots, the alleyway and courtyard became the property of the larger buildings adjacent to mine. These buildings straddle the courtyard, extend all the way to the sidewalk, and have recently been purchased by the Rejewski group. By restricting access to the courtyard, they can effectively turn my building into an island, unreachable without crossing the property of the other buildings.

How this bizzaro property arrangement came to be, Leonard explains, is that at the time the properties were split up, no one really cared. Aside from Way-Point, my building had been vacant for several decades. I purchased it from the grandson of the original owner, who had sold the other properties decades earlier. And in my rush to buy the building, I didn't have time to do any due-diligence at all. So, I guess this one's on me.

"This can't be legal, Leonard," I say, digesting all the information he has provided. "You can't have property without some point of entry or egress."

"True," Leonard replies, "but it's been in the city books like that for the past fifty years. No one has ever cared enough to correct or even identify the issue since so many of the buildings on that block were either in disrepair or unoccupied. And you pulled the trigger on the purchase so fast that there was no way we would uncover something like this."

"So how do we fight it, then?"

"We don't, Dan. You know how slow things move in city planning. It would take forever to even address this thing from a legal perspective. And in the meantime, the Rejewski's have the right to restrict access to the property that they legally own."

"This is crazy. How can I own a building but have no access to it other than through someone else's property?"

"You've got the waterfront behind the building... maybe build a dock?"

"I'm serious, Leonard. This doesn't make any sense."

"I'm not saying it makes sense, Dan. But there it is."

"There it is," I echo.

"Anyway, what difference does access make to you? Your building is in the dead center of the block they're trying to re-gentrify. The Rejewski's will pay whatever you ask for it."

"I don't want to sell the building to the Rejewski's. What are my options?"

"You've only got two options, Dan," Leonard says calmly. "Either sell to the Rejewski's or own a building that you cannot get into or out of for the foreseeable future. Sorry, son, but it looks like that's the way it is."

I hang up the phone, look around the wide courtyard. This is so ridiculous. I turn around to head back into the building and drop Linda's phone in a startle when I see Trevor standing in the doorway. How long has he been there?

"Sup?" I say, stupidly.

"Sup, Mr. P," Trevor replies. "You break Miss Park's phone?"

"Nah. Looks like it's okay," I say, picking up the phone and turning it over in my hands.

"That's good," Trevor says. "Miss Parks would have been pissed if you broke her phone."

"Yeah," I reply. "So, ah, how's it going?"

"It's going good. You?"

"Good, good. So, uh, how long you been standing there?"

"Here?"

"Yeah."

"Not long."

"Long enough to hear my phone call?"

"Some of it," Trevor says, looking at his shoes.

"How much?"

"Some."

"What did you hear, Trevor?"

"Hey, want to go double or nothing on another game of chess, Mr. P? It sounds like you can afford it."

As if I didn't have enough problems right now. I think for a second while Trevor alternates between staring at me and looking at his shoes. I don't have the energy to lie my way out of whatever Trevor has heard. And anyway, there are already too many lies to keep track of these days.

"Hey, Trevor. Can you keep a secret?" I ask conspiratorially. At this point, an ally might actually be a good thing. Even if it's just a twelve-year-old ally. We walk back into Way-Point and I tell him everything.

"So, you're rich?"

"Rich is a relative term, Trevor. But, yeah, I've got money."

"I don't think I've ever had a conversation with a rich person before, Mr. P. Much less beat his ass in chess three games straight."

"You manipulate the substitute pieces in between games. I'm on to you."

"That's home field advantage. It's not like I'm cheating."

"Anyway, it's the least of my problems," I sigh.

"Why'd you lie to Miss Sarah in the first place?"

"I told you, I didn't lie. I just, kind of, walked into a lie and didn't fix it."

"Why not?"

"I didn't know I was going to, you know…"

"Crush on Miss Sarah?"

"Who said I was crushing on Miss Sarah?" I ask, defensive, like I'm a fifth grader or something.

"Give me a break, Mr. P. Everyone knows you're crushing on Miss Sarah. You make googly eyes, like, whenever she's around."

"I do not make googly eyes."

"You're making googly eyes now, even just talking about her."

"You're not helping, Trevor."

"And I'm the only one you've told about all this?"

"You and the O'Shaughnessy boys, yeah."

"Are those guys really going to kill themselves?"

"If the right opportunity presents itself, yeah, I suppose." I obviously have no idea what you should or shouldn't talk to tweens about.

"That is so wicked cool," Trevor says.

I'd immediately regretted telling Trevor about the suicide club – unsure what impact that kind of weirdness would have on a twelve-year-old – but he seemed to accept it without much more than raised eyebrows. I think he was more blown away by the fact that they got themselves into huge amounts of debt by getting advanced degrees in philosophy – to which he responded "that there is rich people stupid." To Trevor, the statement suicide thing seemed like a pretty logical conclusion.

"You know that suicide is, like, not something that a kid your age should be thinking about, right? I mean, there's nothing wicked cool about suicide. You know that, right? You should never think about hurting yourself, no matter how bad things ever get," I say, assuming this would be something a responsible adult might say.

"You're going to try to talk to me like you're a grownup after everything you just told me?" Trevor cocks his head, squints his eyes at me.

"I am a grown-up. Just not a very good one. And I thought it was an appropriate thing to mention."

"You don't have to worry about me, Mr. P."

"Good. I'm glad to hear it."

"Still, it's wicked cool how those guys backed themselves into a corner, life-wise I mean, and then decided to go out with a bang. It's like, when you're down to only your king in chess, you know? When there's no way that you can win and all of your moves are just holding out against an inevitable loss?" What twelve-year-old uses words like inevitable, I wonder. "Who wouldn't want to see their king, like, blow up or something. Instead of the slow surrender of checkmate. I dig it!"

"Okay, I agree. There's something totally noble about a last great act of defiance."

"Totally," Trevor confirms with a nod.

"But there's nothing noble about suicide," I re-confirm, "outside of this specific context, right?"

"Sure." Trevor shrugs.

"So, let's wrap commentary on the O'Shaughnessy boys and get back to my problems."

"Okay."

"Okay, so what do you think I should do?"

"Sounds like you're backed into a corner. I think you should kill yourself and leave all your money to me."

"Thanks. That's not an option."

"Okay, well, what problem are we talking about? The fact that this rich people group is trying to cut off the building? Or are we talking about how you get out of lying to Miss Sarah?"

"Both. Either. Any ideas on anything would be helpful."

"Why don't you just sell the building, take the money and use it to buy a new place for Way-Point?"

"Obviously I've thought about that. But the building is so close to the school and the clinic and the subways, we'd never find another location that's as convenient for what Way-Point does. And, most importantly, big money people shouldn't be able to walk into anywhere and just take what they want. Am I right?"

"I have no idea."

"Well, they shouldn't."

"If you say so," Trevor mumbles, out of his element. "So, okay… about you lying to Miss Sarah?"

"About that, any thoughts?"

"I'd say, about that, you're pretty much screwed."

I thank Trevor. We bump fists. I walk out the door of Way-Point and run right into Clancy. What the hell?

CHAPTER THIRTY

"Hey, baby!" Clancy shouts, then shushes herself dramatically. "Oh, right. We're setting each other free. Don't worry. I'll give you your space."

You have got to be kidding me. Why would Clancy, along with a whole bunch of private equity and investment banking suits, be milling around the courtyard in front of Way-Point?

"You missed it, you know," Clancy says.

"I missed it," I reply flatly. "Missed what?"

"The fundraiser thingy! Don't worry. I took notes. And Gwen can give you her presentation in private, if you want. And this is business, right?" She gestures at the cluster of dark-suited men behind her. "So it's not like we're spending time together in a relationship way. So, it's fine, right?"

"Clancy, I have no idea what you're talking about. What are you doing here?"

"Like, why am I still here? I'm involved now, baby. Officially, I mean. I'm helping with social media for the launch party this Saturday. I'm going to blow up the Internet for the re-gentrification project," Clancy giggles.

"Your fundraiser thingy was here?"

"Not here, silly. Over there."

Clancy points to one of the buildings at the mouth of the courtyard. One of the buildings that the Rejewski group owns. My mouth drops as the pieces fall into place. I can't believe it never occurred to me that this Gwen thing is one and the same as the re-gentrification project that is threatening Way-Point.

"I'm not here for any fundraiser thingy, Clancy," I say, steadying myself.

"But if you didn't come for the fundraiser thingy then what...? Aw, baby, you came to see me! If you love something, set it free. If it comes back, it's yours forever. You came back, baby. You're mine forever!"

What a horribly disturbing thought.

"Clancy, I didn't..."

"The wedding's back on!" Clancy screams, right into the face of Gwen, who seems to have appeared out of nowhere. The two of them lock hands and holler shrilly into one another's faces, bouncing up-and-down in sync with the kind of over-enthusiasm that can only be achieved by former cheerleaders.

"Oh, my God, congratulations!" Gwen shrieks.

"And congratulations to you, too!" Clancy responds in kind. "Who's ready to start designing my penthouse again?!"

"Oh, my God. I'm going to be tied up for months on this thing," Gwen pouts, waving her hand at the courtyard.

"Don't you worry! We're going to be engaged for a year, so there's plenty of time for you to finish this thingy and still design my space, too!"

"You'd wait for me?" Gwen asks, her eyes welling with tears.

"Of course, I'll wait for you. I would never have anyone but you design my place," Clancy responds.

The two of them are still clutching hands, but the bouncing has stopped. The way they're looking into each other's eyes, it totally looks like they're going to make out. I glance left and right. All the suits have halted their conversations and are staring open-mouthed at Gwen and Clancy. Behind me, one suit whispers urgent and unconsciously, "Come on, do it, come on, please..."

Well, that all escalated pretty quickly.

"Ladies, there appears to have been a misunderstanding," I say.

The two unlock eyes and turn their faces towards me.

"You suck, dude!" shouts one the private equity suits.

"Let 'em have their moment!" shouts another.

"We are not redesigning my apartment," I say and Gwen gasps. "And we are not getting married." And Clancy gasps. Then both ladies look at me and deflate, like I'm that wrong guest who walked into a surprise party and got everyone excited over nothing.

"Danny, you are the world's biggest buzz kill," Gwen snarls. She knows I hate it when people call me Danny. "Who do you think you are, playing with Clancy's emotions like that?"

"Right on, lady," says one of the suits.

"Scumbag," says another.

"Whatever," I reply, to no one in particular. I know from experience that there's no way to untangle myself from the center of this kabuki theater. But I also know from experience that the Clancy and Gwen show burns out very quickly when I refuse to engage. I wait it out.

Thirty seconds later, life starts up again. Aside from furtive glances from a few of the suits hoping for a sequel, it's like the whole scene never happened.

"So, Danny, why are you here, then?" Clancy breaks the silence, cool and composed, as if the past few minutes were no more important than a Mountain Dew commercial. I can't believe there was a time I wanted to marry into this noise. The highs and lows of Clancy – the emotional equivalent of base jumping.

"Huh?"

"Why are you here, Danny?" Clancy sometimes calls me Danny instead of baby when she's trying to be frosty. Far as I'm concerned, both names suck.

"Why am I here," I repeat. I need to think about that one.

So Gwen's project, which is apparently now Clancy's project as well, is the same project that is threatening Way-Point. How totally random, given all the re-gentrification real estate projects going on in the towns approximate to Manhattan. And as much as I want to smack Gwen in the face, figuratively speaking, with the information that I own the building that has been giving her project so much trouble, I think the smarter move would be to use this interval to gain some further insight into the plans of Rejewski's re-gentrification team.

"Okay, fine. I do want to hear more about this project," I say truthfully.

"Yay! I knew you'd come around, baby!" Clancy shouts, frosty to warm in a heartbeat. I wonder if she might have a dissociative identity disorder. "Where should we go?"

"My place," I offer, because it's not too far a walk.

"Uh, no," Gwen replies icily.

"Not after the incident, baby," Clancy whispers at me, even though I'm no further from her than Gwen. "Oh, I know!"

"I'm not going into Manhattan," I say, as Clancy pulls out her smart phone.

"Hey, it's me. Can Danny, Gwen, and I use your place for a little business meeting? Sure, sure. Maybe in fifteen minutes? No, you don't need to change your clothes. We're intruding on you, silly. What? I don't know," Clancy looks at Gwen. "Black pumps, black stockings, tight black leather skirt – why?" She's talking to Sluggo, obviously. "Hold on a second." Clancy reaches the smart phone towards me. "He wants to talk to you."

"No," I say, taking a step back. As far as she knows, I still don't do digital, the bitch.

"Okay," Clancy shrugs, puts the phone back to her face. "He doesn't want to talk into the cell phone. I know. One step at a time. Anyways, see you in a bit. And thanks, Sluggo!"

"He asked what I was wearing?" Gwen's tone suggests that she'd rather find another place to meet.

"He was just fooling around. You know Sluggo. He's such a rascal. Tell her, baby."

"Sluggo is undoubtedly the most shameless pervert who has ever walked this earth."

"Danny, that's your best friend," Clancy pouts. "And anyways, he's been so nice to me ever since you had your breakdown."

"Sluggo is not my best friend, and I didn't have a breakdown."

"Whatever," Clancy says with a wave of her hand and looks at Gwen. "Sluggo's a good guy, hon. He's just got a twisted sense of humor, but underneath it all he's actually a real gentleman."

"What color is the sky in your world?" I ask Clancy.

"You know Sluggo's loaded, right? He's from an old money family," Clancy says to Gwen, raising her eyebrows and giving me a glimpse of their conversations when I'm not around.

"Gross," Gwen replies. "Anyways, I'm seeing someone, remember?"

"Is Jack out on parole already?" I ask, cruelly. Gwen dated an investment banker who got collared for insider trading a few years back.

"Danny!" Clancy shouts. "We don't talk about that."

"Jack might be in jail, but at least he's still living," Gwen jabs back. "Which is a lot more than I can say for a caveman like you."

"Come on, you two. We're all friends, here," Clancy says, trying to de-escalate rising tensions. She locks arms with Gwen on one side, me on the other, and we walk back to my building.

Chapter Thirty-One

"Good evening," Sluggo says warmly, opening wide the door to his apartment. He is – no joke – dressed in a red silk robe with black trim, leather slippers. He's actually wearing an ascot. It's like he's dressed up as Hugh Hefner for Halloween.

"You know that look doesn't work without a pipe," I say.

"It's in the living room. Clancy, my dear," Sluggo says grandly, giving her a kiss on the cheek, "and Gwen, how nice to see you again. Welcome, welcome."

"Are you even serious?" Gwen asks.

"I mentioned to Clancy that I was already in my leisure wear. I can change if it makes you uncomfortable," Sluggo says gallantly.

"Don't bother," Gwen replies, probably fearing whatever alternative garb Sluggo might select instead. I wouldn't be surprised if he's got a leather gimp outfit somewhere in the apartment.

"A moment, Dan?" Sluggo says, extending his palm towards the kitchen.

"Sure."

"You ladies please make yourselves comfortable in the living room. There's Veuve on ice, as well as bottle of Blue Label if you're interested in something a little stronger."

"Aw, champagne! Sluggo, you're a darling!" Clancy shouts.

"Is there any way we can test this stuff for Rohypnol?" Gwen asks.

"Both bottles are unopened," Sluggo replies as we walk into the kitchen and he shuts the door behind us.

"What are you doing?" I ask.

"What am I doing, what?"

"How exactly do you see this evening playing out?"

"Okay. Actually, I'm glad you asked. So, you know I've got this thing for the Disney princesses, right?"

"A fetish is what it's commonly called."

"Right, whatever. Well, obviously, Clancy's got that princess thing sewn up tight. The innocence, the bubble…"

"The bubble?" I interrupt.

"Yeah, like, the whole bubbly sweet thing she's got going on."

"Calling it the bubble sounds disgusting."

"Fine. Whatever. You know what I mean. And the innocent way she has of accidentally, well…"

"Showing her body?"

"Right, that."

"You don't really think she's doing that unintentionally, do you?" I ask pointedly.

"Hold your tongue! Of course it's unintentional. She's just careless is all."

"No one has that many accidental slips, Sluggo."

"Wawawawawa," Sluggo replies, shaking his head and covering his ears so as not to hear my blasphemy. "Don't ruin it for me, Dan. Please!"

"Okay, fine. Go on."

"What do you mean, go on? Are you telling me that you've never noticed?"

"Noticed what?"

"Come on, man. Don't be dense. I'm talking about Gwen."

"What about her?"

"She's the flip side of the coin, man. She's Clancy's sexy evil twin. Her dark side."

"Gwen is Clancy's dark side," I say flatly.

"Are you kidding me? Look at the facts. Clancy dresses ultra-conservative, but you can always catch a glimpse of something naughty. Gwen dresses naughty – intentionally sexy, I mean – but you can never see anything. I mean, I've never once been able to look up her skirt or down her shirt. It's like she's Fort Knox, the way she hides all the good parts. Clancy's got the bubble…"

"Please stop saying that."

"…and Gwen's a bitter pill if I ever met one. They're mirror opposites of one another. Snow White and Maleficent. Cinderella and her sexy stepmother. And do you know what happens when you put mirror opposites together in the same room and add alcohol?"

"Clancy and Gwen were college roommates. They were alone in the same room with alcohol all the time."

"Stop interrupting. This is my world I'm talking about. Do you know what happens in my world when you put mirror opposites together in the same room and add alcohol?"

"Okay, no. What happens?"

"I have no idea, but I'm sure it will be awesome."

"Why are we in the kitchen, Sluggo?"

"I wanted to thank you, is all."

"You're welcome. Listen, I don't want to make this an all-night thing and I actually do need to understand some stuff about their project, so give me a little talking space, huh?"

"I'm just a fly on the wall."

We walk back into the living room. Clancy and Gwen are both drinking the Veuve, their coats slung across the back of a particularly fluffy and low-seated couch. The low seating has caused the hem of Clancy's sensible white minidress to somehow make its way up around her navel, high enough to see a band of skin above her very tight, white satin panties. Gwen, although seated on the same couch and wearing a much more aggressively sexy miniskirt, has managed to retain her modesty by keeping her thighs in a vise-tight clench.

"See," Sluggo whispers to me. "Conservative-sexy and sexy-conservative. It looks like Gwen has even figured out my couch – which is a first. My step-mom couldn't even figure out my couch. I call it the skirt-buster." He's talking an octave or two below the music, so I can hear him but the girls can't.

Sluggo pours the Blue Label, one for himself and one for me. He presses a button to ignite the gas fireplace and turns the dimmer knob to lower the lights. Walking back to the center of the room, he eyes Clancy's legs and panties in the half-light, squints, returns to the dimmer knob and cranks the lights back up to full power. He hands me the old-fashioned whiskey glass filled with Blue Label, raises his own to toast me and the girls.

"O'Shaughnessy!" I shout. There is no response.

"Dude," Sluggo groans. "You're spending way too much time with those guys."

"Let's talk real estate project," I say to the girls.

Gwen leans forward, carefully pinning her legs together under the watchful gaze of Sluggo, and gives me the full rundown. She walks through the property values of the neighborhoods surrounding the block where, unbeknownst to her, my new building sits. She outlines how the re-gentrification committee purchased five buildings on the block using different shell companies to camouflage their intentions to upgrade the entire site. Gwen really hits her stride when she describes the exterior and interior architectural plans, all designed to create the next generation of a self-contained living community for the super-rich twenty-five-to-forty Manhattan set. I'm flashing back to when I worked with Gwen on my brownstone, the next gen of next gen day-to-day tech living, yada, yada, yada.

"And here's the great news," Gwen says, leaning closer while simultaneously tightening her thighs and holding her low-cut top in place. "This morning we figured out a work-around for the last obstacle standing in our way."

"What obstacle?" I ask innocently.

"You know the building at the center of the block? We don't own it yet. It's abandoned."

It's not abandoned, you self-absorbed bitch.

"Sure, the one at the back of the courtyard. It didn't look abandoned," I say.

"It's abandoned," Gwen says again, "there's some kind of squatter charity using the space, but no long-term tenants. Anyways, the building was just bought out by some mysterious shell company, and the new owners have been holding out on us. Even though we're offering to buy it at fifty points higher than the previous sale, which was, like, a couple days ago."

"Why won't they sell?" I ask innocently.

"Who knows? Probably they're just trying to bleed us, the scumbags. We're not even talking to the owners. Everything goes through their attorneys."

"Okay, go on."

"Yeah, well, this next part is off the record. I mean, you can't tell anyone because it will probably impact the offering price. See, it turns out that the courtyard isn't part of the building's property. It's split down the middle, belonging to the properties on its left and right. And these are the properties that our side owns. So, if the new owners want to play hardball, we can too. We've already informed the attorneys representing the other side, and our lawyers are handling the paperwork as we speak. We're going to freeze them out."

"Freeze them out," I say flatly.

"Yeah, they can't get into or out of the building without trespassing on our property. Once the documents are in place, we'll post security guards at all access points. The building will remain empty until the new owners sell."

"I thought it was already abandoned."

"It is, but we're taking away any prospect of the new owners using or even developing it. And who's going to buy a place with no entry or egress – aside from our people? So, what are they going to do, just sit on a worthless piece of property? Give it a little time, we offer them a fair price and they'll jump on it, believe me. In the meantime, we go ahead with our development plans for the rest of the block."

"Makes sense," I say. "When do you think you'll have the paperwork done to freeze out the building?"

"Our lawyers think we can get it done by Friday, Saturday morning at the latest. Just in time for our media launch event on Saturday night. That's when we will make public exactly how much of the real estate we already own and announce our re-gentrification and upgrade plans for the whole block."

"That's the event I'm doing social marketing for!" squeals Clancy. "I'm going to blow up the Internet! It's my big break."

"Saturday," I mumble.

"But that's not the best news. We haven't told any of our investment partners or prospects that we've solved the problem with that building that we don't own. And we're not going to tell them until all the legal paperwork is in place, which our lawyers assure us will be very shortly. So, Dan, if you want to pull the trigger and invest before we share this information, you can buy in at what will end up being a big discount."

"Two things, Gwen," I say. "First, that sounds a lot like a variation on insider trading, what you just offered me. Second, you keep saying 'we' – I mean, I know you're involved in this project, but it's just on the interior design side, right? Why are you talking to me like you've got the power to make a deal?"

"My boyfriend is the lead investor."

"Your boyfriend?"

"Well, actually… you've got to swear you won't tell anyone, okay?"

"Okay," I say. Clancy nods. Sluggo is hypnotized by Clancy's panties and doesn't seem to have heard a word that Gwen has said.

"Actually, he's my fiancé. He hasn't told his family yet, so we're keeping it under wraps."

"Gwenny!" Clancy shrieks, grabbing her around the shoulders, tumbling backwards on the low-seated couch in a bear hug that finally allows Sluggo a glimpse between Gwen's legs.

"Niiiice," Sluggo sighs.

"I can't believe you didn't tell me, hon! I'm your best friend in the world!"

"I wanted to tell you *so* badly," Gwen says, leaning on her elbow, cupping Clancy's cheeks as they lay on their sides, facing each other, "but I promised I wouldn't. Can you forgive me?"

"I can forgive you anything, hon," Clancy whispers, her lips so close to Gwen's that they're almost touching. This is too much. Either they really are about to make out or at some time during their years of friendship they practiced how to amp guys up because, what they're doing, it's too perfect not to have been choreographed in advance.

"Oh, my God," Sluggo whispers.

"Uh, ladies?" I say, clear my throat.

"Shut up, Dan! Jesus Christ, they're having a moment!" Sluggo screams, loud enough for people across the Hudson to hear.

"I'm so happy for you, Gwenny," Clancy giggles, embraces her friend and they both lift themselves back into a seated position.

"You ruin everything, Dan," Sluggo says, shaking his head. "You're my freaking apocalypse."

"So, Gwen, about your fiancé?" I ask.

"Yeah, so, his family is the lead investor."

"Wait… you're engaged to a Rejewski?"

"How did you know the Rejewski's were leading the project?"

"I'm a property owner in Jersey City," I say, thinking on my feet. "There's a grapevine."

"Oh. Well, yeah. Fourth generation, oldest son. He's the Managing Director of the LLC they set up to handle the re-gentrification of the block. And he's a lawyer, too, so he knows what the legal team is onto when they talk about freezing out the new owners of that building."

"Okay. And what about the insider trading stuff I mentioned earlier? You know you shouldn't be sharing this information with a potential investor." You'd think Gwen would be more careful about this kind of thing after her ex-boyfriend got jailed for insider trading.

"Come on, Dan. I've been bugging Clancy to get you to invest in this project since before I even got the job. There's a string of e-mails going back months – before we even *had* a problem with the new owners of that building. Anyone can invest at the current buy price. Why shouldn't you be able to? There's nothing even remotely suspicious about it."

"She makes a valid point, stupid," Sluggo mumbles, still bitter about my intrusion on Gwen and Clancy's moment.

"Okay, I get it. Now tell me about this launch party next Saturday."

"It's going to be a total media blitz," Gwen says proudly, "network, print and social. All the top heads that talk and hands that hack will be there. It's going to be huge. Everyone in Manhattan will want to move into our new development, just you watch."

Chapter Thirty-Two

"I'm not going to say it."

"Say what?" I honestly have no idea what she's talking about.

"It doesn't make me feel any better to say it, you know," Sarah says, uncharacteristically upbeat, especially given our current situation.

"Say *what*?" I've got too much on my mind for these riddles.

"I will not say I told you so. That's what I'm not going to say."

"You just said it."

"Yeah, but only in the context of not saying it."

"Tell me something, Sarah. When you wait around for bad things to happen, is there something redeeming about when those bad things do actually happen?"

"Don't be ridiculous, Bill."

Sarah actually seems happier than she did before we found out about the plan to freeze us out of the building, back when everything looked so perfect for Way-Point. I feel there's something about Sarah that can't relax unless everything is falling apart.

"Seriously, you were a mess when everything was going our way with the building. And now that we're being frozen out, it's like a weight's been lifted off you."

"There might be something to that," Sarah sighs, rolling her eyes.

"Like what? I mean, I'm interested if you want to talk about it."

"I guess, well, you know how I told you I was homeless for a while, right?"

"I remember that conversation, yes."

"Well, it was like my whole world was turned upside down, you know? I was only a kid, and everything that was supposed to be stable and solid in my life just, like, evaporated. I don't know if things really were great before we lost the farm, but I sure remember them that way. So now, it's like I'm always edged up when things are going well, like I have to prepare myself for when they'll inevitably go off the rails. On the other hand, when things are going wrong, I instinctively put on a brave face and adopt a positive attitude. That's what I had to do to make it through when I was homeless."

"That's not a great way to live, you know. Unhappy when things are good and happy when things are bad."

"It's not like I'm trying to be this way. It's just how I am."

Sarah stops, hands me a little plastic bag. I lean down to pick up Cujo's poop. I decided not to walk the rest of Bill's dogs today and instead am just accompanying gimp-arm Sarah and Cujo.

"I'm just saying, once we get things resolved with Way-Point, you might want to talk to someone about the good-unhappy, bad-happy thing."

"I'm talking to you about it," Sarah offers optimistically.

"I brought it up."

"Yeah, that's true. Okay, I promise that I'll make a serious effort to figure it out when we get some daylight. Is that fair?"

"That's fair," I reply. I don't know why it matters so much to me, though. By the time Sarah gets her head straight, I figure she'll want nothing to do with me. Because, at some point, she will find out I've been lying to her. And the worst part is that it's such a stupid, meaningless lie.

"They told Linda that Way-Point has to be out of the building by Friday, latest Saturday morning. Actually, what they said is, our guests don't have to leave the building, but if they stay past noon on Saturday, they won't be able to get out without being fined for trespassing."

"It sounds like that re-gentrification consortium is made up of some pretty compassionate people."

"That's right, they are," Sarah says sarcastically. "In fact, they're having a big party on Saturday night to celebrate getting over on the little guy yet again."

The launch event. The media blitz. The event that will make everyone in the greater New York City area want to live in their new ultra-modern, high-tech development.

"You're sure there's nothing we can do, from a legal perspective, I mean?" I'm just throwing Sarah a bone. I've been through this with Leonard six ways till Sunday and there's not a legal way out. Not in the short term, at least. Not before Saturday.

"We'd have a better chance of taking down a tank with a squirt gun. They've got a whole team of tier-one lawyers. All we've got is me."

"I'd rather have you on my side than a whole team of tier-one lawyers, any day."

"I'm not even sure if that's a compliment," Sarah sighs.

"Yeah, corporate attorneys are a soulless lot. They should never be compared to good people."

"You really think I'm a good person, don't you, Bill?"

"Sure, I do. I mean, you're, like, my inspiration. Ya make me want ta' be a better man," I grunt in my best Jack Nicholson impression.

"Stop it, Bill."

"What?"

"I, um, I don't feel like a very good person when I'm around you."

"I'm sorry… *what*?"

"That came out wrong. I just, I feel like we might be getting a little too close."

"And the problem with that would be?"

"Don't be an idiot. The problem with that is you're a married man with a child. And I'm not the kind of person who is okay having feelings for a married man, especially a married man with a kid. Look, I know your marriage isn't the greatest, okay. I know you're not happy with Betsy and that you wouldn't be with her if it wasn't for Bitsy. But that doesn't make you any less married."

Did she just say she has feelings for me?

"I think we need to take a break," Sarah says.

She definitely said she has feelings for me. Wait... what was that last bit?

"Not spend so much time together," Sarah continues.

"Sarah, that's crazy talk." I should just tell her now. This is a perfect opportunity to come clean.

"It's not crazy talk, Bill. You know I have this thing about hardcore honesty. And you've agreed to be honest with me so I'm going to be honest with you. And if I'm being honest, I'm starting to not trust myself around you. I feel like I could be talking to you and at any second I could kiss you – like it would just happen and I wouldn't be able to stop it."

Wow. That has got to be the coolest thing that a girl has ever said to me.

"And I'm definitely not going to get into a dishonest relationship. I mean, if you even feel the same way about me."

"Sarah, what if I told you that there was a little misunderstanding happening here?"

"You don't feel the same about me. Oh, my God, I'm so embarrassed." Sarah covers her eyes with her hands.

"No, no, no... not that. I, uh, totally feel the same way about you. Probably more so."

"So that's why it's got to stop," Sarah sobs.

"No, no. The misunderstanding, remember? What if I told you – and just kind of keep an open mind about this until I can explain, okay – what if I told you..."

"Hello there, Bill."

This cannot be happening.

"Hello, Sarah," my brother says casually, walking towards us with his pack of dogs and a stroller full of Bitsy.

"Hey, Dan," Sarah says, wiping her eyes. "Long time no see."

"Little brother's been taking over dog duty for the past few days, as you well might know. I'd congratulate you for losing the air-cast on your leg, but you seem to have replaced it with something even more menacing." Bill is talking in a way that reminds me of the Thurston Howell character from *Gilligan's Island*. I can only assume this is the wealthy persona he wears for the dog park crowd. It's kind of interesting to experience it, firsthand.

"The jig is up, dude. I'm telling her, right now."

"Dear boy, I don't know what you're talking about."

"You're telling me what?" asks Sarah.

"Far out, man! This is the first time I've seen the two of you here together!" shouts the spandex cowboy, walking up to us with his pack of dogs. "Dan and Bill Johnson, the prince and the pauper. Man! Oh, no offense, Bill – that's kind of what we call you guys around here. Hee, hee. Whoa, Sarah, what's up with the arm?"

"I have to keep my hand elevated for two weeks," Sarah says.

"Bummer," the spandex cowboy says. He appears to have no intention of asking why.

"Hello there, Rolf. I hope you're feeling well," Bill says majestically.

"I am stoned off my gourd," the spandex cowboy replies. "So, yah, feeling good."

"Your daughter, my good man," Bill says, out of nowhere handing me a sleeping Bitsy. Because my only alternative would be to drop my niece on the concrete, I take her in my arms. Thankfully, Bitsy doesn't wake up.

"What did you want to tell me, Bill?" Sarah asks as I nuzzle my sleeping niece against my chest.

"Uh, I…"

"Well, if t'isn't the brothers Johnson! I've not seen the two of you together in the park before. Sure, it's a lovely day for a walk, though."

You have got to be kidding me.

"Siobhan, my dear, how perfectly wonderful to see you," Bill says grandly.

"It's clear to see that you love your daughter very much," Siobhan says to me gravely, grasping my shoulder above Bitsy's sleeping head, her knowing eyes locked on my brother. "And that is all that matters, isn't it?"

"Yeah," I reply, "whatever."

"Bill, what…" Sarah asks urgently.

"Jamie! Jesus and all the saints! Do not put that in your mouth!" Siobhan screams at her charge, who's hunched over a steaming pile on the lawn. It's the smudge of poop on the child's chin that makes me vomit in my mouth.

Enough, I think. That's enough. I let out a defeated sigh, hand Bitsy back to Bill.

"Bill?" Sarah says.

"Another time, Sarah. It was nothing. I'll tell you some other time."

I nod at my brother, the spandex cowboy and Siobhan in rapid succession. I tell Sarah that I'll see her tomorrow. And I walk out of the park. I walk straight into the guts of Jersey City.

Chapter Thirty-Three

"Twas the universe conspirin' against ye, mate."

"Twas that, indeed," I reply, not caring that I have slipped into a brogue.

"Tis na necessarily a bad thing. Just means t'was na the right time, boyo."

"Not the right time," I nod, shooting a Jameson and following it with a swig of Guinness.

"Yer followin' yer heart, boyo?" Cleary asks.

"I am, yeah."

"Well, then. Ye gotta trust the universe. It knows what it's doin', sure. And do ye ken who taught us all about trustin' the universe?"

"O'Shaughnessy," I respond flatly. Then, deciding not to be a total jerk, I raise my Guinness.

"O'Shaughnessy!" Toasts the hoard of suicide-apparents at the bar.

"I was going to tell her. It was the perfect time."

"Twasn't," Cleary replies.

"You weren't even there."

"Does na matter. The time wasn't right, ye feckin' gobshite."

"And you say this because…"

"Because ye didn't tell her. So, tweren't the right time. Ye got to give yerself up, boyo. Let go an trust the force, like young Luke Skywalker did."

"Do you really believe that?"

"Course. We live it, do we not? We been waiting in this bar for going on two years now, trustin' the universe'll give us an opportunity to snuff ourselves in a meaningful and spectacular way. In a way that would make that dear, feckin' genius O'Shaughnessy proud."

"O'Shaughnessy!" toasts the bar.

"Okay, so *what* makes you believe that the universe will make that happen?"

"I am a doctor of philosophy, am I not?"

"I've never actually seen any corroborating evidence of that point, but I'm willing to accept it as truth, yes."

"Me an dem boyos, we was the most serious students of philosophy. Sure, we was fooked up most of the time, but tha's na such a bad thing when yer a student of philosophy. An do ye ken the most important thin' tha we learnt in all those years?"

"I do not, no."

"T'was a rhetorical question, ye eejit. What we kenned is, the problem with philosophy is all the bloody thinkin' philosophers do about it," Cleary says, disgusted.

"Ah. So, you would suggest a practice of philosophy that does not involve so much thinking, then?" I ask with a heavy dose of sarcasm. These people continue to get weirder and weirder, and yet I have no urge to dismiss their advice. I wonder if it's only morbid curiosity on my part.

"Aye, tha's exactly what I'd suggest, ye sarcastic fecker. And don't think we all are unaware of the irony. Do ye know that every philosophical concept tha these famous philosophy buggers wit their too-thick-to-read books came up wit, do ye know that every single one of them concepts can be found in poems writtin' hundreds o'years before their own efforts."

"What are you even talking about?" I ask.

"Every single thick-book philosophy concept that was ever defended, not a one was an original thought. You can find every single philosophical concept that ever existed in the works of the poets so many years before this shite they call modern philosophy."

"Wait, seriously?"

"Twas the topic of O'Shaughnessy's dissertation, it was."

"O'Shaughnessy!" toasts the bar.

"All them buggers with their mathematical thinkin', spendin' years of their lives ta unearth something that had already been discovered hundreds o'years before by people who thought not with their heads, but with their hearts."

"Seriously," I say flatly.

"O'Shaughnessy cited examples from every major branch o' philosophy, boyo. Hundreds o' them, not a stone unturned. Sure, philosophers, they put their arguments forth in a way that a scientist might understand, but not a one o' them philosophical concepts was new. Twas was all in the poetry of the past, clear as day."

"Meaning?"

"Meaning philosophy is a load o'crap, ye eejit. It's no more than a masturbatin' of the frontal lobe to ejaculate answers that the heart has known the whole time. An we," Cleary addresses the bar, "bein' doctors o' philosophy, should have a rather keen insight into O'Shaughnessy's opinions."

"O'Shaughnessy!" toasts the bar.

"So, O'Shaughnessy and the rest of this crew... you all lost your religion, so to speak?"

"Aye, and twas the best wasted years of our lives before we lost it."

"And that's why you decided to kill yourselves."

"Nah, boyo. We decided to live."

"By killing yourselves."

"Yer getting fresh, ye maggot. What were the lot of us ta do? We weren't going to teach philosophy or write books about it, leading others down the crooked path we'd followed. So, what? Work at Starbucks or Wal-Mart? Nah, the universe provides a way out if you keep the faith. It did for O'Shaughnessy, sure."

"Because he killed himself."

"Shut yer gob, eejit. O'Shaughnessy's grand gesture was the most spectacular suicide in the history o' the world. He inspired the lot of us. Would he have accomplished that much working retail? Was he the type o' guy who would continue playin' Super Mario Brothers when he'd lost two lives in the first couple of minutes, or was he the type to reset the game and start over?"

"Super Mario Brothers?"

"We played a lot o' video games in grad school. The analogy holds if ye think about it."

"Okay. So, I'm assuming he's the type of guy who would start over."

"Sure, he was. But he didn't just quit, did he? O'Shaughnessy recognized the opportunity to make a statement. O'Shaughnessy, he was a true prophet of the Old Testament type, he was."

"O'Shaughnessy!"

"He was a prophet because...?" I ask.

"Set us on our course, he did. Ya need ta forget about what society thinks – aye, thinkin' being the main problem of society, as we well know – ya need ta trust yer heart and know that the same power that gave them brilliant insights to the poets will provide for ye as well. Long as ye have the faith."

"Faith that the universe will provide an excellent reason for you to kill yourselves in a spectacular fashion," I say, trying to summarize, "because this would be far more meaningful than if you were to shrug off your advanced degrees and live ordinary but discounted lives – discounted, I mean, because a doctorate in philosophy will never get you the type of job you'd need to pay off your crushing student loans."

"Aye, tis the choice we've made and we trust the universe to deliver its end of the bargain."

"Okay, I get it. And in a twisted sort of way, it holds up."

"Thank ye. Not many people understand."

"It's my pleasure. Anyway, I get where you guys are at. So, do you have any advice for me at this point?"

"Sure, stop swimmin' upstream and just trust the universe the way we do."

"This is the same universe that just buggered me at the dog park."

"One man's buggering is another man's honeymoon. Ye just need to change yer perspective. Didn't we tell ye not ta explain things to this Sarah girl until you knew the time was right?"

"And more importantly," I'm surprised to hear myself say, "what about Way-Point? These families have hit the skids and are trying to turn their lives around – with a lot more fortitude than I've ever had. Am I supposed to trust that the universe will find a solution for them, too?"

"It will if ye believe it will," Clancy says solemnly. "All the pieces are there. Ye just need a different perspective to put them together in the right way."

"We're totally shut out from a legal perspective."

"Donna trouble yerself about the law – that's the world o' yer head. What do laws mean ta the heart? Jus' listen to yer heart and the universe will offer to ye the opportunity for a grand gesture that'll cure all yer ills."

"You really think if I just stop thinking so much about these problems and instead – I don't know, be open? – you think if I do that, then out of the blue I'll somehow receive the know-how to fix my relationship with Sarah *and* save Way-Point?"

"Just as did the poets of old, O'Shaughnessy would say. Like George Michael sings, ye got to have faith, boyo."

"You really believe all this, don't you?" I ask gravely.

"I'm bettin' me life on it, ye gobshite!" Cleary shouts. "All of us are, then, aren't we, boys?"

"O'Shaughnessy!" toast the suicides-in-waiting.

Chapter Thirty-Four

"I had nothing to do with Rolf and Siobhan showing up, you know."

"I never said you did, Bill."

"Hell, I wasn't even expecting to run into you guys. It just happened."

"I know, Bill. I'm not blaming you for anything," I say honestly.

That stuff about the poets, O'Shaughnessy's dissertation, how all the conclusions of advanced philosophy could be found in poems hundreds of years prior, maybe that's what pushed me over the edge. Or maybe it's that my head hasn't gotten me anywhere in terms of my current problems, so what have I got to lose just following my heart and trusting the universe?

God, I've always hated New Age people, and now it's like I'm one of them.

"And you said nothing about telling Sarah the truth yesterday. I mean, if you'd given me a heads-up maybe I could have prepared or something, you know? But I just walk up on the two of you and of course I'm going to be in character… what would you expect?"

"It wasn't the right time anyway, Bill. I'm okay with it, really."

"And then Rolf and Siobhan show up out of nowhere? I mean, I've never really had to deal with more than one of the dog park people at a time. They usually respect a paired-off conversation, say their hellos and walk off, which is why I've been able to create so many different plot lines at the dog park. I've never seen them congregate like that before."

"Why did you create so many different plot lines?"

"Creative expression, I guess. I've got a lot of regret bottled up inside of me. Telling different stories to different people was kind of a way for me to release some of my internal tension. Frankly, I was amazed where my mind went. Sort of became, like, an addiction. Plus, I was pretty stoned most of the time so I wasn't really considering potential consequences."

"You ought to try writing down some of those stories, man. Maybe start a fiction blog or write a book or something. Channel your creative expression into something less, you know, socially combustible."

"Are you kidding?"

"What?"

"Mister zero-tolerance for digital technology is telling me to start a blog?"

"I have no problem with technology, Bill. I just didn't like the way it was distracting me so much, especially after I sold my company. Something wasn't right with my life back then, and I felt like the constant distraction of new technology just made it easier and easier to avoid setting myself straight."

"And you think you're setting your life straight now?"

"Maybe."

"Even though you're in love with a girl who thinks you're me, and the homeless support group you're all into is about to become homeless itself."

"I admit there are some external conflicts that need to be resolved. But inside, I feel like I've become more the person I want to be – the person I would want to have around in my own life. I've never really felt that way. Before, it was like I was just someone who was taking up space – pursuing goals that never really mattered to me. Essentially, just killing time."

"You made hundreds of millions of dollars, Dan. Cry me a river."

"I'm not complaining. I'm stating the facts. I had everything that normal people would ever think they wanted, and I wasn't happy. So, I unplugged – from technology, from Clancy, pretty much from the world – so I could figure out what makes me happy. Is that so hard to understand?"

"And now you've figured out what makes you happy?"

"I think so. I mean, Sarah makes me happy. When I'm with her, I feel nothing like the way I feel when I'm with Clancy. Sarah makes me feel whole, you know? And Way-Point makes me happy. I like helping people who deserve to be helped. That's who I am… as far as I can tell."

"Okay, you win," Bill sighs.

"Win what?"

"I'm done pretending to be you. I'll talk to Sarah and the rest of the dog park people. Come clean. Tell them you were only trying to help your seriously disturbed little brother because you were worried about the emotional trauma that might ensue if you pulled the rug out from under my fantasy life."

"You don't have to do that, Bill."

"I want to. You've inspired me. I want to make things right."

"Thanks, man. But seriously, I want you to hold off a little longer. Things are too volatile with the Sarah situation – emotionally, I mean. I need to tell her at the right time. Then, any help you can give me would be much appreciated, believe me."

"Okay, we can wait to tell Sarah, but once we do, I'm going to gather up everyone in the dog park and tell them all at the same time. It will be easier that way. Give them a bit of the shock and awe treatment, align their collective perception around a single truth. That way the mob can unload some of the tension on each other and it won't all be directed at me. And then – blammo! – in an instant their perception of me will be changed forever. Mobs are self-reinforcing that way."

"Blammo," I whisper, in the midst of what might be an epiphany. "In an instant, how they think of you will be changed forever."

"Don't rub it in, Dan. This is my catharsis."

"Little brother," I say thoughtfully, "you might have just helped the universe plant a seed that could grow into a whole lot of catharsis."

"What do you mean by that?"

"I'm not sure yet." And it's true. All I've got is a flicker of an idea triggered by what Bill just said. A flicker, but it's glowing brighter and brighter by the second. Because so much of the re-gentrification project depends on public perception.

And... I've got it. It never mattered that we had no legal recourse to halt the re-gentrification group's freeze-out. What we should have been working on is spoiling the public's perception of the project itself. Freezing us out of the building may technically be legal, but that doesn't mean people would like it – if we can make them understand what's actually going on. And why stop there?

Chapter Thirty-Five

"What are you even talking about, Bill?" Sarah asks me.

"We protest, take to the streets. Think Occupy Wall Street."

"Oh, yeah. Think about Occupy Wall Street. It doesn't work against Wall Street types. And the real estate moguls coordinating this re-gentrification project make the people who actually work on Wall Street look like lambs. We can protest all we want. They won't give a damn."

"It doesn't matter if the re-gentrification people ignore our protests, we're not aiming at them. Our target is the media. And the re-gentrification project has already done us the favor of rounding up a huge representation of the media for us – at their launch party on Saturday. And we've got the element of surprise on our side. We can smear the project in front of the media, don't you get it?" I say, still thinking it through as I speak.

"Sounds great," Sarah says flatly, "only one small problem."

"What's that?"

"People. We don't have them."

"Well, we've got the families from Way-Point, right? And I assume we can get some support from the other shelters and organizations that you and Linda know. Anyway, it's not so much the quantity of the crowd, it's the quality. With the number of media people at that party, even a small crowd can have a big impact. And it's not like we're going to have some kind of debate with the re-gentrification project people. We just need to publicly smear the project so that people won't want to buy the condos and live there. That gives us a lot of flexibility in terms of how we can play this out. I'm thinking waves of flash mob protests," I say, the idea pretty much coming to me as I say it.

"You're not really making any sense."

"Sorry, I'm a little hyped up. So, let's take it from the top, okay?"

"Okay," Sarah replies in a voice that one would typically reserve for a very young child with very severe special needs. I ignore her tone.

"The re-gentrification project is having a launch event on Saturday, yes?"

"Yes."

"They have hired a major PR firm and several independent PR agents to make sure that this launch event receives the maximum media attention possible."

"I'm not sure where you're getting your information, but yes, that sounds reasonable."

"Great. And their objective? To make a huge splash in the real estate market and establish their re-gentrification project as the hot new place to live for rich young families ready to move out of Manhattan but remain within an easy commute."

"Sure."

"And they have no reason to suspect that anyone would want to sabotage their event."

"Sabotage?"

"Classic sabotage. We want to use their own efforts and momentum as a means to achieve a result that is diametrically opposed to their original intention."

"You're sounding crazy again."

"Hear me out. So, that's the situation. What are our advantages?"

"You tell me."

"Well, the first and most important advantage is surprise. They have no idea that anyone is planning to sabotage their event, so we can expect them to prepare for the event in a way that leaves them completely exposed, correct?"

"I suppose."

"So, we need to capitalize on that advantage by closely guarding the element of surprise. Anticipate their reactions. Counter with the unexpected."

"Such as?"

"Such as, phase one. With no prior warning, five minutes following the start of their launch party, a seemingly spontaneous protest of people – belonging to or associated with the homeless population – surrounds the event. They have signs, bullhorns, air horns. We make sure that they're equipped to make a ruckus. And the best part is, they're protesting with good cause, the re-gentrification project's intention to freeze Way-Point out of their building."

"I doubt we'll be able to gather enough people to surround the event."

"That's okay. We can use some people from phase two."

"Phase two," Sarah sighs.

"Phase two," I repeat. "Confusion. Now I know you've got this thing about rigid honesty, Sarah, but for this plan to work we're going to have to rely a bit on a little white lie."

"I'm not sure I want to hear this."

"But you have to, Sarah. I mean, do you have any other ideas to save Way-Point?"

"No, I don't," Sarah replies, defeated.

"No, you don't. So, if this last grand act of defiance is going to work, we'll need to compromise our principles and be just a little bit dishonest."

It's not my primary motivation, but I hope that introducing some collaborative dishonesty into this equation will soften Sarah's firm stance on honesty, especially regarding the relatively unrelated matter of me not being Bill.

"What do you mean?"

"Well, for one," I say, thinking on my feet, "we could tell some of the dog park people that the re-gentrification project is being funded by the largest animal testing facility in the country."

"No way," Sarah gasps.

"Yes. The re-gentrification project is playing dirty by trying to freeze out Way-Point. So, we can play dirty too. We can play the PETA card. Think about how that would rile up some of the people you know at the dog park. They'd cause havoc at the gentrification project's launch event."

"But the gentrification project has nothing to do with animal testing. They're real estate people."

"I know," I say. "That's what's will be so confusing. You get a bunch of dog park people and their friends sloshing red paint all over the private equity, investment banking, and media people – they won't have any idea what's going on. None of them, especially the media. And even though the television, print and social media people will be completely blindsided, you've got to expect they'll be all over this circus run amuck because it's a sure bet that whatever content they get at the event will end up going viral. And, obviously, media people's priority will be to make sure that their audiences do not perceive them as sympathetic to the people PETA is attacking. That would be a nightmare for anyone trying to keep an audience."

"But you're throwing all the dog park people under the bus. I mean, it's eventually going to come out that the re-gentrification project is in no way associated with animal testing labs."

"Sarah, you want to make an omelet, you've got to break some eggs. Anyway, I've talked to my brother and I think he'll take the brunt of outrage from the dog park people."

"What does that mean?"

"It means he's got some unresolved issues with the dog park crowd, but he intends to resolve them in the near term. Taking responsibility for the misinformation about animal testing, it'll help him balance out… in a karmic sense."

"I don't have any idea what you're talking about."

"You don't have to. So, where were we? Right. We've got a blatant social injustice being righteously protested by members and/or representatives of the homeless community. That's strike one. And we follow it with a surreal, unrelated and totally unwarranted uprising by people against animal cruelty. That's strike two. And all of it is being blasted out by insecure media people who don't want to have a thing to do with anything that's on the wrong side of the fence."

"What's strike three?"

"I'm still thinking about strike three. It's a work in progress."

"You must have some idea."

"Strike three needs to be an indelible stain. It's got to salt the earth, make people not want to live there. Like I said, I'm working on it."

"Bill," Sarah says haltingly.

"I don't know what it's going to be yet," I lie. I have some idea.

"No, that's not what I meant. What were you going to tell me yesterday at the dog park?"

"Nothing. It was nothing. Forget about it."

"You seemed pretty amped up is all."

"I was having a problem with Bill," I hiccup. "Dan, I mean. I was having a problem with Dan, not you. Sorry if I was short."

"What kind of problem? And did it have something to do with me?"

"Why would it have anything to do with you?"

"Because you said – a couple of times – that you had something to tell me. And then you walked away without telling me anything."

I can't lie to her anymore.

"Bill?"

But that doesn't mean I have to tell her the whole truth.

"Bill."

"Sarah, Dan's accounts haven't been frozen by the IRS." I mean, she's going to find out soon, anyway. "He's the one that bought the Way-Point building. He's the one that extended the lease and is refurbishing the building."

"What?!"

"It's true."

"But Dan never even showed the slightest bit of interest in Way-Point," Sarah gasps. "Why would he do something like that?"

"Honestly, I wish I could tell you." I can't lie to her anymore.

"So just tell me."

"Dan has feelings for you," I say, which is technically, totally the truth.

"Your brother has feelings for me?"

"That's not what I said," I speak before thinking.

"That's exactly what you just said."

"Okay. I'll give you this and then we're going to end the conversation," I say, hyperventilating slightly. "Dan has recognized what a selfless person you are. Whether you know it or not, the good you do for other people has changed Dan's perspective on life. You've had an impact on him – you and a bunch of suicidal faux-Irishmen, but they're beside the point. Anyway, Dan cares about you and what you're doing with Way-Point. He just has some obstacles when it comes to showing his feelings." Some pretty major obstacles, I might add.

"But I don't even know Dan. I mean, he walked Cujo when I hurt my leg, and he dumped a whole load of his life on me about the IRS freezing his… wait, you say that part wasn't even true?"

"Nah. Why he told you that story, I guess he wanted to buy the building and get Way-Point out of a jam without you knowing it was him." Technically, aside from the part about the motivation for my brother's storytelling, nothing I'm saying here is a lie.

"Wow," Sarah sighs.

"Yeah," I sigh back.

"I mean, I'm grateful and all… but, Dan? I never had any emotional connection with him, you know, like romantically? I mean, he could have been my brother for all I'd felt about him."

"I know. I feel the same."

"He is your brother."

"Yeah, so I, like, know how you feel."

"I'm not attracted to Dan, you know."

"Let's put a pin in that one – at least until we've gotten through the re-gentrification shindig on Saturday, shall we?" I say, desperately trying to change the subject. "Now are you in or out?"

"I still don't know if it's a good idea."

"Give me your top three options to save Way-Point before Saturday and we'll go from there. Come on, don't think about it. Just speak."

"I don't have any other ideas."

"See. Then we can both agree that my currently unfinished idea happens to be the best option we have to save Way-Point before Saturday. So, can you reach out to the homeless support organizations for an impromptu protest?"

"I guess."

"You guess?"

"Yes, I can gather up all the homeless and support personnel who would be interested in doing a flash-mob protest on Saturday."

"Great. Really, that's all I need from you. You're, like, the lieutenant in charge of phase one. Remember, it's a flash-mob protest, so they don't show their hand until they get the signal."

"What signal? You've given me, like, no detail or timing or anything."

"Dan will send you an e-mail."

"Dan doesn't use computers or the Internet."

"Dan is reconsidering his position on technology. Here, this is Dan's e-mail." I pull out my wallet, find a business card. As far as I know, my business e-mail still works. "Shoot him an e-mail and he'll respond with all the details for phase one. If you can't get through, just call or come over. No, actually, don't come over. Just call if there's a problem."

"Why shouldn't I come over?"

"Dan's having the halls of the building fumigated for bedbugs. Not sure when it starts. People can't go in or out of their apartments for six hours tomorrow. Bad timing, eh?"

"He's fumigating the halls, but not the actual apartments?"

"Right. None of the apartments have complained about bedbugs." I really don't know how to lie. Bill would have come up with something so much better than bedbugs.

"So, why's he fumigating the halls?"

"Conscientious foresight. I mean, he's very committed to the comfort and security of his tenants. And, you know, this bedbug epidemic has been all the talk in Manhattan. People are worried. Why shouldn't he take advance steps?"

I reach back into my pocket and hand her a wad of hundred-dollar bills, six or seven I imagine.

"What's this for?" Sarah asks.

"Uh, Dan wants you to have it. For, like, legit signs and other protest paraphernalia. Remember, the media will be there so we need to make this protest look as robust as possible. Have them burn a flag or something. If you need to spend more, go ahead. Dan will pay you back. Just remember, we only have one chance to get this thing right, so don't skimp on the props… or the direction to any of the recruits you can find."

"What about the dog park people?"

"Bill, uh…" Jesus Christ on a bicycle! "… Dan! Dan will take care of the dog park people. He's in charge of phase two." Just let me have a heart attack and get it over with. "We've got three days. Do you think you can get a crowd from the homeless and support community?"

"I'll do my best."

"That's all I can ask. Except, remember, if you don't pull through, the plan might fall apart and the Way-Point families will be out on the street."

"No pressure there. You ever think about being a motivational speaker?"

I was, in fact, offered substantial amounts of money to speak to university and commercial groups on many occasions. Never did it, though. Probably because I never really had anything to say back then.

"Just do your part," I say, turning and walking out the door of Sarah's apartment before I break down and ask her to go steady or marry me or something.

Sometimes you just recognize the person you're supposed to be with for the rest of your life. And here's a bit of advice. When you recognize that special someone, it's best if you hadn't spent the prior two weeks lying to her about being your own brother.

Chapter Thirty-Six

"You're sure you know what you're going to say?" I ask.

I negotiate the leashes of four dogs while Bill strides purposefully beside me, leash-free. In Bill's jacket are five envelopes, each containing five hundred dollars cash. We'd decided that was appropriate working capital for applicable recruits to use for protest paraphernalia. Additionally, inside each envelope is a printed outline of the timing and access details for the re-gentrification launch party.

"I know what I'm going to say. Don't be so anxious. It will be fine."

"It's just that, this is, like, super important."

"Have I given you any indication that I think otherwise?" Bill replies, way too casual.

"You've done your research, then?"

"I know more about animal testing than I'd ever want to know. It really is disgusting what these laboratories do to those poor, helpless creatures. I'm glad to be on board. This is something I can be proud of. I loaded up some really horrifying pictures on my phone. No playing, this cruelty has got to stop."

I halt abruptly, grab Bill's shoulder with my free hand, turn him to face me.

"Bill, you realize that there isn't any real connection between animal testing and the re-gentrification project, right?"

"Sure. Why?"

"You just seem a little too into the nobility of what you're about to do."

"If you haven't noticed, I have a habit of immersing myself in make-believe worlds. Don't worry. It'll work to your advantage in this case. Wait until you see the other stuff I've researched."

"Other stuff?"

"You didn't think we were just going to go with the one-size-fits-all animal cruelty thing, did you?" Bill asks incredulously.

"I did, as a matter of fact."

"You're such a rookie," Bill replies. "Just follow my lead, okay?"

"Fine, whatever. And it really doesn't bother you to lie to these people?"

"Seriously?" Bill asks, rolling his eyes. "That ship sailed ages ago. Just relax. This is my field of expertise. I know what I'm doing. Ah, here we go!"

I see the spandex cowboy, towed by six dogs, walking casually towards us. He doffs his cowboy hat in greeting.

"You think the spandex cowboy is right for what we're doing?" I ask.

"Are you kidding me? I mean, Rolf probably doesn't have much of a network, but are you telling me you don't want *that guy* showing up to protest your event?"

"Good point."

"Anyway, Rolf is easy. He can be, like, a test run. Now let me get into character." Bill takes a deep breath and expels it slowly, puts on a jaunty expression and shouts, "Rolf, my dear boy!"

The conversation that follows is honestly one of the most ridiculous I've ever been a party to. Bill explains to Rolf – in a fairly straightforward manner, I might add – how the re-gentrification project plans to freeze out Way-Point. Then he explains how the re-gentrification project is being driven by capital representing the interests of a consortium of animal testing laboratories – which is a little less believable, but still pretty straightforward. From there, things go way off the rails.

"So, the PETA people, they're involved in this?" Rolf asks anxiously.

"Not the PETA people… the people behind the PETA people. Let's not be ignorant, Rolf. The real war going on right now is a financial war. A war for control. It's like how the Americans and Russians were backing the contra and contra-contra groups in Nicaragua back in the late seventies."

"Are we the contras, or the contra-contras, in this scenario?"

"We'd be the contra-contras in this scenario, but that's neither here nor there. We're the good guys is all."

"Right."

"And I guess you can figure out why the animal-lab-funded 're-gentrification project' is planning to lay siege to Way-Point."

"Something bad," Rolf says, indignant.

"Something bad, indeed. Our intelligence suggests that they plan to develop a huge animal testing facility in the labyrinth of tunnels that exists beneath the Way-Point block."

"The bastards!"

"And why would they build this facility beneath a homeless support organization, in the middle of a city with a fairly substantial homeless problem? Can you think of a reason they might do that, Rolf?"

"Subsidies!" Rolf shouts. "The bastards are getting state subsidies!"

"No, not subsidies, Rolf. The bastards are planning to expand their lab testing operations to include a new species. A species that no one will miss."

"You mean rats!" Rolf shouts, as indignant as he would be if Bill were to suggest humans. Of course, even a five-year-old could deduce that human testing is exactly what Bill is suggesting.

"Sure, Rolf, they'll test on rats. But what I'm talking about is the homeless population. Our intelligence suggests that they plan to test their drugs on homeless people."

"Mein Gott," Rolf whispers.

"We know of similar facilities that exist in South and Central America, Central Asia, Russia, West Africa and, of course, the coal mining regions of Central Pennsylvania. It was obvious to our intelligence team that the next logical step would be to set up shop in Jersey."

"Of course," Rolf nods introspectively.

I crane my neck and glance at Rolf's pupils to see if they are over-dilated because I can't imagine anyone would buy this story unless he were tripping balls on mushrooms or some other psychedelic drug.

"Our intelligence only discovered the location and timing of the re-gentrification project's event yesterday, so we don't have time to mount a full counter-attack by Saturday. We've been instructed to gather pure-hearted local citizens sympathetic to our cause as a means to engineer a skirmish at the Saturday event. The main obstacle we've encountered, given our tight timeframe, is finding these concerned citizens…" Bill lets the statement hang.

"I could see where that would be a problem," Rolf says sympathetically. Bill stares at Rolf. Rolf continues to stare back at Bill, nodding. This goes on for about thirty seconds.

"Might you be one of those sympathetic individuals, Rolf?" Bill asks, finally giving up on Rolf snapping up the bait on his own. A small nuclear explosion seems to detonate behind Rolf's eyes.

"I am!" Rolf bellows, sticking his finger into the air like John Travolta in *Saturday Night Fever*. "I am one of those peoples you are looking for!" The emotional outburst has brought out his German accent substantially.

"And might you have like-minded friends, Rolf? Friends you can trust?" Rolf rolls his eyes upward, stroking his soul patch in deep thought.

"I may have friends, a special group," Rolf says finally. "This skirmish, it would not involve the efforts of Interpol or the FBI?"

I seriously do not want to know why the involvement of Interpol or the FBI would matter to Rolf or his special group of friends.

"No, this protest skirmish has to happen outside the law for now. You know, because of all the red tape involved with the legal bureaucracy."

"Wunderbar," Rolf whispers. "My special friends would be perfect."

"That's what I'd hoped, Rolf," Bill says. "Now listen. We will be trying to recruit several cells, each of which will operate independently. There is to be no communication among the cells prior to the event on Saturday."

"Spies could be anywhere," Rolf nods knowingly.

"Okay, sure. Remember, there is to be no violence. This skirmish is only intended to expose the evil roots of the re-gentrification project to the public. There will be plenty of media in attendance to capture and communicate your efforts. How you plan to execute those efforts – creatively speaking – is entirely up to you."

"Now, I must go," Rolf says, giving Bill a grand military salute.

"Wait, Rolf. One more thing, and it's extremely important. You must tell no one where you got this information. Before, during, or after the skirmish. You must not reveal your source."

"You are, I think, a double agent? That is how you obtained this information in the first place?"

In response, Bill gives Rolf a dramatic wink. Then he hands Rolf an envelope containing the logistical details about the event as well as the five hundred dollars in cash – for protest expenses, he explains. Bill repeats that Rolf seriously can't tell anyone where any of this information or money came from.

Rolf, unphased by the cash, gives him another salute and walks rapidly away behind a handful of leashes. If it weren't for the comment about Interpol and the FBI, I would have assumed Rolf's special group of friends as likely to be canine.

"Tell me you will not try to use that story on any sane people," I say when Rolf is out of earshot.

"Different stories for different people, man. That's my bag. Just trust me."

"I'm trying to trust you, but that last bit would have been more believable in cartoon form."

"It worked for Rolf, though, didn't it? And imagine what kind of freak show he'll be bringing to your party. I hate it when you underestimate me, Dan."

"My apologies. Allow me to congratulate you on your bizarre but effective work."

"You ain't seen nothing yet," Bill says with a wink, then scans the dog park until he glimpses his next target. "Come on."

Over the course of the next hour, Bill works his magic with the grace and efficiency of a true sociopath. By the time we leave the park, he has assembled a team of recruiters highly motivated by unique and outlandish back stories regarding the re-gentrification project, each specifically crafted to inspire outrage on a highly individualized basis.

For hardcore left-wingers Jane and Janet Meadow, the re-gentrification project is being secretly financed by a group of Southern State White Supremacist Neo-Nazis seeking to establish a militia stronghold approximate to Manhattan. The ladies promised strong representation from the LGBTQ community, even on such short notice.

For Irish nanny Siobhan McCoy, the re-gentrification project is being funded by the Orange Order of Northern Ireland Protestants seeking to establish a beachhead geared at neutralizing the New York fund-raising activities of Sein Fenn. Siobhan was quite sure that the people in her Irish community would have something to say about these "bugger Orangemen" organizing so close to home.

For Virginia Waddle, pet rescue zealot, the re-gentrification project is being financed by an international consortium of puppy farmers seeking to create an urban breeding complex to better serve the Five Boroughs.

For Zev Frankle, unofficial head of Jersey City's intolerant vegan community, the re-gentrification project is being financed by Kentucky Fried Chicken.

Bill delivers these stories in the same conspiratorial fashion and with the same request for secrecy to protect the implied "insider position" that allowed him to obtain the relevant information in the first place. My brother is a master of prefabrication, even if the dog park is kind of a Special Olympics playing field.

"I'm impressed, little brother. You're a true artist. You really ought to think about how you might use your talents for the good of humankind."

"I thought that's what I just did, big brother," Bill replies.

We bro-hug. Bill takes the leashes from me and starts walking back to my building.

Me, I've got another stop to make.

CHAPTER THIRTY-SEVEN

"You realize what I'm asking, then?"

"Yer nay askin', boyo. Yer givin'. Yer the universe come here to present ourselves wit the very thing we been waitin' on for two years now."

"I'm only putting this out there because it seems like the right thing to do. As wrong as I think it is, I mean."

"Yer listenin' to the universe, mate, actin' on its behalf. None o' this is happenin' by accident. Aye, boys?" Cleary lifts his pint.

"O'Shaughnessy!" toasts the bar.

"But I got to tell you, I'm uncomfortable even talking to you about this."

"I'm a doctor, ye gobshite. No need for discomfort."

"Well… you're not, like, a real doctor. I mean, you're a Doctor of Philosophy, sure, but it's not like you're licensed to practice anything." I digress, which happens sometimes when I'm drinking.

"License or not, I've got a degree that says I'm a doctor. An' ye'll be mindin' yer P's and Q's in front o' me from now on."

"Not meaning to offend," I say, "but you understand my situation, right?"

"Course. Ye said it about five times now, didn't ye?"

"And I want to make sure, like, for the record," I look back and forth along the bar, "that I am in no way condoning or suggesting anything. All I've done here is to relate an opportunity wherein a benevolent non-profit company that supports a deserving homeless population is in danger of being pushed out of its residence, right?"

"Keep talkin' all tha head-talk and shortly I'll be spewin' chunks on the bar," Cleary replies.

"My point is, Cleary, are ye sure?" I ask.

"Look around the bar, boyo."

I look around the bar. It's not a pretty sight.

"Okay."

"What do ye see?"

"Uh… I don't know. You guys."

"What ye see is a lot tha wuld be lucky to make next Christmas. Christ, it's a wonder two or three of us ain't petered-off already. Look at my eyes, boyo." I look into Cleary's eyes. The parts that are supposed to be white are yellow.

"Ye don't look great," I say.

"We're dying on the vine, ya gobshite."

"On that, I'd have to agree." I scan the bar for a single healthy-looking person and find not one. Even so, this isn't an easy ask. Or offer. Or whatever it is. I shoot a Jameson's and swig my Guinness.

"Here, not ta be disrespectful now, but ta give ye some perspective – sure, yer the universe finally come callin' – but the universe could'a just as well been that there cockroach on da floor, or that there mouse by the ladies room, or that there pile o' ants at the corner of the bar." And despite the fact that I'm fairly well drunk, I'm just now noticing how unclean this bar actually is. "Yer nay special, mate. Yer a gift ta us, whether ye know it or not. But it ain't about you, now is it? Tis about us. Don't go losin' any sleep over it."

"Okay – and I feel weird for even mentioning it – but if you want to help, well… It's got to be pretty dramatic, you know? Not that I'm advocating anything…"

"Dramatic? Ye gobshite, nothing could be more dramatic than O'Shaughnessy's suicide waltz. We ken what we're doin', believe you me."

"So yer gonna, like, do what O'Shaughnessy did, then? Not try to improve on it or add anything, are you?" I ask in false, but addictive Irish brogue.

"Ye remember the story of O'Shaughnessy, boyo?"

"I do, yeah."

"Could you improve on killin' yerself beyond the grand gesture made by himself?"

I think for a minute… or maybe three. I'm drunk.

"Nay," Cleary finally interrupts my introspection, "a gombeen like ye couldn't improve on it in ten years of thought. Hell, we're all Doctors of Philosophy and we could think of nothing to compare in the past twenty-four months."

"But if yer just gonna imitate O'Shaughnessy, then why did ye wait this long?" I ask.

"O'Shaughnessy was a prophet, ye gobshite. His job was ta show us the way. Our job – tanks ta ye and the universe – is ta help save an organization devoted ta helpin' people in need… in addition ta endin' our lives in a spectacular fashion as a statement to our not believin' in the core tenants of our chosen field of philosophy, like O'Shaughnessy himself. But mostly, I hope, t'will be remembered as a grand gesture to help those who are deservin' of help."

"I understand."

"That said, I will be countin' on you to take up responsibility for the communication of O'Shaughnessy's cause when we are done for," Cleary adds, as if communication of O'Shaughnessy's cause had been something that he and the boys had actually engaged in over the past two years.

"Sure," I reply. "I'll do as good a job as you all have ever done."

"Boyo," Cleary says, grabbing my collar and pulling me close enough to smell his rotting teeth, "in ancient Japan, the Samurai used to say that life is only a dream within a dream. Everything that seems to matter so much, it simply dissolves when ye wake up. And it's twice so in a dream within in a dream, which is this thing we consider to be our lives."

"That's nice. Japanese philosopher?"

"James Cavell. Read it in *Gia-Jin*, I tink. Not his best book, but all of his novels are worth a go, especially *Shogun*. Ye remember the mini-series with Richard Chamberlain? Brilliant. But in terms of books, really any of the novels in his Asian Saga series will make do nicely."

"I'll check them out. So, anyway, I take it you guys are up for the task at hand, then?"

"Grateful for the opportunity, is what we are."

"And – again assuming this is something you want to do – are you sure that you've got enough lead time? I mean, you'd need to get your supplies and hide out inside the Way-Point building in," I look at my analog watch, "like, less than twelve hours."

"Plenty of time, mate. And our supplies are already got and waitin' for us."

Why am I not surprised at that?

"So, you're sure you want to do this?" I can't help double covering my ass on this aspect of the plan.

"Aye, and then some. Tis a great gift more yer givin' us, on behalf of the universe. I hope people will understand what you want 'em ta understand from it, because very few are likely ever to ken the whole story."

Chapter Thirty-Eight

I wake up Saturday around three p.m. The prior evening turned into a very long drinking session with the O'Shaughnessy boys. Special occasion, I think. Irish wake.

After I finally left the no-name bar, Cleary and the others dragged their drunken asses to the Way-Point building. I'd already told Linda Park to give them whatever access they needed.

I unzip the front of my Ozark Trail Twelve Person Three Room L-Shape Instant Cabin Tent and step into Hooverville. This is going to be a great day, I believe. I stretch in the early afternoon sunlight streaming through my huge windows. I take a long, deep yoga-breath…

"Hey, baby!!"

"Jesus! God damnit!" I startle, then I start to whine. "Come on, Clancy. What about setting each other free?" I hate when she makes me whine, especially when I'm hung over.

"What? I thought I'd get ready for the event over here. It's about logistics, not about us."

"How'd you get in?"

"The door was unlocked."

"Yeah, but how'd you open it?" I'm not sure why I ask when I already know the answer. Sluggo walks out of my Double Layer Waterproof Dome Tunnel Tent, zipping his jeans.

"Yo, Dan! You're up," Sluggo looks from me to Clancy. "Wow, cutie-pie. You are a vision."

"Thank you, Sluggo," Clancy says, pouting at me. She is wearing a very short, black, sleeveless cocktail dress, made of semi-rigid material but so tightly fitted that it's obviously not off the ready-to-wear rack at Nordstrom's. Clancy raises her hands to check her hair and the top of the dress rises with her breasts, so no nipple slip, which is surprising. Then I notice Sluggo's panting bulge-eyed stare, directed a bit lower than my own. Ah. Not only does the top of Clancy's dress rise with her arms, the bottom does as well.

Somehow, the semi-rigid, flared hem of Clancy's dress has flipped up with the upper-body movement of her hand to her hair. Below the thin rim-peek of Clancy's tight belly, her totally sheer pale pink panties — tight like they're painted on — seem to accentuate, rather than cover up, her vagina.

"This is so weird," I mumble, not realizing that I'm speaking out loud.

"What's so weird, baby?" The front of her dress is still flipped up. Sluggo might as well be a cartoon wolf with eyeballs popping out of its skull, and Clancy is speaking to me with a look of doe-eyed innocence.

That's it. I'm done.

"The fact that Sluggo and I are both looking at your vagina," I say flatly.

Clancy shrieks and appears genuinely surprised when she looks down at herself. She flips the hem of the cocktail dress with such force that her right breast pops out. Inevitable, I think. Sluggo makes a sound like a low moan.

"Sluggo, give us a minute," I say.

"Uh-uh," he replies, shaking his head, trance-like.

"Dude, if you're not out of my place in like, five seconds ago… then you're out of the building." I'm done with this best-friend's-girlfriend's-best-guy-friend thing, too.

"What's your problem, man?" Sluggo asks, peevish.

"He didn't do *anything*, Dan," Clancy whines, maybe wanting Sluggo to stay in order to avoid a one-on-one conversation with me right now.

"Out," I whisper to Sluggo, pointing at the door.

"You gotta lighten up, man," he replies, sluffing out of my apartment.

"Bye, Sluggo!" Clancy waves, hand high in the air, hem of her cocktail dress flipped up to again reveal all of her vagina. Sluggo looks back, sighs ambivalently, waves.

"Stay just like that!" I shout.

Clancy looks at me, lowers her arm.

"No," I say, walking into my Double Layer Waterproof Dome Tunnel Tent, returning quickly with a six-foot, full-length mirror, which I set in front of Clancy. "Do it again."

"What, Danny?"

"Wave again, like you did at Sluggo."

Clancy cocks her arm at the elbow, limply jiggles her wrist.

"No, big wave, like you just waved to Sluggo!"

Clancy complies, a little taken aback.

"Stop," I say. "Perfect. Just freeze. Now look at yourself."

"What?" Clancy asks, looking at her lipstick, her eyeliner, her perfect hair.

"Look down."

"What… oh, whoops." Clancy giggles, flips down the front of her cocktail dress, adjusts the hem. "What?" she asks again.

"Whoops," I repeat flatly. "Like that was an accident."

"Of course it was an accident. What else would it be?"

"Clancy, the frequency with which your private parts become public is a total contradiction to the probabilities typically associated with the term 'accidental.' I mean, come on. We dated for four years and were engaged for ten months," I say, calming myself with a deep breath. "I'm not trying to attack you here. I just don't get it. And I've never had the nerve to ask you about it."

"You don't get what, baby? You know you can ask me anything," Clancy says sweetly.

"Okay, so I'm asking you. Why is it that almost every time I see you, I'm able to make direct eye contact with parts of your body that, on every other girl I've ever known, typically remain covered up?"

"Why would I be worried about covering up around you, Danny? It's nothing you haven't seen before."

"No, no, no. It's not just me. Don't you think it's a little strange that every one of my friends and family members – every single one – has seen your vagina on multiple occasions? That's not normal, Clancy."

"Don't be ridiculous, Danny. My body is no one's business but yours. And all of this, it's just in your head."

"Seriously, Clancy, I don't care. No judgments. I mean, if you get off on showing yourself, that's fine. There are lots of weirder things that people are into. But this has been bothering me for years now. I just want to understand it. Like I said, no judgments. You say you want to be close, to be intimate, right? Well, intimacy means talking about stuff that makes you feel vulnerable, stuff that you don't feel comfortable talking about with other people. That's what intimacy is." I can't help thinking about Sarah, telling me about the year she spent being homeless.

"I have no idea what you're talking about," Clancy says, not looking at me.

"You know how it bothered you when your mother's breast popped out the other day at Applebee's?"

"My mother's breast didn't pop out at Applebee's!"

"What do you mean? Of course, it did. You told her to cover herself up."

"I did not. I've never told my mother to cover herself up."

"Clancy, I've heard you tell your mother to cover herself up literally hundreds of times."

"You're insane, is what it is. First you ditch our plans for the apartment, then you disconnect from anything technology, then you pull away from me and now you've finally lost your mind. You're making up stuff about me and – you sicko – my mother!"

For the briefest second, I wonder if all of this *is* in my head.

But, of course, it's not.

And that's when I finally realize the biggest reason I've wanted nothing to do with Clancy for the past year. It's because, if we ever got married, I'd be forced to live in Clancy's reality. The world inside of *her* head. Because that's the only world she knows. And it's not necessarily a bad world, at least from her perspective. But it's not real. And I choose reality. Reality is where I want to live from now on.

"Why don't you go get ready for the launch party at Sluggo's?" I ask nicely. "You and I need a little space right now."

"My thoughts exactly," Clancy huffs, gathering her things. At the door, she stops. I walk over, open the door for her, and she turns to me.

"Don't be mad at me, baby. I'm not mad at you. This is just a setback. All couples have them. We're going to be okay. We'll work through your insanity together, and in the end we'll be stronger for it. I'm not giving up on you."

"I'm sure we'll both be fine, Clancy," I say as I duck her approaching lips and give her a peck on the cheek instead. This time, it really feels like a kiss goodbye. "I'll see you at the launch party."

Chapter Thirty-Nine

"Wow."

"Jesus, Bill," Sarah says, blushing. "What?"

"Wow. Just… wow," I whisper.

Sarah is wearing a fitted cocktail dress that is in no way slutty, but definitely shows off a figure I had not seen before. She is stunning. I mean, really beautiful. Even with the awkward arm-brace thing that's holding up her smushed hand.

"Stop it," Sarah says shyly, "I know how to clean up, okay?"

"Wow."

"Please, stop. Do you want to come in for a minute?"

"No," I say quickly. "We should go."

"Bill, I think we need to talk. Anyway, it's only five-forty-five. The launch party doesn't start until six."

"We should get there a few minutes early, you know, to make sure everything's on track. We can talk after the party."

The last thing I want right now is alone time with Sarah. I'm too tangled in a web of lies, I've got too much to say, and I'm hoping that whatever weirdness happens tonight will give me some clarity on how to resolve this situation. No, I'm not hoping. I'm open. I'm open to the universe providing the clarity necessary to resolve this situation.

That's what I am. Open.

"Okay. Let me get my wrap." Sarah turns back into her apartment. We're both awkward, the way two people are when stuff needs to be said between them. Sarah returns, wearing around her shoulders a very unattractive shawl-type-of-thing. Seriously, it's like something straight out of the Trail of Tears.

"Dude, no," I say, because she should not go out wearing that shawl thing, especially when she looks so great underneath it.

"It's not so bad," Sarah blushes.

"No, it is so bad. Come on, you can wear my jacket," I say, pulling off the top half of a suit I haven't worn since my brother's wedding. "It's, like, seventy degrees anyway."

"This wrap is lucky for me," Sarah says, looking at the ground. I don't know if it has anything to do with her year living in an RV, but I'm not going to ask because I'm sure the answer would break my heart, whatever it is. And anyway, right now we need all the luck that we can get.

"You know, when you step into the light, it isn't so bad," I comply.

"Shut up."

"Really."

"It was my great-grandmother's. She was indigenous."

"You mean, like, Native American?" Is there anything not fascinating about this lady?

"Indigenous people don't like to be called Native American. America is a name given by the foreigners who took this land away from the people who originally lived here."

"I didn't know that. But it makes sense, not wanting to be named by the people who stole the land from you," I say sympathetically.

"They didn't steal it, actually. Land ownership wasn't what the indigenous people were about. They'd fight battles to protect their hunting grounds, but they never felt like they owned the land. They were just grateful for the opportunity to live on it."

"I'm sorry," I say. It sounds like I'm apologizing on behalf of Western culture.

"I'm only one-eighth indigenous. The other seven-eighths is the same European scum that took the land away from indigenous people in the first place, so you don't need to apologize to me."

"Okay, how about one-eighth of an apology?"

"Apology one-eighth accepted," Sarah says, giggles, then turns serious. "Bill, the other day, when you told me that Dan was attracted to me, that he had spent so much money trying to help Way-Point. What was that all about?"

"Let's talk about it after we wreck the launch party and save Way-Point."

"Is Dan going to be there?"

"I don't think my brother is going, no," I say truthfully, swallowing an absurd stab of jealousy. "Why? Did you want to see him?"

"I mean, I want to thank him, of course. But I guess I was just worried about it being awkward. I had no idea he felt that way about me. I wouldn't know what to say to him."

"Why? Do you think there's any chance of something developing between the two of you?" I shouldn't be pursuing this conversation, but I'm so morbidly curious as to how she'll answer.

"I wish there was a chance, actually. He's obviously a great guy – what with everything he's tried to do for Way-Point – but, well…"

"Well, what?"

"I don't want to offend you or anything, but, well… Your brother's kind of weird, you know? He's got that whole Thurston Howell thing going on, you know, like on Gilligan's Island."

"Totally! Thurston Howell is totally who he reminded me of at the dog park!" I shout. It is so cool, how in sync Sarah and I are.

"What do you mean, at the dog park? Isn't he like that all the time?"

"Sure, I guess he is. But, it's like I just made the Thurston Howell connection for the first time, the other day at the dog park."

"No matter how great a guy he is, I don't think I could ever be with someone that reminds me so much of Thurston Howell." Sarah giggles shyly. "You're not going to repeat that, are you? Not to be conniving or anything, but I don't want to offend Dan after everything he's done for Way-Point."

"Oh, I will definitely mention it to Dan, you know, the fact that more than one person has noticed how he's channeling Thurston Howell. But I'll keep your name out of it."

"Thanks," Sarah says, bumping her shoulder against mine as we approach the courtyard that fronts the Way-Point building.

Up and down the block, I notice many small clusters of people, some of whom I recognize from Way-Point, others I don't recognize at all. Either way, it looks like the blocks surrounding the Way-Point building are at least ten times more crowded than they would be on a normal Saturday. I take this as a good sign.

"Good turn-out," I whisper to Sarah, "and it looks like everyone is keeping the protests on the down-low, which is great."

"Weird, man," Sarah whispers back. "Look at all of them. It's spooky. Like an eerie calm before the storm, you know?"

"I know," I reply. Anticipation weighs heavy in the air, like barometric pressure before a hurricane. I wonder if the re-gentrification people or the media can sense any of it. Probably not. I'm sure none of them are very familiar with Jersey City, much less this specific block. If anything, I imagine all they're feeling is the normal rich-person-invading-a-poor-person's-neighborhood kind of tension. The type of tension they must be used to – media and investors alike. They expect nothing, I think to myself. Sarah and I make our way past all the little people-clusters lining the block and approach the courtyard.

"Tickets, please," asks a neckless security guard as we veer left towards the Way-Point building. The courtyard is fully decked out for a high-end party. Linen-covered tables border the outside of the space, with trays of hipster appetizers and three open bars serving only the top shelf of top shelf liquor. A fistful of investor and media types are congregated in the center of the courtyard, maybe a hundred people, tops. Not a big crowd compared to the clusters forming outside the courtyard. That's a good thing.

"She's with me," I say, indicating Sarah with my chin while handing the guard the ticket I procured from Gwen earlier in the week. The guard nods, glancing at my ticket, obviously instructed to cause no problems to the potential investors attending this launch party.

I see Clancy at one of the bars, talking to Gwen and some guy in a suit. I steer Sarah in the opposite direction in a fleeting attempt to delay the inevitable. I think about what Cleary said about the grand gesture, how the brain can only process so much information, how the impact of my big reveal to Sarah would be diluted by the shock and awe of simultaneous events. Between meeting Clancy and the coming waves of inane protests, I'm thinking Sarah might not even blink when she finds out I've been lying to her about being Bill.

Still, I feel a strange sense of peace which is totally inappropriate, given what's about to go down. But there it is. I'm completely letting go and putting myself into the hands of the universe, fully trusting that everything will work out how it should. It's a different feeling for me. I like it.

Chapter Forty

"Hey, baby! You made it! Who's she? And what is that she's wearing?" Clancy looks at Sarah like she's something scraped from the bottom of a shoe. Here we go.

"Clancy, this is Sarah. She's a friend of mine."

"You've never said anything about a friend named Sarah. What's with her arm?"

"I'm right here, you know," Sarah says.

"Sarah has to keep her hand elevated. She punched a wall."

"That doesn't sound like a very smart thing to do," Clancy replies directly to me.

"Still right here," Sarah says.

"Oh, look! There's Gwen!" Clancy shouts, as if she hadn't been with Gwen five minutes earlier. Clancy raises her hand to wave Gwen over, causing the front of her cocktail dress to flip up. Sarah looks at Clancy's sheer panties, then looks at me and raises her eyebrows.

"Where'd you find this one?" Sarah asks me quietly.

"Long story," I reply and Gwen stomps over, giving me dagger eyes. "Hello, Gwen."

"You've got a lot of explaining to do, buster," Gwen says to me fiercely.

"This is Sarah," I say.

"Whatever," Gwen replies. "So, we just found out, from Max's lawyer, who bought this warehouse we're standing in front of. What do you have to say for yourself?" Gwen is waiting for me to reply as one of the suits walks over to us.

"Is this the guy?" The suit asks, nasty, glaring at me. Then his face suddenly turns shock white as he glances to my left. "Oh… oh, my God. Sarah?"

"Hello, Max," Sarah says coldly.

"Uh, yeah it's, ah, been a, uh, long time," Max stutters.

"Yup," Sarah replies.

"What happened to your hand?" Max asks awkwardly.

"She punched a wall," Clancy replies, not wanting to be left out of the conversation.

"You two know each other?" I ask Sarah.

"We were engaged," she replies. Ah, that Max.

"You were *engaged* to *her*?!" Gwen asks Max.

"It was a long time ago, honey," Max says to Gwen.

"That's right," Sarah says. "What was I, Max? Engagement number three?"

"You've been engaged *three times*?" Gwen shouts.

"I'd imagine there have been more in the past couple of years," Sarah adds.

"We were just kids," Max backpedals to Gwen. "It was a complicated time in my life. I don't think we were even technically engaged."

"You gave me a ring and asked me to marry you. Then we slept together. Then you totally ghosted me. From what I understand, it's a pretty typical pattern for you," Sarah says.

Gwen's mouth drops open as she stares at the ring on her own finger.

"Don't worry, sweetie, it's not the same ring," Sarah says to Gwen.

"You didn't sleep with him until after you got engaged?" Clancy asks, as if that's the oddest thing about this whole conversation.

"Look, I can't talk about this right now. They're about to unveil the architect's model of the new development for the media," Max says to Gwen, regaining his businessman composure. Then he turns to me. "You're the one who bought that building?"

"He didn't buy the building," Sarah replies. "His brother did."

"Bill?" Clancy asks, confused.

"Yes?" I reply, as if Clancy had addressed me directly, which further tangles her thoughts.

"You and I need to talk. Or your brother and I need to talk. Whatever. But right now, I've got to go handle the media," Max says haltingly. He looks at Sarah, then at Gwen, as if he's about to say something, but he just exhales, slumps his shoulders and walks away from our little group.

"Small world," I say.

"You were *not* engaged to Max," Gwen says to Sarah accusingly.

"Believe me, if I had the chance to do it all over again, you'd be right," Sarah answers.

"I don't know what's going on here. Why is this girl even here?" Clancy asks me, raising a hand to her forehead in a way that flips up the front of her cocktail dress again. It's like the hem of her dress is spring loaded or something. I can't figure out the physics behind it.

"I don't know if I would have gone with the sheer panties when wearing that particular outfit," Sarah says to Clancy, who quickly flips down the hem of her dress. "Anyway, I'm here because Bill invited me. I do pro-bono legal work for Way-Point and he's been helping me out for the past few weeks."

"What exactly is a Way-Point and what does Bill have to do with any of it?" Clancy asks.

"Way-Point is the homeless support organization that's leasing this building. You know, the one that you guys are planning to freeze out by blocking access to the courtyard," I say.

"You're kidding," Gwen says.

"Uh, uh."

"Well, I'm sorry to tell you, but we're about to turn this shabby waterfront block into the hottest near-city living space in the country. Just look at the media turn-out we've got here tonight," Gwen says. "And, sad for you, homeless people are *not* part of the plan. As of today, anybody trying to get into or out of that building will have to pass through our security team. We own the courtyard and all points of entry and egress. Too bad, so sad, you lose."

"Your friend is a scumbag, Bill," Sarah says to me.

"Gwen's not really my friend," I reply, lift my face and show Sarah my scars. "She gave me these, actually."

"Did she just call you…" Clancy starts to ask me, but Gwen interrupts her.

"Come on. Max is starting!" Gwen grabs Clancy's arm and yanks her towards Max, who has just started speaking to the media at a podium in front of the architectural model of the soon to be re-gentrified block, press conference style. Somehow Gwen's tugging has activated Clancy's spring-loaded dress and the entire hem, front and back, has flipped above her waist so she is effectively bottomless as she walks towards the media. I glance around the crowd and see businessmen's jaws dropping to the ground.

"Where'd you find indecent-exposure Barbie?" Sarah asks. "I always wanted one when I was a kid."

"She does that on purpose, right? I mean, there's no way that anyone could show that much skin accidentally, right?"

"Why are you so interested?"

"I've known her for a long time. She was part of my old life."

"She's beautiful," Sarah says.

"Yeah. Not so much on the inside as on the outside."

"Still…" Sarah says, and I'm wondering if she might be a little jealous right now. How cool would that be?

"Oh, hey, it looks like the show's about to start," I say.

Sarah and I both look past Max's press conference to the front of the courtyard. Seemingly out of nowhere, a full-on protest has erupted to contest the treatment of Way-Point by the re-gentrification project. There are signs, there are banners, there are bullhorns shouting the truth about how the re-gentrification project is planning to exploit a loophole to freeze out Way-Point. Sarah's people have assembled maybe a hundred recruits – enough to cover the mouth of the courtyard two or three deep. To the media people surrounding Max, it might as well be a thousand people.

"Nice work," I say to Sarah.

"The timing was perfect," she replies. "I'm impressed."

I look at Max. An impromptu but well-organized protest, appearing out of thin air, is definitely not something that he had been expecting tonight. He is sheet-white and struggling to keep the attention of the media people. They've turned en masse to look at all the protesters who'd surrounded the courtyard just seconds earlier. I'm definitely feeling the flash-mob vibe.

We walk closer to Max's podium. The media people have digested enough of the flash-mob protesters' message to start asking Max questions.

"What's Way-Point?"

"How are you freezing them out?"

"Did you know that your project would displace an organization that supports the homeless?"

"These protestors allege that your re-gentrification committee is using a legal loophole to shut down Way-Point's operations! Can you comment on that?"

"I have no knowledge of any organization called Way-Point," Max says into his microphone. "These people are mistaken. This is all just a big misunderstanding, and I'm sure it will be cleared up in no time. Please, let's not let this distract us from the plans to re-gentrify this block, a major step forward for not just Jersey City, but for all of New Jersey."

"He's such a liar," Sarah says. "I can't believe I ever fell for his bull crap."

"I have a feeling he's not going to lie his way out of this," I reply.

"He will. The flash-mob thing may have surprised him, but people protest development all the time. He'll get the media people back on his side, Max is a master liar."

"Yeah, but even a master liar needs to know what he's lying about. I don't know Max as well as you do, but from what I've seen of him, I'll bet he can't hit a curve ball."

Chapter Forty-One

Like a true corporate attorney, Max smooth-talks his way through the Way-Point protest surrounding the courtyard. He repeats that he has no knowledge of the organization, promises to look into the matter immediately, and verbally commits the re-gentrification project to donate whatever it takes to right any inadvertent wrongs. He speaks with eloquence to both the media and the protesting crowd, soothing the flare-up in a way that makes me think of a hemorrhoidal remedy cream.

"Told ya," Sarah says to me.

"That was only batting practice," I reply. "Let's see how he does when the real game starts."

Just then, about two dozen naked vegans sprint through the web of security guards at the mouth of the courtyard. This is not a pretty sight. It looks like each of the vegans is carrying the plucked carcass of a chicken, neck in fist. Some are carrying two chickens, one in each fist.

A wave of naked vegans carrying dead chickens is a good start, I think.

A surprisingly well-hung Zev Frankle breaks from the crowd – for a second, I think he's carrying three dead chickens, one between his legs – he sprints to the podium and smacks Max in the face with a limp, bald bird. He grabs the microphone while Max gives him a very wide berth, disgusted for so many reasons.

"New Jersey is no place to farm mutant chickens!" Zev Frankle screams into the microphone. "These people are playing God with what our children are eating! Do not allow this facility to be built! Do your research! As long as there are slaughterhouses, there will be battlefields! Never again! Never again!"

The naked vegans cheer. I drop my head. I haven't been online in over a year, and even I know that the whole mutant chicken thing with KFC is a total urban legend. I find it hard to believe that none of these militant vegans have ever Googled KFC mutant chicken, or maybe they just think it's a cover up related to whatever meat-eater conspiracy theory they subscribe to. Anyway, I should have kyboshed that mutant chicken angle with Bill immediately, once I understood that he was using it to incite Zev Frankle. Companies have a hard-enough time as it is without people making up stuff about them. And chicken-shaming people isn't my idea of fair play.

Still, it looks like Max is thrown for a loop, so that part of the mission is a success. A security guard finally makes his way to the podium and gently removes Zev Frankle and his plucked chickens. Max returns to front the media.

"Well, folks, we're certainly getting our share of crazy tonight," Max says into the microphone, adjusting his tie like Rodney Dangerfield.

"That was as ridiculous as it was pointless," Sarah asides to me.

"Ridiculous, yes. But not pointless. Look at the media people," I say. "This launch party is in danger of going off the rails. It just needs a few more nudges."

"If you say so," Sarah sighs, as maybe a hundred dogs suddenly bolt through the courtyard, crashing into linen-covered tables and attacking trays of hipster appetizers.

"Stop the cycle of violence and cruelty!" Virginia Waddle shouts into a bullhorn, facing Max's podium from the mouth of the courtyard. "By supporting this organization in any form, you are personally contributing to the genocide of man's best friend! Deplorable living conditions – neglect, starvation and extermination in the millions – all in the name of profit! These people are engineering a modern-day holocaust as we speak! If you support these people, you might as well be supporting the Nazi party!"

"Lady, what are you even talking about?" a dumbfounded Max asks into his microphone.

"This will be good," I aside to Sarah. "I love it when people try to dialogue with pet rescue fanatics."

"Oh, that's right! That's right! Pretend you don't know how much suffering your puppy mills are responsible for! But we can see through you! We can all see the evil muck deep down in your beady little eyes!"

For an instant, Max looks like he's taking personal offense to Virginia's comment about his eyes, but then he looks at the media people capturing all this insanity on their smart phones and his anxieties shift to larger issues. Most of the security guards hired by the re-gentrification project are still trying to catch and evict a bunch of naked, chicken-wielding vegans. Max looks helpless. I could almost feel sorry for the guy, if I didn't know what a bastard he is. Karma is truly a bitch.

"There are millions of dogs – good, loving, obedient dogs – in need of adoption, in need of a caring home! These people, with their cycle of abuse for profit, are stealing this opportunity from the most innocent of God's creatures! For shame! For shame!" A burly security guard has finally made his way to Virginia Waddle and is struggling to take the bullhorn as she ducks and dodges. "Do not support these people! Do not support this evil! Jesus was a dog! Jesus was a dog!"

"Did she just say that Jesus was a dog?" Sarah asks me.

"I think she means metaphorically, you know, like the suffering part," I reply.

The security guard, finally ripping the bullhorn from Virginia's hands, is struggling to pull her plump, kicking, and screaming body from the courtyard.

"She's got a lot more energy than I would have thought," I say.

"Yeah," Sarah says, "those animal rights people can go a little berserk when you get them riled. What's next?"

"Check it out," I reply, jutting my chin to the mouth of the courtyard where a dozen men in army boots and black skull caps are holding a huge cloth banner bearing the words "AN IRELAND UNFREE WILL NEVER REST".

"So, you got the IRA involved?" Sarah asks.

"I think they're mostly just amateurs. My brother might have mentioned some affiliation between the re-gentrification project and the Orange Order of Northern Ireland Protestants."

"Clever," Sarah says.

The black-clad Irishmen take a position against a brick wall, standing in silent protest.

"Uh, hey, guys," Max addresses them from the podium, still struggling to maintain some modicum of control. "Can we, uh, help you with something?"

"We want ye off our land, both here and back home!" shouts one of the Irishmen.

"I, uh, I truly do not understand what you're talking about," Max says into the microphone.

"We're talkin' about hundreds o' years of civil unrest, an we won't be havin' ye bring it to our backyard here in Jersey! We're not gonna make this pleasant for ye, so I suggest ye move along!"

A few of the braver media people approach the gang of Irish to try to figure out exactly what is going on. I also notice other media people talking to the vegans and pet rescue people outside the courtyard. That's positive.

"Seriously, guys…" Max pleads, only to be interrupted by Jane and Janet Meadow leading what looks like an entire LGBTQ marching parade into the courtyard, carrying the standard rainbow flags and all kinds of poster board signs condemning every variety of White Supremacist Neo-Nazi intolerance. Both Jane and Janet are carrying bullhorns, both leading chants of "haters go home!"

"Oh, come on!" Max whines from the podium.

"Oh, *you* come on, you white supremacist bastard! We know what you're trying to do here, and we're not having any of it!" Jane shouts into the bullhorn. She starts a chant of "We are queer and we are here!" and the LGBTQ parade picks it up immediately.

Max looks doubly upset with this latest protest group, given the critical importance of the gay demographic to the success of the re-gentrification project. I have to keep reminding myself of how he treated Sarah, and his intention to freeze out Way-Point, to avoid feeling sorry for him. Max slumps into a seat behind the podium, giving up any hope of controlling the pandemonium in front of him.

As people from the other protest groups join the LGBTQ parade in their chant, I scan the courtyard.

"Are you looking for something?" Sarah asks.

"No," I say. "Well, yeah, actually. I'm just wondering what happened to the spandex cowboy."

"Rolf?"

"Yeah. I was kind of interested in what his team might bring to the table."

"You got Rolf involved, too?"

"He was our first recruit."

"Did he know it was Saturday?" Sarah asks over the din of the crowd.

"He got the same directions as everyone else," I reply.

"No, no. I'm sure he knew that the media launch party was happening on Saturday. What I mean is, does he know that today is Saturday? Did anyone tell him?"

"Did anyone tell Rolf that today is Saturday? No, that was not an agenda item."

"Well, there's your problem," Sarah says, smiling. "What kind of organization did Rolf think was backing the re-gentrification project?"

"Animal testing labs secretly trying to expand their range to humans. Homeless humans, actually – it synced up nicely with Way-Point," I say.

"Makes sense," Sarah replies, "as much as any of this makes sense, I guess. We might want to come back here tomorrow or Monday around this time. I'm sure Rolf's cooked up something special."

"It's a date," I say.

Sarah looks into my eyes for a second, then turns her head.

"Anyway, it looks like this media launch party is something that the re-gentrification people are going to seriously regret. The last thing any media people will talk about is turning this block into the most desirable near-city living space in the country," Sarah says.

"We're not done yet," I reply, as eight spotlights suddenly illuminate the roof of the Way-Point building.

My emotions regarding phase three of this plan are more than a little mixed.

Chapter Forty-Two

"Hey, look! There are people up on the roof," Sarah says to me.

"Yeah."

"Isn't that a little dangerous?"

"I can't argue with you there."

"What are they holding?"

"Those would be straight razors."

"What are they doing with straight… oh, my God. Oh, my God, that's blood on me!"

"Me, too."

"What are they… what is that?!"

"That would be bleach, I think."

"Oh, my God, they're drinking it!"

"Yeah."

"What are they… we can't just let them… we've got to do something!"

"Yeah, I think that train has pretty much left the station."

"Why are you so… *oh, my God!*" Sarah screams as the eight faux Irishmen drop semi-full bottles of bleach from their mouths and tumble from the roof. At this point, Sarah is not the only one screaming. Every smart phone in the place is pointed skyward as the falling men are pulled taut by the nooses around their necks.

"Oh, my God. They hung themselves!"

"Give it a second," I say, as the ropes break in unison and the bodies drop towards the asphalt below. Sarah's jaw drops as all but one of the falling bodies burst into flames. Patrick – I think it was – the poor guy's incendiary device didn't work. Or maybe he was gone before he could trigger it. It's not likely I'll be able to ask him.

It's like car crash slow motion how these fiery meat sacks, excepting Patrick, seem to take forever to hit the ground. And when it does happen, it's what you'd imagine a bunch of flaming watermelons would sound like, hitting the pavement after a five-storey drop. Better late than never, Patrick's body bursts into flames just as it hits the ground. Good on you, Patrick.

And suddenly, the courtyard is silent.

"I can't believe what I just saw," Sarah gasps, wide eyed.

"No one can, it looks like."

"Why are you so calm?"

"It's a long story. I knew those guys. They were friends of mine. Believe me, it's what they wanted." My eyes are filling up in a way that makes me feel like I might cry. But I'm not sad… not exactly.

Sarah, same as everyone else, is too shocked to register any emotion. I reach over to one of the linen tables, grab a champagne flute because there isn't any Guinness, raise my drink to the burning sacks of meat that used to be the O'Shaughnessy boys.

"O'Shaughnessy!" I toast quietly. "Sure, didn't his boyos know how ta do it right."

"What are you even doing right now?!" Sarah asks as I take a long swig of champagne. The surrounding crowd – the suits, the media, the protestors – all of them gaping in shocked silence.

"Two things, Sarah. First, I believe Way-Point will have no more problems with the re-gentrification project."

"How can you even think about Way-Point after what we just saw?" Sarah asks, then hesitates, taking a second to actually think about Way-Point. "Wait, what do you mean?"

"What I mean is, there's no way anyone can create the hottest near-city living space in the country on the sight of the most spectacular mass suicide in history. Especially not when it's all been recorded by so many members of the media. The re-gentrification project is over. In fact, we can probably get these two buildings on either side of the courtyard for cheap, if we're looking to expand."

"I can't think about that right now," Sarah says.

"Yeah," I say, "but it's important. It's a gift that the O'Shaughnessy boys gave us. We have to appreciate it. We have to appreciate how we got it."

"The O'Shaughnessy boys?"

"The dead guys on fire over there," I explain.

"I can't understand how you can be so calm about all this," Sarah says, as the surrounding crowd slowly unfreezes from the shock of what they just saw. "What's the other thing?"

"What do you mean?"

"Just a minute ago, you said two things. What's the other thing?" Sarah looks pale, really shaken, like she's just hanging on by a thread. Most of the people in the courtyard look the same.

"Oh, that. Right. Well, I'm not exactly sure how to put this – and I don't want to upset you more or anything – but there's been a bit of a mix up vis-à-vis me and my brother."

"What's that supposed to mean? What are you talking about?"

"I'm sorry, Sarah."

"Sorry for what?"

"For not fixing this whole mess before I fell in love with you," I say and extend my hand. "It's nice to meet you, Sarah. My name is Dan."

Sarah instinctively reaches out to shake my hand, then pulls back like I'm a hot stove, holds her palm up facing my chest. Sarah's green eyes show a bunch of different emotions banging around inside her all at once. She opens her mouth as if to say something, and then rocks a bit, and collapses in a dead faint.

Luckily, I'm able to catch her before she hits the ground and does more damage to her already smushed hand.

I don't think she fainted just because I told her who I am. I think this whole evening was a little too much for her. I mean, there are people fainting all over the courtyard right now. I think Cleary and the O'Shaughnessy boys gave me sound advice about telling Sarah who I am in the midst of a grand gesture. I don't know how she will react when she wakes up, but everything that went on tonight has got to have a diluting effect on any negative emotions she'll have towards me.

"I'll keep an eye on Sarah. You've got other fish to fry right now."

"Bill," I say as my brother walks towards me and the unconscious Sarah, "when did you get here?"

"I've been here. You didn't think I would miss this thing, did you? Act Two was, like, my masterpiece. Unfortunately, Act Three blew it out of the water. Where did you find a bunch of guys willing to kill themselves?" My brother, never easily rattled.

"I didn't find them, they found me. Or maybe I did find them, I don't know. But the whole suicide thing, it definitely wasn't my idea. They were waiting, en masse, for an opportunity. The universe just, kind of, put us together. That kind of stuff can happen, if you're open to it."

"Okay, Buddha, whatever. We can talk about it later. Now, why don't you go take whatever heat you've got to take from that crew over there. I'll take care of your girlfriend, here."

"I don't know if she's my girlfriend," I say, following Bill's line of vision to Max, Gwen, and Clancy, who are marching towards me with purpose. I turn and walk to meet them halfway.

"Some launch party," I say casually.

"What did you do?" Max whines. "*What* did you do?"

"Me? I did nothing," I shrug. "Sure, apparently some of these impromptu protest groups might have been misinformed, but they all acted on their own volition and as far as I can tell, none of them did anything illegal. I mean, free speech, right? And I'm sure you're not suggesting that I had anything to do with eight guys offing themselves – in a most spectacular fashion – at your launch party. Just saying it out loud, that kind of suggestion sounds insane."

"*What* did you *do*?" Max whines again.

"Well, from twenty-thousand feet, I'd say I did just what you did, Max."

"What is that supposed to mean?"

"You know how you found a loophole to exploit against Way-Point? Taking away their entry and egress capabilities, I mean. Well, it looks like someone found a bigger loophole to exploit against your re-gentrification project. That loophole being, nobody will ever buy high-end condos on the same site that played host to the most spectacular mass suicide ever recorded by the media. I don't know if that was part of your risk assessment planning, but it probably should have been."

"We've put over fifty million dollars into this project," Max says to no one in particular. "My father is going to kill me."

"Max, it's not your fault. Your father will understand," Gwen says, shooting me dagger eyes and grabbing Max's arm.

"Don't… don't touch me," Max says, shrugging off Gwen's hands. "I… I need some space right now. I need to figure out what I'm going to do about this. Just give me some space."

Max walks away. Gwen freezes for a second, trying to decide whether to go berserker on me or chase after Max. Happily, she decides on the latter, darting after what I believe is soon to be her ex-fiancé. I sigh, take a quick look at Sarah. She's still unconscious. And then I look at Clancy.

"Dan," Clancy says, "we need to talk." That might be the first time in our relationship that she's called me by my grown-up name.

Chapter Forty-Three

"I never thought you'd sabotage me, Dan."

"Excuse me?"

"I never thought you'd be the one to stab me in the back."

"What exactly are we talking about here, Clancy?"

"Stop it. You knew this was my big opportunity. You knew the re-gentrification project hired me to do a huge part of their social media. I'm on their payroll, though I doubt I will be tomorrow. You knew how important this was to me."

"Wait, you're talking about your job?"

"It was more than a job and you know it. It was my big break!"

"Clancy, eight people took their own lives tonight. How about we get a little perspective here?"

"I didn't know *them*!" Clancy shouts. "But *you* knew how important this was to *me*. And you know what? I just figured something out about you, Dan."

"Really, what's that?"

"You're a saboteur, that's 'what's that.' You're the only one who can have any kind of success. You're the only one who can make it. Anytime someone close to you has a chance at a big break, you undermine it. Just look at what you did with Gwen and your penthouse."

"I really don't like to call it a penthouse. I mean, it's only four floors and a double high."

"Make jokes if you want to, but I feel like I'm seeing you for the first time tonight."

"How do I look?"

"Small and mean and petty."

"Huh. It's the suit, right? I probably look like all the other small, mean and petty corporate scum at this thing. I should have just gone with jeans and a t-shirt." I should stop making jokes right now. It feels like things are coming to a head with Clancy.

"You ruined my shot. You ruined Gwen's shot *again*! And you ruined Max's project. All because you have to be the only one in the spotlight. All because you can't let anyone close to you achieve any kind of success on their own," Clancy shouts into my face.

"Don't be ridiculous, Clancy. If all I wanted was to be in the spotlight, why did I step back from the world when I sold my company? Why did I ditch technology and pull away from everything that was my old life – if being the most successful guy in the room mattered so much to me?"

"You did it for attention. I can see that now. I used to think you'd just lost your mind, but now I realize that you did it to make people think you were so special – this mysterious tech-money hermit who gives up technology. You did it because you were afraid to keep competing with people who might end up being more successful than you."

Oh, my God. I can't believe I was engaged to this person. She literally knows nothing about me. She's never done anything but fit me into a box that's part of the warped reality that spins around her alone. I should feel offended by what she's saying, but, really, I don't feel anything.

"Okay, Clancy. It sounds like you've got it all figured out, then."

"You bet I do."

"So where does that leave us?"

"Danny," Clancy says, "Dan. There can't be an 'us' anymore. Your problems, the way you need to keep everyone around you down, there's no way that I can shine in that kind of relationship. I'm sorry, Dan."

"Wait a second… *you're* breaking up with *me*? Are you breaking up with me?"

Holy cow! This is so awesome! And I didn't think tonight could get any better.

"We're finished, Dan. You're toxic to me. And I've given enough of my life to this toxic relationship already."

Man, I am so stupid. I spent all that time trying to break up with Clancy when what I really should have been working on was getting her to break up with me. Wow, I could have been so much worse to her over the past year. Live and learn, I guess.

"I understand, Clancy. And you're right. I'm probably never going to change."

"I thought our lives were intertwined, Dan. I pictured myself singing 'You're Still the One' at our fiftieth anniversary party." God, how I hate that song. "You took my best years, Dan."

"Yeah. Sorry about that. But you're still young and you'll be better off without me, I guess. And I'll just try to muddle along on my own. At least I'll know that I'm not weighing you down."

"Thank you, Dan. I assume you realize that we will have to stop all contact, right?"

"I realize that, yes."

"Are you going to be okay?" Clancy asks with what seems to be genuine concern.

"Probably not," I reply, so ready to be done with this kabuki show that is Clancy's life, "but even though I'll never get you back, you can feel good about the fact that you've taught me something. That you've made me a better person." I am vomiting in my mouth.

"That's all I ever wanted," Clancy says. "Goodbye, Dan."

And with that, Clancy turns and walks out of my life. Naturally, the back of her cocktail dress has flipped up as she turns to walk away. And I take one last look at the sheer panties covering her fantastic bottom as she sashays away in the revolving red lights of the ambulances that have arrived to take away the bodies of O'Shaughnessy's boys. I feel like a part of my life is ending, forever this time. And I can't remember when I've felt so good.

Chapter Forty-Four

"You okay?" Sarah asks. I'm still looking at Clancy's bottom as she walks out of the courtyard.

"Huh? Oh, geeze, Sarah! You're awake. I'm doing great. How are you?"

"You're doing great? That sounded like a pretty heavy break-up."

"Nah, I broke up with Clancy over a year ago. She just never got it through her head. Until now, that is. So, yeah, I'm doing great." Sarah gives a look that reminds me of how I've been lying to her about being Bill for the past few weeks. "I mean, I'm doing great, other than with you. With you I realize that I have some major explaining to do. And I hope you can forgive me. Really, I do. But, other than that, I have to admit that I'm doing great."

"I'm glad to hear it. And I talked to Dan… Bill, I mean." That can't be good. "He explained why you lied to me about being him. It's okay, I get it. I mean, I'm not sure if I totally forgive you right now, but at least I understand why you did it."

"What did Bill tell you?"

"He told me you were worried about him. How – when you found out he'd been lying to everyone at the dog park about being you – how he threatened to kill himself if you outed him. I mean, I get it. He's your brother. What were you supposed to do?"

Why is everything about suicide these days? And Bill. Man, he's pathological. I need to intervene and get him on a better track, but soon.

"Sarah, that's not true."

"What do you mean?"

"Bill never threatened to kill himself when I found out he'd been pretending to be me. I was just, I don't know – I didn't think any of it through, I guess. I figured, what's the harm in perpetuating Bill's fantasy world by pretending to be him? Then I met you, and I never imagined how I would end up feeling about you, you know? And by the time I was in too deep, you'd already told me the how's and why's of your brutal honesty policy. And – I mean it – I never wanted to lie to you. But I also didn't want to lose you."

"Why are you telling me this? I mean, why not just go with Bill's explanation and leave it at that?"

"Because, other than pretending to be my brother, I don't think I've ever told you anything that wasn't completely and totally true. I didn't want to break my streak, I guess."

"So, when you told me that Dan has feelings for me?"

"True. Totally true."

"When you told me that Dan bought the Way-Point building because something about meeting me had changed his life?"

"All true. Completely true."

"And – just to be clear – you would be Dan in this situation?"

"In this situation, and going forward, I am Dan, yes."

"And you're not married. You don't have a baby."

"I am not married and I don't have a baby."

"And you're not engaged to indecent-exposure Barbie?"

"I *was* engaged to indecent-exposure Barbie, but I ended that over a year ago. And, no offense, but I don't think you've got the high ground when it comes to criticizing anyone else's ex-fiancé."

"That's low, man."

"Just saying."

"Okay, fair point." For the first time since this whole circus erupted, Sarah smiles at me. She really smiles at me. And, wow, those green eyes. "And you think you'd actually want to get into a relationship with a mostly pro-bono human rights lawyer, once homeless, who is brutally honest, has a sometimes-violent temper and takes relationships far slower, I bet, than anyone you've ever been with?"

"Desperately. I am painfully, soul-crushingly desperate to be in that exact kind of relationship," I say truthfully.

"Really?"

"Really. And I have a pass, so we're all good."

"How's that?"

"You gave me one free pass… to act like a jerk. Back at the apple orchard, you know, when you accused me of stealing some of the funds I'd raised for the day trip. Funds I'd raised from myself, incidentally."

"Oh, yeah," Sarah blushes. "That's a little humiliating to think about now."

"Yeah, but the pass is still good, right?"

"I never welsh on a free pass," Sarah says, stepping towards me. "You're in the clear."

"Good," I say, trying to negotiate my arms around her hand brace, feeling like my legs will give out, feeling like I don't care if they do.

People who have been happily married for, like, fifty years or more – I want you to remember the first time you kissed the person with whom you would blissfully spend the rest of your life. Because that's how I felt when I kissed Sarah for the first time. And every time since.

EPILOGUE

"You left the toilet seat up again! My butt got wet."

"I refuse to apologize for something as ridiculous as sitting down when the toilet seat is up. I mean, I have occasion to sit down on a toilet, too, and I've never not checked to see if the seat was down. What is with you people?" This was never a problem with Clancy. But I have to remember that Sarah's never lived with a man before, aside from her father.

"By 'you people,' I assume you're referring to women in general."

"Correct. Women in general is who I'm referring to."

"Women in general assume that other people have a minimum degree of consideration in terms of a shared bathroom."

"Right. That's why I raise the seat when I go to the bathroom, so you don't have to sit down on any pee that I might otherwise have sprinkled on said seat."

"Can't you just make the effort? Try to remember to put the seat down? For me?"

"For you," I say, pulling her into my arms. "Yes, I will try to remember to put the seat down." Every time I kiss her it reminds me of the first time I kissed her, at the re-gentrification project's launch party, almost two years ago.

"I have to get to work," Sarah says, pulling away from me slowly, as if away from me is not where she wants to be.

"Me, too," I say, pulling her back into my arms.

"We can walk together, then?"

"Like we do every morning, yeah."

"I don't want to take it for granted," Sarah says. "I love it too much."

"Still waiting for the other shoe to drop?"

"That's the girl you married."

It turns out Sarah didn't have any year-and-a-half engagement rule, like Clancy did. I mean, we took it slow, believe me. But when I proposed to her after about fifteen months, we got married a mere four months later. I would have been fine if it had been a week.

My top floor, double-wide, double tall apartment has rooms now. Drywall along most of the brick circumference, but no ceilings. Sarah made it a condition of agreeing to marry me. For her I would have put in split levels, but she likes the open floor plan. She just doesn't like tents indoors. All marriage is a compromise, I guess.

And I've got a smart phone now, because Sarah needs to know where I'm at, like, all the time. Not that she's checking up on me, but just in case her water breaks or something. She's in her third trimester. But she's still working, which I have advised against time and time again. It's just that her platform to help accelerate the homeless job acquisition process launched less than three months ago, and it's her baby. Her other baby, she says. Somehow, the new platform isn't my baby, even though I financed its development. That's fine. I'm more interested in the baby that's a month or two away, anyhow.

And I'm sure you've all been following Clancy, right along with the rest of America. Yeah, my Clancy is the same Clancy who holds a record five-hundred-forty-three modesty blurs on last year's season of *The Bachelor*. Public outcry, primarily from the male demographic, all but demanded that she be chosen as next season's Bachelorette. I'm sure Sluggo has his DVR already programmed to record every episode.

Sluggo moved out of my building shortly after Clancy and I ended everything. He said he couldn't share floors with the same person who ruined the best relationship that he's ever had. I'm sure he's found another best friend with a hot girlfriend by now, but I have a feeling that Clancy will always occupy a special place in his heart.

As for Gwen and Max, I'm pretty sure there stopped being a Gwen and Max on the night of the re-gentrification launch party. But really, who cares? I haven't heard and I haven't asked.

Another bit of good news is that my brother Bill has split up with Betsy – joint custody of Bitsy. I gave Sluggo's old apartment to Betsy so she can be close to Bitsy, because as much as I hate Betsy, that's what you do for family.

And on a final positive note, Bill has stopped smoking pot (mostly) and he's stopped telling other people that he's me. Instead, he's channeling all of his creativity into a career as a novelist, where he just writes about being me – and all kinds of unrealistic nonsense that his rich brother gets himself into. Some of it is based on the truth, though. The important parts, at least. But the main thing is that he's happier now, trying to be a writer instead of just smoking so much pot and lying to the dog park people. You ought to check out his novels.

In fact, he just finished one.

THE END

About the Author

Award-winning author Joe Barrett has spent the past twenty-five years as a chief executive of entrepreneurial organizations ranging from private, venture-funded companies to large publicly listed multinational corporations. He has been a frequent speaker at National Retail Federation conferences and has sat on the boards of several for-profit and non-profit companies. His short fiction has been published in *Iconoclast*, *The Storyteller* and *The Palo Alto Review*. He lives with his wife and two children in Tampa.

Note from the Author

Word-of-mouth is crucial for any author to succeed. If you enjoyed *Unplugged*, please leave a review online—anywhere you are able. Even if it's just a sentence or two. It would make all the difference and would be very much appreciated.

Thanks!
Joe

Thank you so much for reading one of **Joe Barrett's** novels.
If you enjoyed the read, please check out his first book!

Managed Care by Joe Barrett

Kirkus Reviews says Joe Barrett's writing is,
"Witty, occasionally crass, and an unqualified delight."

Authors Reading calls Joe Barrett,
"A master storyteller and humorist."

View other Black Rose Writing titles at
www.blackrosewriting.com/books and use promo code
PRINT to receive a **20% discount** when purchasing.

www.ingramcontent.com/pod-product-compliance
Lightning Source LLC
Chambersburg PA
CBHW011132100726
47898CB00009B/2951